Barker got off the remaining two rounds and again worked to reload. There was no way he could wait for the twilight to deepen and hide his escape. The gang was circling him, waiting for him to make a run for it. He clicked the gate on his six-shooter closed, took a deep breath, and got his knees under him. With a surge, he came to his feet, stepped over the log, and let out a screech like a banshee as he ran forward toward his attackers.

Rather than burn through his six rounds as fast as he could, he fired with measured speed, each discharge like a peal of doom. His unexpected frontal assault caused the gang to hesitate—that would afford him a few seconds more of life, and that was all he could hope for.

Then the air filled with more whistling bullets than he could track. It took Barker a second to realize these were not heavy leaden pellets coming to kill him but carbine fire from behind.

Sturgeon and his buffalo soldiers had heard the gunfire and had attacked.

This buoyed Barker up but he kept running and firing. A distant grunt hinted that someone had been hit in the gang's camp, but Barker ignored this small victory. Step after step carried him closer to the edge of the woods. He heard the road agents running away ahead of him and the pounding of horses' hooves behind.

"Get down, you fool. Take cover. We'll get 'em!"

Sergeant Sturgeon thundered past on his horse, his men flanking him in a precise battle line that quickly fell into disarray when they reached the edge of the woods. Barker slowed to a walk, reloading as he went and realizing he was out of bullets. What he had in the cylinder was it. Six rounds. He had to make them count.

THE
SONORA
NOOSE

JACKSON LOWRY

BERKLEY BOOKS, NEW YORK

THE BERKLEY PUBLISHING GROUP
Published by the Penguin Group
Penguin Group (USA) Inc.
375 Hudson Street, New York, New York 10014, USA
Penguin Group (Canada), 90 Eglinton Avenue East, Suite 700, Toronto, Ontario M4P 2Y3, Canada
(a division of Pearson Penguin Canada Inc.)
Penguin Books Ltd., 80 Strand, London WC2R 0RL, England
Penguin Group Ireland, 25 St. Stephen's Green, Dublin 2, Ireland (a division of Penguin Books Ltd.)
Penguin Group (Australia), 250 Camberwell Road, Camberwell, Victoria 3124, Australia
(a division of Pearson Australia Group Pty. Ltd.)
Penguin Books India Pvt. Ltd., 11 Community Centre, Panchsheel Park, New Delhi—110 017, India
Penguin Group (NZ), 67 Apollo Drive, Rosedale, North Shore 0632, New Zealand
(a division of Pearson New Zealand Ltd.)
Penguin Books (South Africa) (Pty.) Ltd., 24 Sturdee Avenue, Rosebank, Johannesburg 2196,
South Africa

Penguin Books Ltd., Registered Offices: 80 Strand, London WC2R 0RL, England

This is a work of fiction. Names, characters, places, and incidents either are the product of the author's imagination or are used fictitiously, and any resemblance to actual persons, living or dead, business establishments, events, or locales is entirely coincidental. The publisher does not have any control over and does not assume any responsibility for author or third-party websites or their content.

THE SONORA NOOSE

A Berkley Book Book / published by arrangement with the author

PRINTING HISTORY
Berkley edition / February 2011

Copyright © 2011 by Robert Vardeman.
Cover illustration by Bruce Emmett.
Cover design by Diana Kolsky.
Interior text design by Kristin del Rosario.

ISBN: 978-0-425-23976-6

BERKLEY®
Berkley Books are published by The Berkley Publishing Group,
a division of Penguin Group (USA) Inc.,
375 Hudson Street, New York, New York 10014.
BERKLEY® is a registered trademark of Penguin Group (USA) Inc.
The "B" design is a trademark of Penguin Group (USA) Inc.

PRINTED IN THE UNITED STATES OF AMERICA

10 9 8 7 6 5 4 3 2 1

DEDICATION

This one's for that ole wrangler, Ken Hodgson

ACKNOWLEDGMENTS

For the many people who helped along the way, including Charles Vane, Alva Svoboda, Martha Martin, Nancy Holder, TJ Cardella, Amanda Capper, and of course, my ever capable, ever helpful editor, Faith Black

1

DEPUTY MARSHAL MASON BARKER WINCED IN PAIN, twisted from side to side without finding any relief, then ran his hand over the spot on his lower back causing him the distress. Riding for the last nine hours after serving process for Judge Terrence Donawell over in El Paso had taken its toll on his body. He was only thirty-eight years old but felt a hundred after such a long junket. Barker stretched in the stirrups to his full five-foot-eight height and then patted his bulging belly. His wife, Ruth, fed him too damn well the times he managed to sit down at the table with her. That gut dangling over his gun belt might be part of the problem with his back, but he wasn't inclined to give up that second helping of Ruth's peach cobbler whenever it came his way. It was too good, especially after living on cans of tomatoes and boiled beans on the trail.

Still, he had to do something about the pain that lanced up and down his spine.

He had been thrown from a captured horse while serving as a scout for Colonel Carson during the Navajo War. Barker couldn't even claim he had come by his injury performing some heroic deed. It had been a danged fool thing to try to ride an Indian pony unaccustomed to a saddle, but no one else had stayed on it longer than a few seconds. He had been younger and cockier then, full of piss and vinegar, and up to any challenge. There had been enemies to stop and worlds to conquer and he had done his best, but he still wished he hadn't taken that header off the feisty horse to land on a mighty hard rock at the mouth of Cañon de Chelly.

"Good thing that sunfishin' son of a gun didn't toss me a few feet farther," Barker said to himself as he stretched more of the kinks away, presenting his back to the afternoon sun for some heated comfort. He had missed a huge clump of prickly pear cactus that would have given him woe enough so that he'd still be picking broken spines out of his leathery hide twenty years later.

And his back would still have been bent at a crazy angle.

He drew rein outside the corral behind the town marshal's office, then dismounted gingerly. Barker moved slowly, putting down his weight a little at a time, as if walking on eggshells instead of dusty New Mexico ground, but the back pain refused to abate. He knew what he had to do as he heaved a sigh and headed down Mesilla's main street toward his favorite watering hole. There were fancier saloons in town than the hole-in-the-wall Plugged Nickel Saloon and Gambling Euphorium, but he appreciated the misspelling of the name as well as the pun. He had pointed this out to Gus Phillips, the gin mill's owner, but Gus hadn't seen anything wrong, even after Barker explained the difference between an emporium and euphoria.

More out of habit than any real need, before going inside he wiped the dust off his deputy's badge hammered out of a Mexican silver peso. Although he was a federal deputy and spent more time tracking down outlaws throughout the rest of New Mexico Territory than he did bellying up to the bar at the Plugged Nickel, the folks here knew him well enough. He thought of Mesilla as his town, his home, the place he returned to after long weeks patrolling the rest of his district. It was as close to a home as he had been able to give Ruth and his son over the long years of being constantly on the move, and for the welcome the folks in Mesilla had given he was grateful.

Barker winced as he stood in the doorway, as much from back pain as from the cacophony roiling from inside. Gus had hired a new piano player, who was even worse than the former one, if that was possible. It had been more than two weeks since Barker had been in town, and in the life of a saloon like this one, that amounted to an eternity. He paused and looked around, taking in the changes. Besides the weasely-looking piano player with his thinning, greased-back sandy hair and long fingers that played bonelessly, there was a new nude hanging behind the twenty-foot-long polished oak bar. It was about time that the old painting be replaced, Barker decided. The voluptuous red-haired woman in the old "masterpiece" had begun peeling in unseemly places, and the paint had faded so much from smoke there was almost no contrast left between acres of bare flesh and background. Worse, the yellowing had made the woman look Chinese, a curious contrast with her flowing red hair. The new painting was a real work of art.

"She's a real beauty, ain't she, Marshal?" asked Gus, coming down the bar, his rag working feverishly to pick up beer spills and return the precious gleam to the wood.

"The piano man over there, he painted her. Watched him do it in less than a day. The man's a genius."

"Glad he's got other talents to fall back on," Barker said dryly as the piano player butchered Stephen Foster's "Nelly Was a Lady."

"A man of many talents, yes, sir," Gus said with some admiration. "Don't know his real worth, neither. Got him singin' 'n playin' for only a dollar a day."

"A steal," Barker said, not indicating whom he considered was being robbed. "I need a shot," he said.

Gus hesitated.

"Trade whiskey's fine," Barker said, knowing the barkeep's reluctance came from not knowing if he was going to get paid. Barker's salary, even as a federal deputy marshal, was sporadic at best. He had heard that Marshal Dakes over in Arizona had never collected a dime of his salary and didn't even know for certain what he was supposed to be paid. Barker was ahead of him in that respect, getting forty dollars a month, whenever the federal marshal's office thought to send it. Mostly he made his money serving process for judges in El Paso, Texas, and several towns throughout southern New Mexico. Of the lot, he was glad he had settled in Mesilla. It had the feel of a real town to him, unlike Tularosa and other supposedly inhabited places sprouting up like vile weeds around the Chupadera to the north.

He fished out a silver dollar and let it ring sonorously on the bar. Gus performed a sleight of hand and the coin vanished, replaced as if by magic with a brimming shot of the powerful antidote for what ailed Barker.

"You want to pay off your tab, Marshal?" Gus asked. He grinned when Barker nodded once, then he passed over the glass so the marshal could knock back the potent concoction of grain alcohol, with gunpowder added for bite and a few rusty nails tossed in to give the proper color. Barker belched as the whiskey hit his belly, but the heat spread through him and centered on the stubborn pain in his back. In a minute the misery receded, and after a second drink, it was almost gone.

The deputy wanted nothing more than to leave the Plugged Nickel and ride home to his Ruth. He had been on the circuit a tad longer than he had expected this time, but finding the miner hidden away in the Organ Mountains and serving him the foreclosure on his property had proven to be a real chore. For a heartbeat Barker had thought the old miner was going to shoot it out, but part of being a federal marshal was convincing men to do what they didn't want to do without resorting to using the six-shooter hanging at your side.

But he knew from the sounds rising behind him in the saloon that going home was out of the question for now. Barker turned slowly and took in the situation. Facing Manuelito and his entire clan of savage, clever Navajo warriors would have been more appealing at this instant. Mason Barker had seen too much sudden death come from situations like the one brewing to be easy about it. He had never killed a man, but that might change fast right now if he wanted to prevent a real bloodbath.

"You cheated me!" shouted a sodbuster that Barker struggled to place. The name finally came to him. Sean Leary had put away one too many drinks—or maybe one too few. Another jolt of Gus's tarantula juice might have caused him to pass out and would have relieved Barker of his duty to keep everyone concerned alive.

"Boys, you saw the cards," said the card slick across the table from the farmer, to the others in the poker game.

"I had two pair—little ladies and deuces. All he had was a pair of kings. Two pair beats one every time, no matter that they're kings."

Barker saw the wild expression on Leary's face. It was as much fear as it was anger and confusion, but he doubted the farmer was afraid of the right thing. The gambler must have rattled when he walked, hideout guns and knives never more than a few inches away from his nimble fingers no matter how he turned in his chair or how relaxed he looked. He sounded peaceable enough, but Barker saw the slight twitch under the gambler's right eye showing the anticipation. It certainly wasn't fear of a drunk pinto bean farmer.

Two quick steps put the deputy behind the gambler. He rested his hand on the man's shoulder and bore down hard enough to get his attention. Barker didn't look at the gambler, but across the table at Leary.

"What's the ruckus, Sean?" he asked.

"Marshal?" Sean Leary blinked as he tried to focus. "Marshal! He done stole from me! That was the mortgage money for my farm! He cheated!" Leary frantically pulled out a black-powder Remington and waved it around wildly. This was what Barker had feared when he had seen the sodbuster from across the room.

"I never—" started the gambler, but Barker's powerful grip tightened, silencing the man. Barker looked around the table and read the facts on the other players' faces. Leary had joined the wrong game. The gambler didn't have to cheat to beat a drunk farmer come to town for supplies and to pay his mortgage.

"Put that hogleg down, Sean," Barker said gently. "You don't want to go shooting it off in here. The smoke from that ole blunderbuss would choke the lot of us till next Sunday." He tightened his grip and found nerves that caused the gambler's right arm to go numb, so he couldn't reach for the derringer poking out from his vest pocket, not inches from the tips of his fingers.

"He stole my money." Leary's anger was disappearing, replaced entirely by fear.

"Your wife doesn't know you were gambling with the mortgage money, does she, Sean?" Barker asked gently. He knew he had hit the nail on the head by the way Leary jerked, as if the accusation was a whip lash across the face. "Put that damned thing down for a moment. Keep it under the table so you don't spook Gus's other patrons, and let me and the gambling man talk about this."

"I want my money back, Marshal!"

"You stay put, Sean," Barker said sternly. "And you, outside." He maintained his steely grip on the gambler's shoulder. If he dug his fingers in harder, he could make the cardsharp's entire right arm go numb for the rest of the day. Guiding the gambler outside onto the boardwalk, he spun him around.

"I didn't cheat him. I—" The gambler never got out another word.

Barker shoved him against the Plugged Nickel's adobe wall, hard enough to cause a small dust cloud, and caught both the man's forearms, squeezing tight as he hunted for mechanical devices. Nothing. A quick look assured the lawman that the gambler hadn't been using cards pulled from his vest or waistband, either, but that didn't mean a whole lot. From the man's nimbleness, Barker reckoned he could deal seconds and stack a deck with the best of them. Maybe he had done that. Or maybe the game had been an oddity in Mesilla: honest.

"A word of advice," Barker said. "Leave Mesilla now."

"You don't want his money back?" the gambler asked suspiciously.

"From the look of it, you won fair and square. You deserve to make a living, like anyone else, but taking Sean Leary's money is like stealing a dead man's boots. There's no challenge to it. Now, you clear out and I'll settle matters with him."

"Thanks, Marshal."

"It's Deputy Marshal Barker." Mason Barker glared at the grateful gambler, who took his advice, mounted a swayback mule, and headed out of Mesilla fast amid a tiny cloud of gritty brown dust. Barker heaved a sigh of relief. A fight with that vulture would have been bloody. But he still had the other half of the battle to win. He wasn't sure but that dealing with a man afraid of what he had done and not willing to fess up to his wife was more dangerous than tangling with an armed and agile gambler.

Hell, Barker knew that it was.

He went back in, a smile on his face in spite of the way Sean Leary waved his six-shooter around. The man had gone from blaming the gambler to claiming the others at the green-felt-covered card table had cheated him. Barker recognized two of the men and doubted they would be in cahoots with the gambler. The others were drifters passing through Mesilla on their way to God knew where, but their expressions told him they'd as soon be on the moon as here looking down the immense bore of Leary's six-shooter. If they'd cheated Leary, they would already be forking the money across to him. Like as not, they had lost to the gambler, too.

"Sean," Barker said in a low tone. "We got to talk. Let's step outside."

"No!" the man said, his knuckle turning white on the trigger. "I want my money back, and I ain't budgin' till I get it. I was robbed, I tell you. Where's that worthless hunk of coyote meat?"

"Don't go doing anything you'll regret," Barker said, seeing that Leary wasn't going to stir from the chair at the card table until he either got his money back or started flinging lead.

"My money, Marshal. I got to have it!"

"This is a bit delicate, Sean," Barker said in a confidential tone. "You see, I have the money."

"Gimme it!"

"I can't, Sean, as much as I'd like to. It's a matter of pride. That gambler can't let it be known he's giving you the money back. It'd ruin his reputation."

"But—"

"He gave it to me because I'm a federal deputy marshal, but I can't let it look as if he did. So I'll sit down in his chair, and we'll play one more hand. I'm no good at cards, so I'll lose. You take the pot, you get your money back, and you get on back to the missus."

"All right," Leary said, frowning as his alcohol-fogged mind worked on what the lawman said. He didn't relax the grip on his six-gun. Barker watched to be sure the farmer wasn't going to open fire and worried that the old pistol might go off accidentally. The potential was still there for someone to get hurt mighty bad.

Barker settled down, now on the receiving end of the pistol. He took the cards and shuffled quickly. The other players tried to edge back and leave, but Leary's threatening six-shooter kept them glued where they were.

"All right, ante up," Barker said, scooting a white chip to the center of the table. The other men also anted up. Barker's eyebrows rose when Leary didn't make a move to put his chip in. "Go on, Sean. Ante up."

"You know I can't, Marshal. He done robbed me of all my money."

"This is a problem," Barker said softly. "You know I can't give you back the money. We got to make it look respectable." He paused a moment, then smiled. "I've got it. Just you and me. We cut the deck. High card wins."

"All right," Leary said.

"But you have to bet something. What do you have that's worth anything?" Barker pushed his chips into the center of the table.

"I . . . I don't have nuthin'."

"The gun. Put it into the pot. It ought to be worth about that much." Barker held out the deck for Leary to cut. The drunken farmer was torn between getting his money back and putting down the pistol.

"I'm gonna win, ain't I?"

"Sure as rain," Barker said, hoping Leary wouldn't consider how dry it was in the desert this year. Not even the droughty Rio Grande a couple miles to the southeast was flowing as poorly as Leary was thinking.

Leary put his pistol onto the table and cut out a ten of diamonds.

"I win," he said, but Barker was quicker. The deputy cut out a queen of spades.

"Nope, I win."

Confusion befuddled the sodbuster for a moment, giving the lawman time to scoop up Leary's six-shooter.

"I was supposed to win!" Leary cried. He looked around wildly, but without a six-gun to use as a threat, he was powerless. Barker wasted no time shoving the farmer's six-shooter into his belt, going around the table, grabbing him by the collar, and half-dragging him from the Plugged Nickel.

Barker raged. "Don't ever, I mean *ever*, gamble money you can't afford to lose. If I see you within ten feet of a bottle of whiskey, I'll clap you in jail so fast your head won't stop spinning for a month of Sundays!"

"But you said—"

"Get your buckboard. I'm taking you home."

"No, you said I'd get my money back."

"It's lost, Sean. You lost it in a fair game."

"My gun!"

"You lost it, too. It's mine and I'm keeping it. Get in that buckboard of yours. Oh, the hell with it." Barker grabbed Leary by the seat of the pants and his collar and heaved, staggering him down the street to the buckboard. With a heave, he dumped the man into the back. "You stay put. I'll be back with my horse in a minute."

Barker saw he wouldn't have to chase Sean Leary down. The man was curled up in the buckboard sobbing like a baby.

In disgust, the deputy got his trusty mare and fastened the reins to the rear of the buckboard, then got the rig moving to the Leary farm outside Mesilla. As he rode, Barker saw the fields of beans and fragrant green alfalfa stretching out of sight. This wasn't the best land in the world, but with irrigation from a well-planned acequia, a hardworking man could make a decent living.

An hour after leaving Mesilla, the sobbing man had finally fallen into a drunken sleep, and Barker pulled up in front of an adobe house needing a fair amount of repair work on it. He figured Leary was more inclined to go into town to drink and gamble than he was to do a proper day's work here, but that was his wife's problem.

"Afternoon, Mrs. Leary," the deputy called. He drew rein and fastened the leather straps around the brake before jumping to the ground. He touched the brim of his floppy black hat in polite greeting, but the tiny woman knew this was no social call.

"What's wrong, Marshal?" she demanded. She wiped flour off her hands as she stepped away from the rounded, head-high, adobe *horno* she had just shoved a couple loaves into to bake. The Indian oven a couple yards from the main house seemed out of place being used by a woman with such a heavy brogue, but in this desert everything but sidewinders and prickly pear cactus was an interloper.

He cast a quick look into the rear of the buckboard.

"He lost our mortgage money, didn't he?" she said, her lips thinning to a razor slash.

"Reckon so, ma'am," Barker said. He hesitated. These weren't rich folks, but neither was he. Still, he couldn't stop himself from saying a bit more. "I've got his six-shooter, but I can't in good faith give it back after Sean waved it around like he did."

"I understand," Mrs. Leary said.

"That's why I got to pay you for it." Barker fished in his shirt pocket and found some of the scrip Judge Donawell had paid him. He unfolded a ten-dollar note issued by an El Paso bank. In Mesilla it didn't mean as much, but the Learys weren't going to starve. He handed it to the woman.

"You're paying ten dollars for that rusty old thumbbreaker?" she asked.

"You see that he stays out of the saloons in town, ma'am," Barker said. "I told him, 'fore he passed out, that I'd have to lock him up if I ever saw him in any of them again."

"Considering how many drinking establishments there are, that's nigh on half the town being off-limits," Mrs. Leary said in despair. "That's good of you, Marshal

Barker. Thank you." Her eyes shone with unshed tears and not a little anger, but it was directed at her husband. Her words of gratitude were sincere.

"You look after him and keep him working," Barker said.

"I will." The cold steel in the small woman's words chilled Barker. He was glad she wasn't *his* wife. He tipped his hat, mounted his mare, and rode off without so much as a look backward when he heard Sean Leary's anguished screech as his wife dragged him from the buckboard. Before this day was over, the man would end up wishing he had been thrown into the calaboose.

Mason Barker rode toward home and his family, feeling good that he had avoided bloodshed. Even better, his back hardly twinged at all.

2

MASON BARKER RODE TO THE SMALL BARN AND shook his head when he saw how badly it needed another coat of paint that would be put off, at least for a few days until he could get rested up. He dismounted and settled his mare in a stall with a nose bag filled with oats as reward for such diligent service over the last couple weeks, did a bit of currying, and only then went to the door of his small adobe house. He hesitated for a moment before opening the heavy wood door, then pushed inside to the cool, dim interior.

"Ruth, I'm back!" he called. The house was modest and his booming voice filled the four rooms.

"Mase?" came the tentative query.

"It's me," he said, going into the main room crowded with a settee, a china cabinet that had belonged to Ruth's aunt, two long tables he had made from a lightning-struck oak tree, and a rocking chair with a smaller table beside it holding their solitary coal oil lamp. The kitchen straight

ahead was empty. That meant his wife was in their bedroom, since he doubted she would be in their son's room
attached to the other side of the house. "Who'd you think
it was?"

Ruth came from their bedroom, a hint of a smile on
her lips. She brushed back vagrant strands of mousy brown
hair from her eyes. The woman stood five-foot-two but
seemed smaller, as if she had collapsed into herself. When
her brown eyes refused to meet his pale blue ones, Barker
knew something was amiss.

"Oh," she said a little guiltily, "I hoped it was Nate."

"He hasn't come home for a spell, has he?" Suddenly
every bone in his body ached. Barker took off his gun belt
and hung it on a peg threatening to pull loose from the
flaking adobe wall. The weight of the leather belt, holster,
and six-shooter was almost too much for the wood post. He
knew how the peg felt. Too much weight over time could
wear down anyone with despair.

He sank into the sturdy oak rocking chair that had come
all the way from Indiana and felt his back try to relax. It
was almost painful. Almost as painful as hearing what
trouble their son had gotten into while he was gone.

"You know how it is with young men," Ruth said, rubbing her hands nervously on her calico skirt. "You sowed
your wild oats before you settled down, Mase." She finally
met his gaze. Barker had become real good at reading what
people meant rather than only listening to what they said.

"How long since he decided to leave?"

"He left just after you did. I reckon he'll be back anytime now that you're home. How did it go?"

Barker sighed and dug around in his shirt pocket to find
what money he had left. He quickly counted it and came to
eleven dollars and eighty cents as he put it on a side table.

It wasn't much, but it would let Ruth get food for another couple weeks. He had earned enough from serving process to pay expenses for a full month, but he had given Mrs. Leary ten dollars for a hunk of rusted iron that wouldn't fetch fifty cents honest money. He shrugged it off. That was only scrip. What he had kept was all specie. Except the silver dollar he had paid to Gus Phillips. That was the way money always went, a little here and a lot more there.

"That'll go a ways toward paying off our bill at Dooley's," Ruth said. Their bill at the general store was always a matter of concern since Hugh Dooley was about the hardest-nosed merchant this side of the Pecos. He didn't let anyone run up an account more than twenty dollars. Sometimes Barker bumped up against that barrier, but seldom did he ever pay off the entire amount due the tradesman. There was always some other reckoning from some other store. At least he had paid off Gus at the Plugged Nickel.

"Nate's not contributing anything to running the household," Barker said. "It's high time he found a job and settled down."

"If he's not here, he's not eating our food," Ruth said. "That's no drain."

"He ought to be fixing up the barn, taking care of the house, feeding the stock." Even as the words left his mouth, Barker knew the same could be said of him. Although his job took him away from home and bed often enough, he was seldom able to do much when he was there, because of his back.

Barker rocked a little and eased the tension mounting across his shoulders. He did what he could to keep his discomfort from his wife. Ruth had enough to worry about, what with their ne'er-do-well son causing such concern. It had been so hard when their younger boy, Patrick, died from infection four years ago. Somehow, they had both pinned their hopes on Nate, and the boy wasn't up to meeting such lofty expectations. Mason's own job as deputy marshal gave Ruth a twinge or two, also, in spite of his assurance that he was more likely to get snake-bit than shot by any of the owlhoots roaming through New Mexico Territory. What little law enforcing he did was in Mesilla, and it was hardly more than a town marshal would do.

He had to smile thinking how he had run the tinhorn gambler from town and taken care of Sean Leary. It'd be a cold day in hell before that sodbuster's wife let him out of her sight again, and when she did, he wouldn't dare even go sniffing after a shot of whiskey. The image of Sean Leary crouched at the front door of the Plugged Nickel, snuffling like a whipped cur at the scent within, made Barker smile even more.

Thinking about the potent liquor made Barker hanker for a shot of his own, but he had left his small half-pint flask out in his saddlebags.

"He's only a boy," Ruth said.

Barker groused, "He's a man and ought to accept responsibility. Where does he go when he's not here, anyway?" He turned as the door opened and his son came in, having to duck to avoid hitting his head on the low lintel.

Nate Barker mumbled under his breath as he headed for his small room.

"Come on back here," Barker said sharply. His keen nose picked up not only tobacco smoke but also beer from the eighteen-year-old's clothes.

"Mase, please. Let the boy—"

"He's not a boy," Barker said to his wife more harshly than he'd intended. The sight of Nate looking as if he had been on a weeklong bender did something to him. It wouldn't take much for Nate to end up like Sean Leary, gambling and losing money he didn't have after drinking himself into a stupor. Mason hadn't worked as hard as he had, spending long hours in the saddle under a burning desert sun catching crooks and serving process, so his son could become a complete wastrel.

"What do you want?" Nate said sullenly. He was an inch taller and thirty pounds heavier than his father, all of that weight muscle. His pale blue eyes were bloodshot, and his dark hair was a greasy tangle no self-respecting rat would have deigned to crawl around in. It looked as if he had lived in his clothes for the entire time he had been absent. Barker couldn't say much about that since he hadn't changed his clothes in two weeks, either, and sorely needed a bath himself.

"For you to pull your weight around here," Barker said.

"You're a fine one to talk. You're never here."

"I have a job that pays for the food on the table and the roof over your head," Barker said, holding down his anger.

"That what you call real money?" Nate said sarcastically, pointing to the money on the side table. "That's chicken feed."

"I earned it," Barker said. "Where's the money you earned? Nate, it's high time for you to get a job since you're not helping with the chores for your mother."

"What are you going to do? Hire me as a lawman? A deputy's deputy?" Nate's tone irritated Barker with its sarcasm.

"There's nothing wrong with being a deputy marshal," Barker said, a tad closer to losing his temper.

"Nate, dear, your father's likely to be made chief deputy before long."

Nate scoffed. "Oh, good, *chief* deputy marshal. Heap big chief."

"I'll get you a job tomorrow in town."

"Doing what?"

"Anything I can find, since you're not inclined to put yourself out."

"As long as I don't have to drag off dead animals in the street, like you do." Nate retraced his steps and left, slamming the door behind him. Barker started to get out of the rocker and order Nate back, but his back tightened in a new spasm that kept him seated. The sound of horse's hooves pounding told Barker his son had left again.

"You don't have to do that, do you, Mase?" asked Ruth.

"That's what town marshals are for," he said.

"There isn't one in Mesilla, not right now, but I heard Mayor Pendleton say the other day at church how he was thinking of hiring one since you're always out serving process. He thinks trouble in town can be held down if there's a permanent marshal."

Barker and the mayor didn't see eye to eye often, but this time he had to agree. A town marshal would take a considerable weight off his shoulders. Barker considered Mesilla his home and felt an obligation to maintain the peace. He might get that promotion to chief federal deputy Ruth had mentioned if he could spend more time riding through the vast arid stretch from Arizona Territory over to the Texas border and ranging all the way north to Socorro. That would mean more time away from home. It would also mean more money, maybe as much as fifteen dollars a month more.

"Are you hungry?" Ruth asked, looking distracted.

"Hungry for you, my lovely young bride," Barker said. He used the forward motion of the rocking chair to get to his feet as he reached for her, but she stepped back just enough to avoid his grasping hands.

"I meant food, Mase. Please, I'm not up to doing anything . . . more."

She hardly ever felt up to performing her wifely duties, not after Patrick had died. Barker accepted a plate of savory beans with green chili mixed in for spice and a fresh-baked flour tortilla with churned butter, instead of lying with his wife in a bed they seldom shared anymore.

Early the next morning he was in the saddle, heading into Mesilla to find his son a job. It might not lighten the guilt he felt for never being home to raise Nate properly, but at least a job would furnish more money for Ruth to run their household.

3

BARKER MIGHT WEAR A DEPUTY MARSHAL'S BADGE on his vest, but he felt like a naughty schoolboy whenever he spoke with Hugh Dooley. The man peered at him through spotlessly clean spectacles, head tipped slightly forward so that he always seemed disapproving. And maybe he was. Barker knew he and Ruth seldom paid off their bill at the general store, but most other citizens of Mesilla were in the same position, especially after the Panic of '73. Still, Dooley made Barker feel as if he were the only scofflaw in the whole danged territory who was a day late and a dollar short.

"This is mighty unusual, Deputy," Dooley said in his clipped, precise tone. His lips thinned to a line, and he shook his head slowly, as if denying everything Barker said and stood for. "Ordinarily, I hire youngsters to help out in the store. Eight, ten years old."

"Nate needs to be whipped into shape, no question," Barker said. Sweat formed on his upper lip. He wished he hadn't bothered to shave this morning. Even a ghost of a mustache would have hidden his nervousness better, but the weather was too damn hot to sport such a lip rug. "You're the one to do it. He needs to learn to do an honest day's work for a day's pay."

"Not likely to pay as well as other places," Dooley said carefully, but Barker saw the sparkle in the merchant's eyes. "Won't pay more than two bits a day, and they'd be long days."

"Just what I'm looking for," Barker admitted. The store owner saw a way to get decent work done for less than he would pay a grown-up. "I hope it won't be for long."

"Long enough to learn what it means to earn a wage," Dooley said, nodding now. "Very well. Get your boy in here tomorrow morning, seven o'clock sharp. I've got a new shipment arriving that will require a strong back and a half day's work."

"Thanks, Mr. Dooley," Barker said, sticking out his hand. They shook.

"That reminds me, Deputy," Dooley said. "You never picked up the book in your last order."

"Book?" Then Barker remembered. He had special ordered a history of Italy from back East. Reading provided about his only decent escape and allowed him to forget his back pain for a spell. "It's a big one, isn't it?"

"Heavy," agreed Dooley, digging around behind the counter to pull out the brown paper–wrapped book tied up with twine. "That's a dollar."

"Put it on my bill. The missus will be in later to pay what's due and get more supplies."

"Very well," Dooley said, his formal manner falling around him again like a shroud. "See that young Mr. Barker is here bright and early."

"That I will do, sir. Thank you again." Barker left the general store, fumbling at the string to get a look at the volume that had traveled so far from Boston to reach southern New Mexico Territory. He grinned when he saw it. Small print, dense, and every page filled with detail. Barker knew many of the folks in Mesilla would wonder about him if they discovered how he buried his nose in a book every chance he got, but then most of them couldn't read, write, or cipher. He had been lucky, growing up with a mother who had been a schoolmarm and a father who encouraged his children to read to widen their horizons, even though he was illiterate himself. Without that support, Barker knew he would never have become intrigued with distant lands, daring explorers, and heroic soldiers, and he might never have gotten up the nerve to volunteer for Colonel Kit Carson's campaign against the Navajo after both his parents and two brothers had died of cholera up in Denver City.

Barker tried to walk and look at the book at the same time and found himself almost run down by a wild-eyed man galloping in from the south.

"Marshal, Marshal!" the man called, reining back so hard his horse dug its hooves deep into the street and kicked up a choking dust cloud. "They done it. They went and done it."

"What're you going on about, Caleb?" Barker asked, scowling. Caleb Young was an excitable sort who managed to find disaster in the simplest problems. Something about him this time warned Barker it might not be a false alarm.

"The stagecoach, outside o' town. Not ten miles back toward El Paso. The Ben Halliday coach. Road agents!"

"Did the stage get robbed?" Barker asked pointedly. "Caleb! Was anyone hurt?"

"Don't know, Marshal. Came right away after I heard the shootin'. I wasn't a mile off."

Barker tucked the book under his arm and hurried to his small office with the adjoining four iron-barred cages that served as cells. He dropped the book onto his desk amid a small cloud of dust and made certain the rifles in a pine-wood case on the wall were chained securely, then dashed back into the street to get his horse.

Caleb Young was holding court, telling anyone within earshot what had happened. Barker wished he had told the man to keep quiet, but that would have been going against his nature. Caleb might have exploded if he hadn't been able to spread the news.

"You need help, Marshal?" asked a man at the edge of the growing crowd.

"Not right now, thanks. If I have to rustle up a posse, I'll pass the word." He looked over at Caleb. "Actually, I'll let Caleb pass the word since he seems to take a shine to doing that chore," he amended.

He gathered the reins and climbed into the saddle, wincing slightly. He settled down so that his back stopped twinging, then wheeled about and shouted to Caleb, "You lead the way."

This served several purposes. It separated Caleb from his audience, quieted the worry that spread like wildfire, gave the young man a reason for going along, so he could report even more to the people of Mesilla later on, and also provided backup for Barker should he run into the road agents. Caleb might not be much of a fighter—Barker had no idea if he could even fire a pistol—but the mere sight of two lawmen coming onto the scene might spook the robbers.

Even if one of the "lawmen" was more inclined to shoot off his mouth than his six-gun.

Barker had to admit the chances were good that the outlaws had already stolen what they could and left.

He pulled his bandanna over his nose to block out the gritty, biting dust from the road and tugged at the brim of his floppy hat to protect his eyes a mite. As he rode behind the frantic Caleb Young, he wondered what he would find ahead. The cutthroat gang of desperadoes over in Arizona calling themselves the Cowboys had been a constant source of annoyance, not to mention death, for the entire territory, but there had been rumors of a gang of Mexican banditos run north of the border by Rurales. If so, those banditos would be about the only ones afraid of the Mexican soldiers. But Barker knew other reasons could bring outlaws from the depths of Mexico.

As flies sought out fresh cow flops, banditos went where there was money to be stolen.

Barker pulled himself back to the reality of the countryside and scanned the rugged, arid terrain for other riders. He and Caleb might as well have been the only men on earth for all the life he saw. Even as this thought crossed his mind, Barker heard Caleb shout and start to wave his arms around like a windmill.

"Don't fall off," Barker called.

"There, Marshal, up there!" Caleb pointed, and the lawman saw the coach ahead, canted at a crazy angle. The six-horse team was nowhere in sight, but Barker saw two men crouched atop the coach, arguing. He guessed they were debating whether the road agents had returned or if help had finally arrived.

"Hallo!" Barker called, not wanting the shotgun guard

to open up on him when he rode closer. "It's Deputy Marshal Barker, from Mesilla. Are you all well?"

"Dammit, Marshal, we been robbed!" shouted a hunched-over man rising up out of the driver's box. Barker recognized Little Tom Goff.

"Tom, keep your gun pointed some other way so I can get closer."

"Get your worthless carcass over here, Marshal," Goff growled, scrambling to the top of the coach with the other men. Even standing, Goff was hardly five feet tall and was bent over like a question mark.

"You stay back till I give you the sign," Barker told Caleb. The man's head bobbed as if it were mounted on a spring.

Barker rode slowly, not wanting to spook the men any more than they already were. He had identified himself, but he took no chances with passengers inclined to have itchy trigger fingers. As he approached, he saw that the stagecoach had lost a rear wheel, causing it to tip precariously. Of the team he saw no trace.

"They done up and robbed us, Marshal," complained Goff. "I seen a man sittin' alongside the road, whittlin' up a storm. He was on the upslope, so I was goin' real slow."

"You didn't see the others, mounted, who came up from the sides," Barker finished.

"You saw them varmints? You saw them shootin' us up and didn't do nuthin'?"

"That's how I'd've attacked," Barker said. "A driver as experienced as you, Little Tom, well, they'd have to make a powerful distraction so's they could take you by surprise. I'll be sure to put in a good word about how hard those owlhoots had to work to rob you."

"There wasn't any effort on their part," groused a passenger on the coach top. "This short drink of water throwed up his hands and gave in without any fight. They stole my pocket watch! It was an heirloom! My granddaddy gave me that watch on his deathbed."

"Whoa, hold your horses," Barker said, seeing how angry this made Goff. "You may not realize it, but the driver might just have saved your life. There only the pair of you?" He saw Goff nod and the two men reluctantly agree. "How many of them were there?"

"Not countin' the road agent doin' the whittlin', there was five of them. Two on each flank and one behind, as if I coulda turned this rig around and beat a retreat back to El Paso."

"Six against three," Barker said, letting the numbers sink in with the passengers. "That would have been a bloody fight, six desperadoes with guns already drawn and ready to shoot. Little Tom knew that and figured losing a watch, even an heirloom, was better'n you losing your life."

"Might have been that way," the passenger said reluctantly.

"Give me a description of the watch. It might be the only way I can bring these sidewinders to justice." Barker listened as the man, a patent medicine peddler, described the watch. Barker allowed as to how it was distinctive and would be a help finding the outlaws.

"They rode up wearing masks," said the passenger, as if this was in the least helpful. "And they had them bright-colored Mexican blankets—"

"Serapes," cut in Goff.

"What he said," went on the passenger, waving his hand in a dismissive gesture. "They had those see-wrap-pees draped over their shoulders so I couldn't tell what kind of clothes they wore."

Barker's eyes drifted southward, deeper into the Chihuahua Desert. He had worried that banditos might have crossed the border to pick up a few dollars before hightailing it back to safety, and he had been right. The deputy took no pleasure in being right, because it meant a long, dusty chase that wasn't likely to come to a satisfactory end.

"Caleb!" he bellowed. "Get yer ass on over here." To the men on the coach, he said, "This here's Caleb Young. He'll do what he can for you, then ride back to Mesilla for help."

"Where're you headin', Marshal?" asked Goff.

"South" was all Barker said, already hunting for tracks. A blind man could have found the trail, since the outlaws had stolen the six horses in the team. A dozen horses, even in the sandy desert, left quite a path behind, but they had to be followed fast, before the restless wind erased all trace. He spent a few more minutes soothing the passengers, puffing up Goff's already big opinion of himself and his bravery. It did no harm and might eventually do some good since Little Tom Goff was almost as big a talker as Caleb.

Almost.

Barker got on the trail and trotted along, keeping an eye peeled for any sign that the outlaws had halted and were lying in wait for a posse after them. He didn't fault Goff for not shooting it out with six armed, determined outlaws. And he certainly felt no shame knowing he would turn tail and run if he found himself facing those same six varmints. His best hope was to find their camp, fetch a posse, and maybe bring them to justice. He didn't think much of his chances, but he was a federal deputy marshal and had to try to enforce the law.

The sun burned down on him from a cloudless blue sky and then turned suddenly cooler as it sank over the mountains in the far west. Just at sundown Barker drew rein and squinted to be sure his eyes weren't fooling him. Six men rode toward him. All six were Mexicans and several wore striped, patterned, brightly colored serapes.

He reached up and pulled off his badge, tucking it into his vest pocket. A quick move took the leather thong keeper off the hammer of his six-shooter, but he knew he would never survive a shoot-out if they caught a hint that he was a lawman. What bothered him most was how they were retracing their trail, going toward Mesilla and not south into Mexico and sanctuary.

"*Hola!*" shouted one rider, waving all friendly-like.

"Howdy," Barker called, turning his mare's face toward the riders. His heart beat faster, and he tried not to sweat more than he had been. In the cooler early twilight, wind blew constantly and chilled him.

The men exchanged quick whispers among themselves and looked furtive, but Barker had the feeling they were more scared of him than he was of them. Curious, he rode closer and saw right away that the six Mexicans were riding the horses that had earlier been part of the stagecoach team. He recognized the Halliday Stage Company brand and the way the horses reacted skittishly to having riders instead of traces guiding them. To emphasize it even more, none of the riders had a saddle.

"Where you headed?" Barker asked.

The six swapped glances, and the one who had called to him said in heavily accented English, "We go to Mesilla."

"Looking for work there?" asked Barker, as polite and interested as he could be.

The men understood and all nodded, grinning.

"What can you tell me about the six men who sold you those horses you're riding?" Barker asked. The one who understood and spoke English the best jerked back, startled. He obviously considered making a run for it and then settled down to bluff through the question.

"What do you ask?"

"Tell me about the men who sold you those horses. *Sus caballos*," he said.

"*Sí*," the leader said suspiciously.

"You traded for them?" pressed Barker.

"Food. Frijoles. Water. *Todo el mundo*."

Barker pieced together what had happened in a few more minutes of roundabout questioning. These six were making their way on foot up from Mexico and had come across the fleeing stage robbers. The outlaws had swapped the horses for enough food and water and everything else the six had to get them across the Mexican border, safely away from American justice. It was only a coincidence that there were six outlaws and six Mexicans hunting for jobs.

"Ships passing in the night," Barker muttered to himself. Louder, he asked, "Were they your countrymen?"

"*Sí*," the leader said, looking uneasier by the minute at these questions. "From Sonora. They say they come from Sonora. We come from Chihuahua."

Barker studied the men closely and believed their story. None carried a weapon more dangerous than a knife, although those blades might be mighty deadly, and other than the horses they rode, they carried no baggage. Although they might have hidden the booty from the stagecoach robbery, they wouldn't have ventured back into the desert without a few supplies.

"Any of you got the time?" Barker asked.

The leader squinted and looked into the setting sun. "It is half hour till the darkness," he said.

"*Tiene un reloj?*" he asked, being more specific now.

"No, no watch," the leader said, frowning at the question.

This satisfied Barker that none of them carried the stolen watch. Ask a man for the time and if he has a watch, it'll come out in a flash without an instant of thought about the action. These half dozen caballeros used the sun and stars to gauge their time and might never have even seen a pocket watch in their lives.

"How long ago did you trade for the horses?"

"Two or three hours," the leader said.

Barker sagged a little. That gave the outlaws plenty of time to have crossed the border. He had never expected to overtake them, but hope sprang eternal.

"Any chance you recognized any of them? Can you describe what they wore?"

It took the better part of ten minutes for Barker to piece together the description. The outlaws' leader had worn a large sombrero with flashing silver *conchas*; all six had serapes covering crossed bandoliers of ammunition with six-guns tucked into broad hand-tooled leather belts. But description of the men themselves was sadly lacking. The six Barker had found had been too awed by the sight of so much firepower and too eager to trade their supplies for the stolen horses to pay much mind to what the outlaws looked like.

About that, Barker had to think a minute or two. Receiving stolen property was a crime, and he didn't doubt for an instant these men had known the horses were stolen and that their benefactors were actually banditos running from the law.

"If you'll accept it, can I give you some advice?" Barker asked.

"*Sí, señor, gracias.*" The man looked as if he was going to be forced to swallow a mouthful of alkali water. The way he shifted his weight away from Barker caused his horse to shy, as he waited for what had to be bad news.

"Don't go riding into Mesilla on those horses. They're stolen and the stage company agent might not believe you had nothing to do with stealing them. They're all carrying Halliday brands, unless I miss my guess. Go west, right into the setting sun, and head for Shakespeare or Lordsburg. They'll recognize those horses as belonging to the Halliday Company, too, but those crooks over there don't pay much mind to such things if you mind your own business."

"They would hang us in Mesilla?"

Barker laughed harshly. It was a hanging offense in New Mexico Territory to rob a train. Stealing a horse was even worse.

"At the drop of a hat. I know." He fished out his badge and pinned it back into place on his vest. "You head on west now, and thanks for your help."

The six lit out like they had fires set under them.

Barker watched until they rode out of sight. He had no problem letting the six keep the stage company's horses. The Halliday agent in Mesilla was a son of a bitch and would have to be content with getting his passengers to the depot without any extra holes in their hides. Barker considered the trade worth it, even if the agent would argue the point. He knew where the outlaws hailed from and had a description that might fit any Mexican, but he might know more about their leader than he had before. All this was a start toward arresting them, however small a step it might be, if they poked their noses back into his territory.

And he reckoned they would. They had committed an easy robbery once. They would assume they could continue breaking the law. Until he caught them.

Frustrated, Mason Barker turned back and rode for Mesilla.

4

MASON BARKER DOZED IN THE SADDLE AS HE RODE.
For close to a month he had ridden the main road, waiting for the Mexican outlaws to show themselves again, and
he hadn't seen hide nor hair of them. It was too much to
believe they had skulked back to Sonora after robbing the
Halliday stage.

It took a bit of work to keep alive the thought of hunting
down the road agents, because he was so tired. The setting sun was like a muzzy cotton blanket swaddling him
in warmth that took him back to his childhood, when his
ma would tuck him between his two bigger siblings on a
cold Colorado night. The blanket always smelled sweet, of
sunlight and herbs and her. He jerked awake when his mare
suddenly reared, snorting in fear. The lawman grabbed
hard at the saddle horn to hang on even as he was search-
ing the parched ground for a sign of what had spooked his
horse. Rattlers came out this time of day, but so did other

predators. He had noticed the coyotes were especially bad this year, owing to the drought that had forced them down out of the mountains into regions where they could dine on the hardy, hearty rabbits and prairie dogs.

"Whoa, settle down. Good girl," Barker said, regaining control of his horse. He frowned when he didn't see what had caused the usually stolid mare to buck like that. Then he lifted his gaze to the horizon and caught sight of light reflecting off brass.

"Let's go see what the army's up to now," Barker said. His horse tried to crow-hop on him, but he persevered and finally got her moving in the direction of the soldiers.

At the head of the column, next to the guidon, rode a newly minted lieutenant, evidenced by the highly polished, unblemished gleam of his bars. Gold bars on a shavetail's shoulders. That usually meant trouble for someone, though even a lieutenant could learn if he lived long enough. Barker waved and then advanced when the officer ordered a halt in what he thought was a commanding tone. The officer was barely old enough so his voice didn't crack from adolescence. As he got closer, Barker saw that the lieutenant led a platoon of buffalo soldiers, Tenth Cavalry by their insignia. The men's sweaty black faces shone like mirrors in the setting sun, but none looked too happy about being in the field. Barker could agree with them on that, especially since they wore heavy wool uniforms in about the hottest summer he could remember.

Barker was glad he wasn't in the army any longer. His eighteen months of service had been hectic, dangerous, and ultimately useful since the Navajos had been removed from their land and put over near Fort Sumner at Bosque Redondo. Barker wasn't sure how he felt when he heard that General Sherman, that red-haired devil incarnate, had allowed them to return to Navajoland. He shrugged that off since it was yet another reason he was no longer in the army. Too many decisions were made back in Washington and not enough by the officers in the field having to deal daily with real problems. General Carleton had a vision for the territory lacking in politicians, and Colonel Carson was about the finest man Barker had ever met.

"Howdy," he called. "I'm Deputy Marshal Barker out of Mesilla."

"Federal?" asked the lieutenant, his tone curt. From his florid, sweaty face and the way he sat, as if someone had jammed a rod up his ass, it was clear the lieutenant was new to command and probably to the West. If he didn't ease up, he would fall out of the saddle, fainting dead away from heatstroke and probably doing it all at full attention. Barker doubted any of the buffalo soldiers would jump to the man's aid, either, not that he blamed them much. Might be they had bets on how long he could sit at attention before keeling over. Barker wasn't much of a betting man, but he would have laid a silver dollar that the lieutenant didn't last another day and maybe not even until noon tomorrow.

Barker looked past the lieutenant and saw a familiar soldier. Sergeant Willie Sturgeon was as soaked with sweat as his superior but had the look of a man able to ride another fifty miles before the sun returned.

"Sergeant, how're you doing?" Barker called. Sturgeon gave him a broad smile but said nothing. Barker turned back to the shavetail lieutenant and said, "Yep, I'm the federal deputy in these parts. I was out serving process. Folks are getting kinda nervy about watering holes because it's been so dry. Better to let them duke it out in court than to start a range war."

Barker fell silent, waiting for the lieutenant to respond with his mission, but the officer said nothing.

"You looking for anyone in particular, Lieutenant, or just riding patrol?" asked Barker, as much to find out as fill the verbal void. He took off his hat and felt a mite cooler as a soft breeze evaporated the rivers of sweat escaping the brim to run down his forehead. After wringing out his blue-and-white bandanna, he mopped at his brow and felt better for it.

"Rustlers," the laconic lieutenant said.

"I chased a gang of road agents a while back. Must have been more'n three weeks ago now. From all I can tell, they were from Mexico." Barker wasn't sure why he wanted to hold his own counsel about being on the trail of those road agents now. It might be he took it as a personal affront that they had robbed a stagecoach so close to Mesilla, or it could be that the lieutenant's attitude annoyed him and he wanted nothing more than to ride on without answering pointless questions.

"Sonora?" asked Sergeant Sturgeon. He was a powerful man but short. Barker wouldn't have known that from the way the sergeant appeared when mounted, but he had seen him on the ground and had towered over him.

"You think the rustlers and my Mexican highwaymen are one and the same? It happens. A gang like them moves in and takes a fancy to an area."

"We're chasing Apaches," the lieutenant said. "Not Mexicans."

"But you must have some reason for asking if the owl-hoots I'm after were from Sonora," Barker said. He ignored the officer and directed his words to Sturgeon. This would only reflect badly on the sergeant, but Barker wanted to round up the outlaws. His outlaws. If a white officer new to the frontier got his nose out of joint because he had to command a company of Negroes, there wasn't anything Barker was likely to do or say that would make matters worse for Sturgeon and the other enlisted men.

"Rumors, suh," Sturgeon said. "We was a day out of the fort—"

"Fort Selden." The lieutenant cut in, obviously irked at being left out of the conversation. "We found a butchered cow. A ranch hand claimed a half-dozen vaqueros had rustled and eaten it."

"Half dozen, eh?" mused Barker. "Might be the ones I'm hunting."

"This was two weeks ago," the lieutenant said.

"Sir," Barker said, sick of the officer's mulishness, "we're on the same side. You don't want this gang running roughshod through the territory any more than I want Apaches rustling cattle."

"I'm sorry, Marshal Barker." The lieutenant indicated that he wished to speak privately, so Barker allowed himself to be led a few yards off. "You seem a decent sort, Marshal."

"Not too many'd make that claim, but I try to be fair-minded."

"Yes, well, you might be about the only one in this godforsaken hellhole willing even to speak to my troopers."

"Because they're black?"

"Yes," the lieutenant said. "We are in serious need of decent food. We requisition meat, and it has maggots in it. The flour is so old it is more like ground chalk. Even the army's commanders back in Washington are less than enthusiastic about supplying Negro units with proper arms and ammunition."

"I've heard tell General Ord down in San Antonio isn't

much of a supporter of the buffalo soldier units," Barker said.

"He gets his orders from General Sheridan, though I suspect he is quite zealous about carrying them out. Neither Colonel Hatch, commanding the Tenth Cavalry, nor Colonel Grierson down at Fort Concho in charge of the Ninth is valued highly by their superiors."

Barker said nothing about the lieutenant's complaints. He could read between the lines what the man was saying. If a colonel with Ben Grierson's outstanding war record was shit upon by higher-ups, what did that mean to a lowly lieutenant with his first command?

"You allowed to purchase from civilian stores?" asked Barker.

"To some extent," the lieutenant said suspiciously.

"Unless you got real pressing business, why don't we all mosey on back to Mesilla? Your men can swill some of the rotgut at the town's saloons while you and me and Mr. Dooley at the general store see if he can do better supplying your post. It's a ways off to Fort Selden, but not that far. Considering his bent, I doubt Mr. Dooley would mind adding to his business."

Barker had another motive for bringing the business to Hugh Dooley. As good as his word, the merchant had hired Nate Barker and had kept him working hard for almost a month. If Barker could return the favor in the form of new business, it might repay Dooley. Even better, Dooley might put Nate in charge of military accounts and let him taste what it was like to be a real businessman.

"We are seldom welcomed with open arms, Marshal," said the lieutenant.

"Well, sir, you haven't been to Mesilla. It's a right friendly town and one where you can do business."

The lieutenant pursed his chapped lips, then rubbed them with his gloved hand as he thought.

"My men don't drink much. They don't have much chance, but as a company they have the lowest incidence of drunkenness in the Tenth Cavalry."

"Sergeant Sturgeon's a good noncom, but I wasn't suggesting that your men would get drunk and hurrah my town. Neither of us'd like that. But a taste of whiskey, just a taste, wouldn't hurt any man in uniform."

"My name's Lieutenant Greenberg." The officer thrust out his hand. Barker solemnly shook it, seeing that the man was slowly coming around to being a tad more human. He still straddled his horse like he had a rod up his ass, but that might be due to the uncomfortable McClellan saddle. Good for the horse, not so good for the rider.

"Let's ride for Mesilla, Lieutenant Greenberg."

The bugler needed a great deal more practice before he hit all the right notes, but he was as enthusiastic as the rest of the company that they were taking a furlough, however brief, in Mesilla. Barker and Greenberg rode along, getting to know each other better.

It was past nine o'clock when they rode down Mesilla's Calle de Guadalupe.

"We've got a fair number of saloons where your men can wet their whistles, Lieutenant," Barker said, "but my favorite's that one."

"The Plugged Nickel Saloon and Gambling Euphorium?" Greenberg chuckled as he read the sign aloud. Barker liked the man even more for understanding the unintentional double entendre in the name.

"Sturgeon can deal with the barkeep. You and I can talk turkey with Mr. Dooley." Barker saw the store owner on the boardwalk in front of his establishment, his sharp eyes counting the soldiers as they rode past. Barker could almost hear the money clinking on the counter and Dooley's poorly hidden gloating because of it.

"If you don't think there'll be any trouble," Lieutenant Greenberg said dubiously.

"As long as they don't pick a fight and keep to themselves, there's not likely to be any cause to worry," Barker said, anxious to get down to negotiating with Dooley. Bring the man business and obligate him to apprentice Nate as a purchasing assistant, so he could learn the business rather than just sweeping up and stocking the shelves—it was simple enough.

Greenberg dismissed Sturgeon and the rest of the company, all of whom went off with whoops of glee. Barker rode to the front of the general store and dismounted.

"You're up mighty late, Mr. Dooley. Waiting for me to bring you some business?"

"Hardly, Deputy," Dooley said in his acerbic way. "I'm not sure I want more army business. The quartermaster at Fort Bayard's slow to pay."

"Might be the one at Fort Selden is better. Why don't you and Lieutenant Greenberg discuss what he needs and how likely you are to get paid?"

"Talk's cheap," Dooley said.

"But it can't hurt," Barker reminded him. He saw that the merchant only wanted to be coaxed. In a few minutes, after the preliminary poking and prodding and feeling out was over, Greenberg and Dooley got down to serious discussion about the type of supplies, quality, quantity, and payment.

Barker enjoyed listening to the negotiating but was distracted by a ruckus down the street. He eased away, not wanting to bother the lieutenant, but the officer saw.

"My men," Greenberg said. He growled like a guard dog. "I should have known there'd be trouble."

"Why don't you stay here and let me take care of it, Lieutenant?" suggested Barker. He felt guilty about inviting the buffalo soldiers to town and then having the rowdier element in Mesilla make life miserable for them. "If you go, it's an army matter. If I do, it's just a local dustup."

"Very well," Greenberg said, displeased.

"Don't you go rooking him none, Mr. Dooley, while I'm gone," Barker said, trying to lighten the mood. It didn't work.

Barker hurried down the street to the crowd gathered in front of the Lost Dutchman Saloon. Two of the soiled doves from inside were egging on the more drunken patrons.

"What's the trouble, Sergeant?" Barker asked in a loud voice.

"Seems they don't cotton to our kind, suh," Willie Sturgeon said. He hardly came to Barker's chin, but the marshal would never have crossed the man. Sturgeon's biceps strained the cloth of his uniform and he barely had a neck, solid muscle going from just under the earlobes straight to his shoulders. Sturgeon radiated power—and more than a little anger.

"By 'your kind,' you mean soldiers?" Barker hitched up his gun belt and turned to face a man dressed in an expensive coat and brocade vest. He had spent more on his boots than Barker made in a year. "Anything wrong with their money, Mr. Delacroix?" he asked the saloon owner, who had one Cyprian on each arm. Barker saw that it was the whores who had sparked this, not the Frenchman who owned the saloon. But Delacroix knew he had to keep both his women and his patrons happy. The buffalo soldiers were interlopers in an otherwise ordered, disorderly house of ill repute.

"Wrong color, might be," grumbled a private who was almost as powerfully built as Sergeant Sturgeon.

"Well then, let's all go to another drinking establishment," Barker said, stepping between a drunk who came up fast, fist cocked, and the private. With a quick belly thrust, the marshal sent the drunk reeling before he could unload his punch. The storm cloud of anger on the marshal's face kept the man from recovering his balance and causing more trouble.

His arm around Sturgeon's shoulders, Barker walked the buffalo soldiers down to the Plugged Nickel.

"Let me go in and make sure Gus has enough liquor for such a thirsty bunch," Barker said. He hurried into the saloon, went to the bar, grabbed Gus Phillips by the front of his shirt, and pulled him halfway over the bar.

"Wh-what're you doin', Marshal?" croaked out the barkeep.

"Making sure my friends get a decent reception here. Seems others in town aren't as willing to roll out the welcome mat."

"Bring 'em in, Marshal," came a cheery voice. "Are they gambling men?"

Barker released Gus's shirt and saw the tinhorn gambler he had run out of town—or thought he had—standing in his starched white, ruffled shirt and looking like a million dollars. He riffled through a deck of cards as he spoke.

"What are you doing back in Mesilla?" Barker asked.

"I'm running the faro game for Mr. Phillips. Do these friends of yours need a bit of instruction in bucking the tiger?" The gambler flashed a feral grin. "I can open the table for penny ante until they feel comfortable with larger bets."

"Sergeant Sturgeon?" called Barker. "Any of your men want to try their luck at faro?"

"Might be one or two. Most of 'em's jist thirsty. Sarsaparilla's good as anything to them boys. We been on patrol for a long spell."

Barker glanced at Gus. The barkeep swallowed hard.

"He's an honest gambler, Marshal. I never seen him cheat."

"You never caught him at it," Barker said. That made for an honest gambler in most parts, but not in Mesilla. Not in his town.

"Never, but I got to get a new keg of beer if you want me to serve that many, uh, soldiers."

Barker noticed that several of the regular patrons slipped out when they saw the color of the troopers, but enough stayed. They might have remained just to see if blood would be shed. The marshal nodded and brought in the company of buffalo soldiers. They filled the place from wall to wall, and some even ordered more than the weak beer Gus served.

The Plugged Nickel would show a profit for the night, and tomorrow no one would remember that the customers were black. More likely, they'd remember the bad piano playing and how the gambler smelled all purty with his violet-scented toilet water and never seemed to lose as the cards flopped over, one after another, on his faro table.

Barker returned to the general store in time to see Greenberg and Dooley shaking hands.

He had to smile. Everything had gone real well this night. Dooley had a new account to supply, and the lieutenant could get decent food for his soldiers. The only thing more he could ask was to catch the gang of desperadoes from Sonora.

And maybe for Nate to get a promotion at the general store. Yes, all had gone well indeed.

5

IT NEVER GOT COOLER. MASON BARKER KEPT HIS face down as he rode toward town to keep the sun from burning his already leathery hide. Not even a hint of breeze cooled him, pulling the sweat off his skin to keep him from feeling as if he had been dunked into a rain barrel. Mesilla stirred in the early morning, working to get chores completed before it got really hot. He touched the brim of his hat in acknowledgment to many of the citizens but didn't stop to talk.

Not till he reached Hugh Dooley's store. The owner of the general store stood in the middle of the street, hands balled and resting on his narrow hips and shaking his head as he studied the window displays.

"Morning," Barker said, stopping a few yards away. "Not liking what you see?"

"Not a bit of it. A display has to reach out and pull in the curious. There's nothing there that draws the eye."

"And opens the pocketbook," Barker finished. He smiled. Dooley didn't. "You been reading 'bout selling merchandise from them merchants back East?"

"I have, Deputy." Dooley turned and scowled. "I should know that a man such as yourself would understand the importance of what is written."

Barker had no call to discuss books or his reading material.

"Might be a flash of color would call attention to your window. Red always makes me look." He didn't say why. Red meant blood, and blood meant somebody had been shot up.

"You might have something, Deputy. You just might. There's a bolt of cloth I haven't been able to sell since I bought it six months back. Using it lavishly, like it was a colored waterfall, would give a flair to the window. Yes, sir, a flair."

"Might be you can put what will actually sell on the cloth, making it stand out all the more."

"You've missed your calling, Deputy."

"Not looking for a job," Barker said hastily.

"Neither is that boy of yours," Dooley said, dashing Barker's hope of building some sort of bridge to the distant store owner. All the work he'd just done talking him up evaporated like snow in this miserable heat.

"You saying that Nate's not working?"

"Not working out," Dooley said, scowling. "He shows up and does what I tell him, but he gripes the entire while. He's driven off more than one customer with his grousing about how hard he's working."

"Not much other place a customer can go," Barker said, immediately regretting the words when he saw the storm cloud that descended over Dooley.

"I pride myself on providing good merchandise at a fair price. I never insult a customer or do anything that would chase one off. Doña Ana isn't much of a town, but they have a general store and it's only four miles away. And Las Cruces? Not much of a store at all there, but they're competitors. A few dollars spent there won't be spent in my establishment."

"You working out supply with that lieutenant?"

"Lieutenant Greenberg is a clever young man, a shrewd Yankee merchant, unless I miss my guess. How he ended up in the army is quite the head-scratcher."

"So he rooked you?" Barker couldn't help but smile. And this time so did Dooley. He had finally cracked the man's dour exterior again with a little joshing.

"He thinks he has. He gets better beef and hardtack and I get twice what you'd pay if you waltzed into my store for the same product." Dooley pursed his lips. "That's assuming you'd ever come into the store, Marshal, since I'd want you to pay on your bill."

"I'll have a talk with Nate about his attitude." He didn't add that it wouldn't be the first time, and he doubted this time would be different. He touched the brim of his hat and rode on to the small marshal's office near the Catholic church just off the plaza.

As he dismounted, he tried to think of business—law business—but couldn't. Nate continued to worry at him like a pebble in his boot. Every time he took a step, he was reminded that something was wrong. The difference with the pebble was being able to locate it

Inside the dim, cool adobe jailhouse, he settled down into his chair and swiped at the dust to clear a spot for his paperwork. It took the better part of an hour to go over the new stack of wanted posters and the letters from Marshal Armijo, his boss. The federal dictum had come down to find the gang of desperadoes from Sonora. The wanted poster, lacking any likeness of any of the gang, sported a fifty-dollar reward. Barker sighed as he thought of how much good that money would do him. Ruth could pay off all their bills and still have plenty left. Maybe he could take her up to one of those fancy spas at Manitou Springs outside Colorado Springs. It would do her spirit a world of good to soak in the mineral baths and partake of the cool, crisp air at the base of Pikes Peak.

Barker heaved a sigh, remembering the one time his pa had taken them there. His ma had been feeling poorly and the sulfur water at Navajo Springs Resort had been just the thing to get her feeling spritely again. Barker ran his finger over the creased wanted poster, knowing that fifty dollars was hardly enough for such a magnificent vacation. Just getting north to Manitou Springs would eat away most of that reward.

Now, if the gang continued to kick up a fuss and the reward was raised . . .

Barker slammed his fist down on the desk, sending paper dancing in all directions. He was a lawman, not a bounty hunter. He shouldn't be wanting the road agents to ply their trade more so their value as prisoners would go up. Settling back in his rickety chair, he knew he should have stopped them after the first stagecoach robbery.

From everything he'd heard all around Mesilla, and from an army scout who had ducked into the Plugged Nickel the night before, the gang was getting nervier. More than rustling and robbery drove them. Barker had seen their like before. Mean, vicious men. It wouldn't be long until they began killing the men they robbed.

The door creaked open. Barker looked up to see a dusty

ranch hand standing hesitantly there, outlined by the brilliant sunlight, with his face hidden in shadow.

"Come on in and close the door. You're lettin' in too much heat."

"Marshal Barker?"

"That's me." He pointed to the solitary chair on the other side of the desk. Too seldom he had visitors. Gus Phillips used to stop by to play a hand or two of gin rummy, but for whatever reason the visits had become fewer, and now Barker couldn't remember the last time he had lost a stack of pennies to the barkeep.

"I work on the Triple B, out to the east."

"Fetched up along the Organ Mountains," Barker said. "I know your boss. How's Mr. Garrison doing these days?"

"Not so good since he lost the missus." The cowboy saw Barker's surprise. "Happened a couple weeks back. She took sick and passed in just a day."

"Sorry to hear that. She was a gracious, lovely lady." The words came easily enough, but truth was, he thought she was a harridan and had been well on her way to worrying Dave Garrison into an early grave. Not that the man was necessarily better off without his wife. Barker had long since stopped trying to figure out why people stayed together—or didn't.

"Well, Marshal, Mr. Garrison, he wanted to complain 'bout some of them buffalo soldiers stealin' his cattle. They rustled two head, and he's concerned they'll come on back for more."

Barker frowned, then chewed a mite at his lower lip. Finally, he said, "Did your boss see them doing the rustling?"

"No, sir, he saw them ridin' away, but two beeves had been all butchered up. They didn't even do a good job at it."

"I've talked some with Lieutenant Greenberg from up

at Fort Selden, and he's got his hands full chasin' rustlers all over the landscape. Said some Mescaleros went off the reservation."

"Ain't seen nothin' of no Injuns. My boss, he'd have for certain sure told me to tell you if he had."

"There's a new gang, up from Mexico, trying to make a name for themselves. They've robbed a stage or two, and the lieutenant is sure they've been doing some rustling. Might have been them instead of Indians." Barker pushed the wanted poster around so the cowboy could read it. He saw right away that the man couldn't read, so he hastily added, "You take this here wanted poster to Mr. Garrison and show it to him. Says there how these banditos are wanted and how the federal marshal's put out a fifty-dollar reward for their capture."

"That's more'n I make in three months," the cowboy said, awed at the amount.

"More'n I'm likely to see, too," Barker allowed.

"But you're the deputy marshal," the cowboy protested.

"I'm stuck here in Mesilla and the buffalo soldiers are out after the rustlers. That's the difference," he assured the cowboy. "I don't think they killed your cows. I think they came across this here gang's theft and got on the trail right away. You tell Mr. Garrison that."

"All right," the cowboy said reluctantly.

"Take this wanted poster. It'll confirm everything you just heard me say."

"Thanks, Marshal." The cowboy coughed and then coughed again, looking almost shyly at Barker.

"Why don't you get yourself a beer to cut the trail dust? That sounds like a nasty cough you've got. Mr. Garrison couldn't say anything about a man taking care of his health."

"You got a way with words, Marshal." The cowboy tucked the wanted poster into the front of his shirt and left.

Barker was sorry to see him go. It got suddenly lonely in the tiny office. He shuffled through the papers on his desk awhile longer, opened the drawer, eyed his lovely book on the wonders of Italy, then slowly closed the drawer and levered himself to his feet. His back felt mighty good today. It must have been the board he put under his side of the mattress. Ruth had complained, but his being able to get out of bed in the morning without a lot of groaning and moaning had quelled her protests.

The sun hadn't gotten any cooler, but then it was hardly an hour since he had gone into his office. It still lacked four or five hours until noon, and then the heat would fry the pimples off a horse's ass until the sun sank behind the mountains to the far west. He knew he ought to make a few social calls on the townspeople, to hear their complaints and maybe share a glass of lemonade or something stronger, depending on who he spoke with, but instead he headed for the general store.

A smile crept to his lips when he saw Nate aggressively pursuing the dust that always piled up on a boardwalk. His broom lacked enough bristles to do a proper job, but the boy didn't seem to notice.

As Barker got closer, though, he understood why Nate wasn't bothered by the puny broom. He was too busy swearing under his breath.

"Not good cussing up a blue streak when customers might hear you," Barker said.

"You're no customer."

"Your ma and me buy from Mr. Dooley."

"Don't do much in the way of payin'. I seen the books."

"He said you're insulting the customers with your attitude."

Nate threw down the broom and squared off, as if he was going to throw down on his pa. There wasn't a six-shooter hanging at his side—and Barker hoped there never would be. With Nate's temper, he wouldn't last very long, even in a peaceable town like Mesilla, if he called out the wrong man. Why, even Dutch Hubert had come through here. There was no telling what other desperadoes might be sucking up suds or downing a shot of whiskey in any of the town's bars.

"You don't have no call to tell me to do anything. For two cents and this—" Nate spat on the boardwalk between them, "I'd quit. No, wait, that's not so. Keep your damned two cents!"

"It's not easy being responsible," Barker said, fighting to keep his temper in check. "You've done good at the work. It's just that Mr. Dooley wants you to be civil to the customers so you don't drive them off."

Nate looked as if he would spit again, then settled down.

"Not like I got better things to do," he said sullenly.

"I wanted to know if the army supplies are getting out all right."

"You workin' for them—" Nate bit off his comment, then shrugged. "Looks as if they're gettin' what they're payin' for. Dooley don't let me handle such exalted chores as that."

"Good. It's not as if I brokered the deal, but I want the lieutenant and Mr. Dooley to both think they've come out ahead."

"I ought to take a break. Dooley said I could come back at ten o'clock," Nate said.

"We can go to the café and . . ." Barker's words trailed

off when he saw Nate pull an ornate watch from his pocket and open the gleaming gold case. His son peered at the face, then snapped it shut.

"That watch have a date etched inside the case? August 20, 1861?"

"How'd you know?"

"Where'd you get it?"

"I don't have to tell you. You always treat me like this."

"Where?" Barker said, a steel edge to his words now. "That watch was stolen from a stagecoach passenger. He described it to a fare-thee-well—that's the date he got married."

"It's my watch."

"You never had one before. You couldn't afford one that gaudy, either."

"I . . . I paid for it. A vaquero. I . . . I bought it off a vaquero for a . . . for fifty cents."

"You had to know that watch is worth more'n four bits."

"He had another, said he wanted to get rid of it. He . . . he'd won it in a poker game. He said."

"Let me look at it." Barker took it from his reluctant son, ran his calloused fingers over the case, and then popped it open to see the date, just as the man had described.

"Where's this vaquero now?"

"I don't know."

"When did you buy it?"

"Last night . . . this morning. Over at the Plugged Nickel. On the way to work I stopped and—"

"Never mind," Barker said, knowing he would get angry about the wrong thing if his son told him he was drinking before showing up for work. "Did Gus see this vaquero?"

"Don't know."

Barker had turned to go to the saloon, when Nate called out, "You keepin' the watch? That's stealin'!"

"It's stealing, sure as God made little green apples," Barker said. "And I intend to find who's responsible." Thought of the fifty-dollar reward fluttered through his mind, but even better was the chance to stop the Mexican gang before they got into serious trouble beyond stage-coach robbing and a little bit of rustling. "What's he look like, this vaquero?"

Nate hesitated, then said, "Not too tall, stocky. He wore a big sombrero with gold thread."

"That describes most vaqueros that come through here," Barker said.

"He had a . . . something wrong with his eyes. They were crossed."

Barker looked at his son, then nodded. This was as good a description as he was likely to get.

"Anything else?"

Nate shook his head, then bent and picked up the broom to continue moving dust from one side of the boardwalk to the other.

Barker reached down and made sure his six-shooter rode easy in the holster at his side. Only then did he head for the Plugged Nickel. He stopped in the doorway, squinted hard to let his eyes adjust to the dimmer light inside, then stepped through. Gus Phillips waved to him.

"Howdy, Marshal. You're in mighty early. What can I get for you?"

"You see a Mexican here this morning? He'd have been talking to my boy."

"Nate?" Gus looked around like a rat in a corner hunting for a way out.

"None other. You see him and a vaquero this morning?"

"Reckon I might have."

"Did the vaquero sell this to Nate?" Barker held up the

watch. Judging from Gus's lack of comprehension, there wasn't going to be any kind of corroboration coming.

"Don't know, but I did see the pair of them together like they was old buddies. Nate, he didn't, well, he didn't have nothin' to drink. Honest."

"Don't care about that. You see where the vaquero went when he left?"

"Didn't ride off, if that's what you mean. Didn't see a horse nowhere near."

"Thanks," Barker said. He turned, then stopped. "It's all right, Gus. You're not in trouble. Neither is Nate."

"But that Mexican?"

"That remains to be seen," the marshal said.

He stepped outside and looked around for a horse outfitted in the Mexican style. Down the street he saw an unfamiliar horse standing in the shade beside the Lucky Lew Saloon. Again he checked his pistol, then went directly to the other saloon. The Lucky Lew changed hands about once a month, or so it seemed. For whatever reason, the owner always ran into a stretch of bad luck. The last two owners had been murdered, and another the year before had been shot up so bad he had retired. The last Barker had heard of him, he was in El Paso working as a telegrapher with his one good hand.

He circled the building, hunting for any back way the vaquero might find to escape. The back door stood half-open to get some air circulating through the long, narrow saloon. Barker went in through it, moving quietly down the hallway, past the storage rooms and to the back of the room, near a billiards table sadly needing new felt. It looked as if the table had the mange, with large green patches falling out.

The piano leaned against the far wall. Somebody had

ripped away half the keyboard, and Barker thought the dark spots on the remaining keys might be blood. But he moved quickly to a spot where, reflected in the filthy mirror hanging behind the barkeep, he could see the vaquero standing at the bar.

The barkeep looked up and started to ask if Barker wanted anything, then clamped his mouth shut when he saw the lawman wasn't there to drink. He licked his lips, then ducked down behind the bar.

The unexpected action caused the Mexican to stand on tiptoe and look behind the bar.

"Where do you go?" The Mexican's gravelly voice trailed off when he looked up and saw Barker in the mirror.

"Don't reach for your iron," the marshal said. "You won't make it."

"I pay for my drink," the vaquero said, pressing his finger down on a silver ten-peso piece. He slid it along so that it screeched as it cut a groove in the wood. Barker wasn't distracted.

"You robbed the stagecoach a month back," Barker said.

"I have only just come to this town. I don't know of this robbery."

"Freeze," Barker said, drawing his six-shooter.

"I do not draw my gun. I only scratch my ass."

"Pull the six-gun with your left hand and leave it on the bar. We're going for a little walk."

"Where?"

"I got somebody who wants to see you."

"I know this man," the vaquero said, pointing up and over the bar to the cowering barkeep. "There is no one else in Mesilla I know."

"We'll see about that," Barker said. He watched the

Mexican leave his six-gun on the bar, then adjust the broad-brimmed sombrero before stepping out into the sun.

"It is a lovely day, no? The sun she shines and the wind is enough to make it cooler."

"To your right. March," Barker said. He stayed several paces behind the vaquero, alert for any trouble. Early on in his career he had learned never to poke a gun into a man's spine. The six-shooter's superiority came from distance, not too far but certainly not close up. He had seen more than one fight in a bar where one gunman had shoved a muzzle into another's belly and fired, more often than not setting the victim's clothes on fire from the flash rather than the bullet doing serious damage.

"We go to the general store?" The Mexican sounded uneasy. "I do not want to buy anything. I have what I need."

"Nate!" Barker bellowed again. His son came out, still holding the broom.

"What do you—" Nate stopped dead in his tracks.

"This the man who sold you the watch?"

"No, I never seen him before."

"You want to show me more of this town, Marshal?" The vaquero looked over his shoulder, a sneer curling his lip.

"You positive, Nate? He was drinkin' down the street at the Lucky Lew."

"He's not the Mexican."

"Reckon I owe you an apology," Barker said, but he didn't put his six-gun back into his holster. Not yet. He waited for the Mexican to turn and face him.

For a moment Nate stared at the vaquero, then spun and disappeared into the store. Only then did the Mexican turn to Barker.

"You have made a bad mistake, Marshal, but I am a forgiving man. I will forgive you."

"Mighty kind of you. What's your name?"

"Why do you ask?" Again the Mexican turned bristly.

"Being polite, nothing more," Barker said. "It's always nice to say a man's name when you're eating crow."

"You should know this," the vaquero said. His eyes were cold, and the sneer returned to his lips. Then he laughed and walked away, returning to the saloon. Barker watched him go, then stared hard at the empty doorway leading into the general store. A cold knot formed in his gut, and he didn't like it one little bit.

6

"MIGHTY GOOD MEAL, RUTH," BARKER SAID. HE
pushed back from the dinner table and rested his hand on
his bulging belly. Once more he had eaten too much, but that
apple pandowdy had hit the spot. He turned a little, and the
momentary pleasure of a good meal followed by even better
dessert disappeared in a twinge that started in his lower back
and radiated upward. There hadn't been anything but water
to drink with the meal. Right about now some medicinal
whiskey would work wonders in returning the sated feeling.

Ruth took the plate from in front of him and scowled.

"You almost licked a hole in the plate. You'd think I
didn't feed you."

"Seems that I spend too much time eating beans and
canned peaches," he said, closing his eyes and drifting for
a moment. The pain receded, and he felt comfortable again.

"All that riding around ought to stop when you get to be
chief deputy," she said.

"You heard something I haven't?" Barker opened his eyes and watched Ruth put the plate into the sink. He'd have to fetch water for her soon enough, but right now sitting motionless suited him.

"The mayor must think you're not going to be around as much," she said.

Barker sighed, then asked, "Has Pendleton finally hired a town marshal?"

"You sound peeved," Ruth said. She faced him and put her hands on her hips. "Why's that, Mase? Mesilla doesn't pay you a penny for your work. Let them hire a marshal so you can spend more time at home."

"It wouldn't work like that," he said. "The mayor doesn't cotton much to me being in town. He's said so often enough. That means he'll throw me out of the office at the jailhouse."

"But this means less work for you."

Barker knew she was right. He got nothing but heartache and headache from keeping the peace in town, and he certainly received no pay. But it was *his* town, and Jacob Pendleton resented the way he tried to mother hen everyone there, thinking it robbed him of influence. For all Barker knew, that was true. It was a matter of some pride for him that the citizens of Mesilla thought more highly of him than they did their mayor.

"I could always ask to take on that job, too. Double salaries would go a long way toward making life easier for you."

"The mayor's already hired someone, or so Miz Warner said."

"She ought to know. She knows everything that goes on in town."

"Now, Mase, you hush up about her. She likes to talk,

but she listens good. Never once has she been wrong on these things."

"It's still gossip, even if it proves true," he said. But his wife was right. Kimberly Warner was a stalwart at the church, and her cobbler was almost—almost!—as good as his Ruth's. She had a way of knowing things before others did and was always the center of attention at the church socials. Barker wished he had a conduit of information as accurate as Miz Warner when it came to the road agents from Sonora.

"Something's bothering you," Ruth said, staring hard at him. "It's not losing a job you don't get paid for."

"Might be I do mind losing it. I can cadge free drinks from all the saloon owners."

"You don't do that," she said, but he saw the hint of uncertainty. She must have smelled some of his medicinally used whiskey on his breath when he'd come home after a particularly hard day in the saddle. About now, he wanted a taste, but it wasn't going to happen, because it would displease her.

He heaved himself to his feet and went to pump water to wash the dishes.

Ruth said nothing until he poured the water into the sink.

"You're worried about Nate, aren't you?"

Barker said nothing for a spell, thinking hard about how to answer. He didn't want to say a word but had to since Ruth wasn't going to let it go.

"I am. He doesn't seem to be working out all that well at the store."

"Mr. Dooley said he didn't know where Nate was when I went in to buy some coffee today."

"I didn't know you'd gone into town," Barker said.

"You don't know everything that goes on in Mesilla," she said.

"That's for certain sure." He heaved a deep sigh. "Why didn't Dooley say something to me? Why to you?"

"I asked." Ruth came up behind him and put her arms around him, pressing her cheek into his broad back. Somehow, the warmth of her body so close to his eased the pain, both in his back and in his soul.

"What's gone wrong? Nate's attitude? I warned him about that."

"He hasn't been home in four days."

This startled him. He had ridden out to serve process the day before, but that meant Nate hadn't been at work for two days prior.

"Not at all?"

"No," Ruth said in a soft voice. "I don't know where he's been, but he's not sleeping in his room."

"He knew that vaquero," Barker said suddenly.

"Who?"

"Nothing, just something that came up last week."

"He's doing something wrong, isn't he? I heard Miz Warner whispering to that nasty old harridan Claire Dupree, and it was about Nate and him stealing."

"From Dooley?"

"I didn't catch that part, and she pretended to be talking about someone else when I got closer. But I read it in her eyes. She was talking about our Nate."

"Our Nate," he said, more to himself than to his wife. Nate hadn't been his—or Ruth's—for years, and he wasn't quite certain when they had lost their only surviving son. It might have been his brother's death that had caused the gulf to grow. Mason hadn't meant to treat Nate any different when Patrick died, but he was only human. The younger boy's death had hit him hard, especially so because he looked so much like his pa and shared so many of Mason's interests. Patrick would have loved the book on Italy that now rested on the bedside table instead of in the top drawer in the marshal's office.

Nate looked more like Ruth's pa than anyone else in the family, and Barker denied that it went farther than that. Ruth's pa had been a rounder, always skirting the edge of danger, smart enough to avoid jail but too drunk and arrogant not to get himself into situations that would get him into trouble.

He hoped Nate wasn't taking after his grandpa. Ruth's pa had been found drowned in an irrigation ditch after going on a weeklong bender a couple months before Nate was born.

"I'll track him down," Barker promised.

Ruth clutched harder at him. He felt her shaking her head.

"Don't. He'd resent you for that."

"Can't resent me more'n he does already."

"He's old enough to make his own way in the world. If he has to take care of himself, well, that's part of growing up."

Memory of how Nate had flipped open the stolen watch haunted Barker. Nate might have bought the watch from the Mexican as he had claimed—they knew each other, Barker was certain, and Nate had lied about it—but Barker worried there was more to it. As much as he tried to deny that Nate could have been one of the outlaws that held up the stage, it was a possibility that haunted him.

But had the vaquero been his partner on the robbery? Why would Nate give such a good description and then deny it? Barker couldn't deny that the vaquero had been a rough customer and that he might have cowed Nate, but there hadn't been that kind of fear on his son's face. When Mason had come up with the Mexican, Nate's expression had been something different.

Like he'd been caught in a lie rather than like he feared the vaquero.

Barker tried to decide what had gone on, but he couldn't. There was a chance that Nate was telling the truth, and only a suspicious deputy marshal misreading his own son's expression was at the center of the furor.

"Wash the plates," Ruth said. "I've got chores to do before it gets much darker."

"Nate ought to be doing them," Barker said, feeling guilty about that and his own inability to do everything he should to help. If he did too much too fast, his back could lay him up in bed for a week. He couldn't let that happen, especially with Mayor Pendleton taking away the city marshal duties and giving them to someone else. If the federal marshal caught wind that Barker was free of those duties, he might send him even farther afield on other business.

Barker knew how Marshal Armijo thought, and in a way, he didn't blame him. It was only through the federal lawman's good graces that Barker had been allowed to patrol Mesilla as much as he had. Las Cruces was an up-and-coming town and needed a strong hand, too. Then there were the towns to the west. Barker shuddered at the idea of having to corral the rowdies in Shakespeare. Even the law-abiding citizens there were more than a handful. The stage driver from Shakespeare had sent for him to keep the peace when passengers bound for Tombstone threatened mayhem after entering the depot for a meal and finding a man hanged inside.

Barker had sorted it all out. The locals had thought it

was great fun watching the passengers' reactions at seeing the body swinging to and fro. Their coming from the bright sun outside had been part of it. The passengers' vision had adjusted to the dim room only slowly, but when it did, they were quick to realize they shared the room with an executed horse thief.

After a lot of smoothing of ruffled feathers, Barker herded the passengers back onto the stage. He had dressed down the citizens of Shakespeare responsible for what they called a prank, but entertainment was hard to come by out in the desert. He didn't doubt that they would find other grisly ways to amuse themselves. Barker hoped he was on the other side of New Mexico when they did.

A full-time town marshal patrolling Mesilla meant Barker would be in the saddle more on federal business and away from home as a result, leaving Ruth to do more of the chores.

He washed the dinner dishes with increasing vigor as his ire rose. Life was going against him and Ruth, and he couldn't help but blame Nate for some of it. The boy . . .

Barker turned when the door swung open.

"Nate!"

His son grunted and started toward his room.

"Hold it, son," Barker said, fighting to keep down the anger he had been working up as he cleaned the dishes. "Where have you been?"

"Why do you care?"

"You had your ma and me worried. She said you haven't been at work for the past couple days."

"Yeah, *she* said. You never noticed, did you?"

"I got other concerns, in case *you* didn't notice."

"No, reckon I didn't." Nate stomped toward his door. Barker stepped back and grabbed his son, spinning him around. They stood, faces inches apart, and glared at each other.

"Why'd you walk away from the job?"

"Job? Sweeping up? That's not a job. Old man Dooley doesn't pay squat. You made me go to work there as punishment."

"Punishment?" This took Barker aback. "What are you saying? I want you to make something of yourself."

"Pushing a broom around while the wind's blowing?"

"What you're doing is learning to—"

"To hate you and Dooley and everything about this stinking town!" Nate shoved him back and went into his room. The door slammed, but Barker wasn't having any of it. He kicked the door open and fought to keep from getting angrier than he was.

"You keep a civil tongue in your mouth," he said. "I don't give two hoots and a holler if you work for Mr. Dooley, but you will get a job and you will pay rent on that bed. If you stay here, you'll help your ma with the chores, too."

Nate started to speak his mind, then saw his father's clenched fists. He fell into a sullen silence and only nodded.

"Get outside and help your ma. Now!"

Barker stepped back as his son pressed past him and went outside. He hoped he had done the right thing having it out like this. The boy was as wild as the spring wind and needed to get his life directed on a better path. Work wouldn't hurt him none. It would build his character.

He went back to cleaning the dinner dishes, wondering if Ruth would find something to give Nate to eat later. Probably. And that'd be all right. Barker wanted his son to know this was his home, no matter what.

Nate packed his gear and left that night.

7

"YOU OUGHT TO WELCOME THE CHANGE, MASON,"
the mayor said. "This'll give you more time to be with the
wife. You're always sayin' how you want to do that."

"Mostly just to hear myself talk," Barker said, looking
past Mayor Pendleton down Calle de Guadalupe. He only
half listened to what the politician said because something
seemed wrong to him. He couldn't put a finger on it, but
over the years he had developed this sense that warned
of things going wrong. If he had developed the opposite
sense—of things going right—he might have been better
off, but what he had kept him alive. More than once he had
chosen not to ride into a canyon, only to find later that an
Apache ambush would have been his fate. More recently
he had gone after a gunman who had shot down a preacher
on the Sabbath, in front of his entire congregation. Barker
had tracked the killer to a patch of rugged country leading
into the Chupadera up north.

He had drawn rein, studied the rugged, lava-rock land-scape, and then ridden to Socorro to tell the marshal of his hunt. He found out that the gunman's gang had turned on their leader and killed him. If Barker had ridden into the dangerous land alone, he would have found only a dead body—and with the gang so incensed about what their former leader had done, they would probably have added him to the bone pile.

"You, Mason, you don't talk to hear yourself speak. Why, you're the most closemouthed man I've seen in years."

"Not like you, Mayor, but then you're a politician and get paid to talk."

"I never looked at it that way, but you're so right. Why—"

"Excuse me, Mayor. Let me know when you have the new town marshal hired and ready to make his rounds. I'll be glad to introduce him around, if he's not from these parts." Barker left the mayor trying to thank him and be outraged that he was walking off without being properly dismissed and maybe a half dozen other confusing things all at the same time.

Cutting away from the mayor, Barker crossed the street and lost himself in the deep afternoon shadows cast by the roof over the boardwalk. He walked carefully so the planks wouldn't creak overmuch and his heels wouldn't click. When he reached the window of Mr. Dooley's general store, he peered in. The owner had taken his suggestion about displaying the silk he couldn't sell and using it as part of a display promoting other products. The harsh New Mexico sun had already faded the silk to a bit pinkish from its original crimson, but Barker looked past it to the vaquero inside.

The Mexican stood, feet planted wide and hands gripping the lapels of his fancy embroidered jacket. His sombrero dangled on his back, hanging from a string around his neck. Dooley's face was turned from Barker, but judging from the set of his shoulders, the owner wasn't liking what the vaquero said to him.

Barker slid the leather thong off the hammer of his Colt, took a deep breath, then walked into the store all natural-like. Inside he was twisted up as tight as a hog-tied calf and twice as nervous. The instant he entered the doorway, the vaquero spun, hand going for the massive pistol slung at his right hip.

"Ah, the town jefe."

"Afternoon," Barker said, his cold eyes meeting those of the vaquero. He had the feeling that whoever looked away first lost, and he was determined it wasn't going to be him. But exactly what would be gained wasn't obvious.

The vaquero slid his fingers back along the lapels of his fancy-ass jacket and half turned back to Dooley.

"I would buy one, if you have it."

Dooley looked at Barker, then nodded curtly. He bent and brought up a tray of pocket watches.

"I would buy *un reloj* to replace the one you took from my good friend, *su hijo*."

"Nate said he didn't know you. So you two are friends now?"

"Oh, *sí, amigos*," the Mexican said. "Our chance meeting has given us the chance to become great friends." He bent to examine the watches. "The best one, the finest for my new best friend."

"How'd you come to be such good friends?" Barker asked, still wary of the way the vaquero stood. If he had a hideout pistol tucked away in an interior pocket, he could get off a shot or two before Barker cleared leather. He wasn't the fastest draw in town and never tried to be, but he was a good shot. An accurate one, given the time to take it.

"This one." A stubby finger stabbed down onto a large watch.

"That there's a hundred-dollar watch," Dooley said. "Don't think you'd—"

"*Solo un cien?* Only a hundred?" The vaquero pulled out a roll of greenbacks and began peeling off tens and twenties. When he got to one hundred, he contemptuously threw another ten onto the stack, adding, "For gift wrapping. You can do this?"

Dooley licked his lips, then said, "What color ribbon you want?"

The vaquero laughed and turned back to Barker.

"You will take the wrapped present and give it to Nate?"

"Why not give it to him yourself?"

The vaquero shrugged.

"My business takes me out of town often. I would have him know the time, since you stole the other watch."

"I returned it to the stage agent so he could give it to the passenger in the robbery." Barker sometimes wondered about the honesty of the Halliday agent in Mesilla, but this time he thought the stolen property would be returned, if for no reason other than it was so distinctive. If the agent flashed that watch around town, he'd be noticed. Besides, although Barker didn't know for certain, he thought a reward might have been offered for the watch's return. The lure of a few dollars would be far greater than knowing what time it was, even using an expensive watch. That little soiled dove that the agent was sweet on would also profit more from a few dollars than getting to look at an open watch case.

"I am sure he was grateful," the vaquero said, with more

than a hint that Barker had kept the watch for himself. "See that Nate gets my generous gift."

"You leaving Mesilla?" Barker asked.

"My business takes me away from here."

"Where?"

"Away." The Mexican slid his fingers down his lapels to get his right hand closer to his six-shooter.

"*Bien viaje*," Barker said.

The vaquero laughed and pushed past the marshal, going into the hot afternoon. The sunlight glinted off the gold and silver chasing on his large sombrero, but the reflection from the embroidered jacket was dazzling, forcing Barker to squint. And then the glare disappeared. The vaquero had hastily moved on.

"What do you make of that, Deputy?" Dooley counted the scrip repeatedly, as if it might disappear if he stopped fingering the bills.

"I reckon you'd better wrap up the watch like your customer said."

"You take it to give to your boy?"

"Keep it here. He might be back to work, if there's a job still open for him."

Dooley hesitated, then his resolve hardened.

"The job's not his. I can't keep workers here I can't depend on. He either shows up and gets paid or he doesn't."

"How much was his last pay?"

"Eighty cents. Still got it here." Dooley fumbled around under the counter and pulled out a small envelope. "You take it to him?"

Barker hesitated. Eighty cents wasn't much, but he couldn't understand why Nate hadn't claimed it. If the boy had gone to drinking, that'd buy him eight shots of whiskey or enough cheap beer to get drunk on.

"Keep it with the watch," he decided. Without another word, he stepped out into the furnace-like air, in time to see the vaquero riding fast out of town. As he bobbed about on his horse, he flashed like a beacon in the bright sun. His sombrero hid his face, but the silver conchas would stand out for miles.

Tracking him would be easy, at least until sundown.

"Marshal Barker, Mason, where are you going?"

Barker turned to Mayor Pendleton, who hurried up fluttering a folded piece of paper as a fan.

"Got business. Law business, might be," he answered.

"Here. I wanted you to see this. What do you think?" Pendleton thrust out the paper, still damp from his sweaty hand.

Barker unfolded it and frowned.

"Looks like a wanted poster, but it says this here's your new marshal."

"I wanted folks in town to know what he looked like 'fore he arrived. He's coming in from over Fort Worth way in a day or two."

"Ed Dravecky," Barker said, letting the name roll around in his mouth. He didn't want to spit, so he figured the new marshal must be all right.

"That's him. He's got a good reputation from working as a deputy for close to a year in Hell's Half Acre."

" 'Fore that?"

"Well, all he'd say was that he worked on a ranch in Indian Territory."

"Doin' what?"

The mayor just shook his head.

"I wouldn't worry about that, Mayor, not if you know he's done a good job this past year in Fort Worth. Those are tough customers there, and if he kept them in line, Mesilla is going to be a Sunday social for him." Barker looked once more at the smeary likeness of the man who was replacing him. "Ed Dravecky. How about that?" He handed the sheet back to the mayor. "You want some advice?"

"Why, yes, of course, Mase. You know I respect you."

"Don't put these up around town. Some of the boys'll use them as targets and might not know the difference when Marshal Dravecky gets to town."

"How should I introduce him?"

"Church on Sunday's a way. He can hit all three of 'em here in Mesilla without any problem. That's what I did when Marshal Armijo assigned me the whole southern part of the territory. Took me a while longer to make the rounds to the rest in my territory, but it worked. I got to know the law-abiding folks 'fore I did the rowdies."

"And they got to know you. Yes, that's a good idea, Mase. You always were a thinker."

That might have been true, but Barker's thoughts were about a mile down the road, following the vaquero who refused to give a name. Anybody flashing such a big wad of greenbacks and mouthing off the way he had was up to no good. Memory of the stagecoach robbery returned to haunt Barker, as well as the army's reports of cattle rustlers. They might think it was Apaches off the reservation responsible—and Barker knew that was a possibility—but he had a gut feeling that the road agents and the rustlers were one and the same.

Ladrónes from down in Sonora.

It took him the better part of an hour to lay in supplies for what might be a long scout, then mount and start from town. He passed by Dooley's store and felt a pang of regret about Nate. If Nate still worked there, he could have told his son to let his ma know there'd be only the two of them for dinner. As it was, Ruth would have to make do on her own. She was a strong woman, but she didn't deserve such a life.

As he left Mesilla behind, Barker wondered if he ought to have argued with Pendleton over the town marshal's job. It probably didn't pay as well as being a deputy federal marshal, but he wouldn't be hitting the trail to follow a will-o'-the-wisp all the time. If he had to justify this trip to Armijo—or to Ruth—he wasn't sure that he could. An arrogant caballero was hardly reason to traipse across southern New Mexico, and yet that was what he was doing.

He rode a little faster. The sun almost blinded him, turning him wary. If the vaquero decided to sit beside the road and wait for anyone trailing him, he would have an easy target. The more Barker thought on it, though, the more he decided that his quarry was in a powerful hurry to get somewhere and probably had too little respect for either him or any lawman to tarry.

When the cold wind began blowing off the desert, Barker had to find a spot to rest for the night. Riding caused his back to twinge, but the cold stiffened it to the point where he couldn't turn. He made a few tentative grabs for the butt of his Colt Peacemaker and found it almost impossible to draw the nearly three pounds of iron.

"That's not good," Barker muttered to himself. He stopped trying to pull his six-shooter and dismounted, leading his horse to the lee side of a sandy hill to fix himself a small fire using dried mesquite from the bank of a nearby arroyo. His horse fitfully nibbled at the grass and found a few seed pods still dangling on the mesquite. Barker fried himself some bacon, made a quick batch of biscuits that were nothing more than flour paste all fried up in the grease, and then washed it down with some water.

As the canteen sloshed toward empty, he knew he'd have to find more. But not now. Not tonight. He scooped out spots for his shoulders and hips in the sand, spread his blanket, snuggled down in the hollows, and fell asleep wishing he were home with his wife beside him.

It hardly seemed an instant until the sun on his face brought him bolt upright. He reached for his six-gun, but again his stiffness betrayed him. Barker lay back down and stared up into the cloudless blue sky, knowing it would be another hot one. For an instant, he considered turning around and going back to Mesilla. Marshal Dravecky would be in town today or tomorrow. Soon. He ought to greet him and show him around, introduce him to the saloon owners and the working girls and the citizens of Mesilla. He ought to.

Groaning as he stretched his sore back and stiff joints, Barker stood, secured his bedroll, and then fixed himself some oatmeal for breakfast, using the last of his water. He needed to boil some coffee to get fully awake, but he had exhausted his canteen.

It took the better part of an hour for him to find a pool of sweet water, let his mare drink, wash his own face and hands, and fill his canteen.

How far ahead was the vaquero?

Barker didn't know the answer. The Mexican might be across the border by now or only a mile down the road. It depended on where he was in such an all-fired hurry to be.

Somehow he didn't think the man was returning to Mexico. Whatever had lit the fire under his tail feathers had to be more important—and a lot less legal.

Barker spotted him from the rise of a hill less than an hour later. The vaquero still rode west but at such a sedate pace that it would be hard not to overtake him.

As appealing as it might have been to beat the information out of him—including his name—the vaquero had to remain unaware he was being followed. Otherwise he wouldn't reveal enough.

Mason Barker was a good tracker, a damned good one, and had learned from the Navajos how to follow a rider and never be seen. He hadn't lost any of his skill over the years—or so he thought.

The tracks stopped abruptly, forcing him to get down to look at the ground more carefully. His first hint that he had grown careless was the crunch of boots on gravel. Then things went to hell in a hurry.

8

MASON BARKER LOOKED UP AT THE RIFLE BARREL
pointed at his head. The man's hand trembled just a mite,
warning that a stray shot might come Barker's way at any
instant if he said the wrong thing.

"Why don't you just aim that in some other direction?"

"Why are you trailin' me?"

"Wasn't," Barker said. "I'm just riding along the road
and—"

"Liar!"

"Now, that's not a neighborly thing to say."

"I seen how you was sniffin' along the road, lookin'
fer my tracks. I outsmarted you and got the drop on you,
though. I'm smarter'n you."

"Seems true enough," Barker said. He tried to twist to
get his hand closer his Colt. Times like this he wished
he carried his pistol cavalry style with the butt forward
or maybe even in a cross-draw holster, so he could throw

down no matter how he was situated. But his back ached, and dragging out the six-gun would be impossible before the trigger-itching finger curled on the rifle.

They said nothing for a spell, making the gunman even more nervous. He finally broke the silence.

"What are you gonna do now?"

"Reckon that's up to you. You're the one holding the rifle on me."

"Why were you followin' me?"

Barker considered letting the man know he was a federal marshal, then decided that might get him killed then and there. Anyone so anxious about being tracked was likely on the run.

"Truth is, I'm following a Mexican fellow." Barker described the vaquero the best he could, then added, "He stole a watch that's been in my family for generations. Can't let a sneak thief get away with my granddaddy's watch."

"A watch? You're not after me?"

"Never saw you 'fore you pointed that rifle at me."

"What's this sneak thief's name?"

Barker shook his head and said nothing.

"You're not Marianne's husband?"

"Don't know any Marianne." There was a ring of sincerity in Barker's words since they were the gospel truth. "Don't even know where I am. Lordsburg is in that direction, but I don't have a map. I lit out after the *bandolero* and that's all I know."

"I seen a rider earlier today. Might have been him."

Barker caught his breath. The rifle lowered enough so any twitchy finger wouldn't send a bullet through his head. Through his horse, maybe, but Barker was likely to get a shot off in that case. He had never killed a man, but if this locoweed killed his mare, Barker likely would add a single notch to the handle of his six-shooter. He got to his feet. The man didn't get any crazier, so Barker asked what he hoped would get the man's mind off his own cheating ways and onto real crime—someone else's criminal ways.

"Tell me about him. Did he shine like he was on fire? He was wearing a silver- and gold-chased jacket, and the sombrero was big, with even more silver decoration on it."

"He did. I thought it was a ghost, maybe." The rifle lowered even more.

"Where'd you see him last?" Barker's voice took on a sharper edge, one of command he had developed over the years. It worked again.

"That way. Off the road, heading down toward the border. You willin' to follow him into Mexico?"

"That watch means the world to me."

"You don't know her?"

"Her?" It took Barker a second to realize the man was still worried about this Marianne's husband coming after him for whatever he had done. Chances were good that he hadn't harmed her or done much more than get her in a family way. Otherwise, he'd be worrying about a lawman on his trail.

"Marianne, but you don't know her." The man lowered his rifle all the way and heaved a sigh. "If I'da knowed she was married, I'd never have—"

"That way?" Barker said, not wanting to listen to the man's confession.

"An hour back, maybe more. But that goes down into the Bootheel. Roughest country this side of hell."

"Thanks for the warning," Barker said. He had been down into the Peloncilla Mountains a time or two and knew how rough the territory was. Once he had caught a fugitive, the other time he had gotten so turned around he was lucky to get out alive, eventually finding a trail leading west into Arizona. It took him a week to travel north until he found the road that led back to Mesilla.

He rode away slowly, the hair on the back of his neck still standing at attention. The itch he felt in his back had nothing to do with the twinges. He just hoped the philanderer didn't take it into his head to remove all traces of his trail—starting with a man he thought had followed him.

Barker wondered where the man's transgression had occurred. This was rugged country, but there were plenty of ranches around. It took close to a hundred acres of this arid land to graze a single cow, but closer to the mountains there were grassier meadows and plenty of water. Not that it mattered how many acres a single cow needed. There was plenty of empty open range here for any size herd.

He rode directly toward a notch in the low hills on the east side of the mountains, thinking the vaquero had made a beeline there. If he hadn't, he'd either camped out or knew of another pass that led deeper into the mountains. Either way, Barker wouldn't find him. But if the Mexican had remained on this trail, he could overtake him before he reached Mexico. Once across the border, not only was he out of Barker's jurisdiction as a lawman, he was likely to blend into the populace so completely that no gringo could ever find him.

If that happened, the best Barker could hope for was a decent shot of tequila and a hasty retreat back north of the border.

He rode steadily until the sun began to set. This close to the western mountains, he knew a couple hours of day would be lost to him. He urged his horse to a trot before twilight shrouded the trail leading deeper into the canyons. As he topped a rise, he recoiled and almost fell from his horse. Not fifty yards away the vaquero crouched by a watering hole.

They spotted each other at the same instant. Barker groaned as he went for his six-shooter, ignoring the sharp pain through his back in favor of dragging out the weapon. The vaquero needed only to reach down and pick up his pistol resting on a rock beside the watering hole.

"Don't go for it!" Barker shouted, knowing the Mexican wouldn't obey, but all he wanted was to delay the man's reach for his six-shooter an instant.

The vaquero still got off the first shot. The bullet ripped through the brim of Barker's hat and caused him to flinch. The snapping of his head more than the bullet sent the hat flying through the air—and that saved him. The Mexican followed his movement and sent another bullet into the hat, giving Barker the chance to fire more accurately.

His slug ripped through the vaquero's left arm, causing a bright fountain of blood to explode outward. The vaquero screamed in pain and twisted, ruining his aim once more.

"I got you in my sights, you son of a bitch. Throw up those hands!"

The vaquero fired again, and this time the bullet did what his earlier ones had not. It sang past Barker's horse close enough to cause the mare to rear. Barker tried to hang on, but the sudden movement and his back worked against him. He went flying through the air and landed so hard he was momentarily dazed. Hardly knowing what he did, he squeezed off another shot. In the dim corner of his brain that was screaming with pain, he knew he had missed. But just as the Mexican's bullet had caused the horse to rear, so Barker's got the man running for cover. If the vaquero had simply stepped up, he would have been able to shoot himself a marshal with no trouble at all.

Struggling to see through the red veil of pain, Barker rocked from side to side, then got enough momentum to come to hands and knees. Again he was helpless—and again firing a shot that went nowhere kept the vaquero running for cover. In the distance Barker heard the clatter of hooves against stone.

By the time he got to his feet and walked to the watering hole, the vaquero was long out of sight. All that remained were two damp spots where he had knelt on the stone by the edge of the water. Barker fired in the direction of the vanished rider, then dropped to a sitting position beside the pool to splash water on his face. The cold, pure water revived him. He stripped off his bandanna, soaked it, and then washed his face and throat. By the time he knotted the bandanna back around his neck, he was feeling almost well. That myth disappeared when he tried to stand.

His back snapped and forced him down to his knees. Gasping, he let the pain abate, then worked his way to his feet, straightened, and tried to ignore what had become a dull ache.

"You can run, but you can't ride fast enough or ride far enough to lose me," Barker said.

He filled his canteen, let his horse drink, washed his face one last time, and by now was shivering with the cold, since the sun had long since disappeared behind the Peloncillas. Barker swung into the saddle, clinging to the saddle horn with both hands. He tapped his heels against the mare's flanks and got the tired horse moving along the vaquero's trail. The sun might have gone, but the starlight was bright enough to see by.

As he rode, he reloaded his Colt.

It took Barker almost an hour to realize he couldn't track in the dark worth beans. When he was younger and riding with Colonel Carson, he might have kept on the trail. Too many years had passed and too many miles had slipped under his horse's hooves for him to entertain such thoughts now. Barker made camp, not daring to start a fire. Instead, he sat with his saddle blanket pulled around his shoulders, shivering so hard his teeth chattered. His shirt and bandanna turned to ice against his skin.

When he began sneezing, he realized he had slept through the night. The sun was poking up over the mountain peak in front of him. Barker worked to orient himself and finally saw a trail angling away to the southeast that had to be the one the vaquero had taken the night before.

Barker dared to start a fire, boiled some coffee strong enough to eat through the enamel in the coffeepot's bottom, then ate some hardtack and jerky and felt strong enough again to whip his weight in wildcats.

A half hour after the sun finally rose full above the peak, he was on the trail, walking slowly, looking for spoor. An hour later he had to admit that he couldn't tell if the vaquero or anyone else had ridden this trail in the past year. He found no fresh horse flop or bright, new scratches caused by steel horseshoes against rock or even a broken twig or thread dangling on a thorn bush. He found nothing at all.

Barker hunted for higher ground, spent another hour riding to the top of a rise, and finally got a good look around. He was as alone as if he was lying in his own grave. Nowhere did he see dust kicked up by a rider or any other sign that the vaquero was nearby.

"Damn," Barker muttered. He had shot it out, gotten a hole shot through his hat, and hurt his back even more, and still hadn't caught his quarry. Rather than leave in disgust, he took out a scrap of paper and sketched the terrain he saw, then added what he remembered from prior excursions into this hellhole. The map took shape under his stubby pencil, and he oriented himself. If the vaquero had taken the path to the south, he was heading for Skeleton Canyon. A couple times before, he had chased outlaws into that canyon, and both times he had given up the pursuit. Too many potential ambush spots existed.

Especially for a solitary rider.

Barker touched the badge pinned to his coat, remembered his oath about keeping the peace, then realized that he would never be able to do his duty if he took a couple bullets to the head.

The Mexican might be heading south of the border, but in his gut Barker doubted it. Whatever had drawn the man up from Sonora would keep him in New Mexico Territory.

With great reluctance, Barker mounted and rode back down to the trail, to retrace his path into the mountains. Two hours later, he realized he had taken a wrong turn, but as long as he kept moving north, he would eventually come out of the maze of canyons and find the road to Lordsburg and then back to Mesilla.

Late in the afternoon he finally left the foothills behind, but his tongue felt twice its natural size, and the grit in his mouth gagged him. He had used the last of his water before midday. That made the small ranch house off to the east all the more attractive to him. Barker angled for it, aware as he rode closer of how run-down it looked.

It didn't matter if the place was deserted, as long as there was a good well and a decent sucker washer in the pump. Before he passed through the gate dangling on a broken hinge, a woman came out onto the front porch of the house. She held her hand at her side, hidden by the flow of her skirts. Barker had seen this before and immediately drew rein.

"Hello," he called. "I'm a federal deputy marshal and am sore in need of water. Can you spare a canteen's worth for me and some for my horse?" He waited to see if she believed him. He turned carefully so the afternoon sun glinted off his badge. From this distance he might be holding a silver dollar for all she knew, but he saw a change in her posture. She relaxed, let the hand holding the six-shooter come from behind her skirt. That she didn't lift the gun in his direction told him he was believed.

"Come on closer, will you, Marshal?"

He rode slowly, keeping his hands where she could see them. From the way she held that six-shooter, she likely was capable enough with it. How good a shot she might be was something he didn't want to find out firsthand. He halted a dozen paces away, letting her make the next move.

"No need to be so cautious, Marshal. I'm not going to shoot." She put the six-gun down on a chair and rubbed her hands nervously against her skirts. "Sweat," she explained needlessly.

"Got no call asking you to tell me anything," he said. Barker gingerly dismounted, keeping the mare between him and the woman not to protect himself but to keep her from seeing how he moved. He felt better, but any exorbitant twist would send paroxysms of pain throughout his body.

"You wounded, Marshal?"

"Just sore from sittin' in the saddle the livelong day." That wasn't entirely a lie, but it still plucked at his conscience.

"What brings you to this godforsaken place? The ranch is more'n five miles from the main road."

"That way?" He pointed north. She nodded. "At least I didn't get that turned around." He chuckled and she smiled wanly.

After a few seconds, she pushed back a strand of fly-away hair and looked momentarily flustered.

"'Round back, Marshal. That's where the pump is. Don't know if there's enough water for your horse, so you might have to do some pumping. The livestock drink from it and . . ."

"That'll be fine, ma'am," he said. He led his horse around and saw the empty trough. Working the pump handle strained him a mite, but soon enough water flowed and he filled the tin-lined trough and stood back, a little dizzy.

"You're wounded, aren't you, Marshal?" He felt a thin arm circle his shoulders. The touch was worse than the vertigo, since it set off a spasm that caused him to jerk.

"Sorry, it's just that I twisted up my back while I was down in the mountains."

"Chasing some outlaw?"

"Something like that. I lost him near Skeleton Canyon."

"That's rugged country," she said. "Why don't you come on inside? I can fix you a decent meal."

"That's all right, ma'am. I don't want to put you out."

"I . . . It's no bother. Having a man for dinner again would do me a world of good. You'd be doin' me a favor if you stayed. For dinner."

"That your husband's grave?" Barker pointed to a cross marker out near the barn. It was a peculiar place for a grave, that near where animals were quartered, and he knew he shouldn't have asked.

"I couldn't dig in the ground anywhere else. The sun bakes the ground harder than a clay pot, and most places you hit caliche less than a foot below the surface. That's like digging into rock. Out there, down by the gate, the spot where it's mostly sand, well, I couldn't dig there, either. The sand kept sliding back down into the . . . the grave."

"Wouldn't be good to bury a man like that. The—" He bit off his sentence. He had almost said the animals would dig in the sand and eat the corpse. From the stricken look on the woman's thin face, he knew that thought had already occurred to her, but that didn't make him reminding her of it any more polite.

"It won't be long 'fore I can throw something together. I don't have much."

"Ma'am, you don't have to put yourself out on my account."

Her look convinced him that she did.

"Why don't I do some chores around here while you fix dinner? You got some wood that needs stacking, and I'm sure the livestock need to be fed. They always do." He hurriedly added that, since he didn't want to make her out to be lazy.

"Too many chores for one body to do," she said, her thin hand going to her throat. She smiled wanly, then went into the house. Barker listened to the sounds of utensils and plates and the smaller noises of a woman fixing dinner.

For her man.

Barker swallowed hard at that, then shoved his face into the trough so the cold water would clear his head. He had seen too many men killed in his day, and more than a few of the surviving women clung to their memories for a spell, then slowly sank without a trace. Trying to keep up the front that there was nothing wrong, that their dead husband would be back anytime now, thoughts that tore away at their souls and drove them slowly crazy.

The ones that didn't remarry right away weren't likely to keep the land under their feet or the cattle out on the range. Looking around, Barker wasn't sure what had kept this ranch going. A few cattle, a patch of alfalfa, determination not to fail, that was about it.

He stacked wood near the back door, then went to the barn. Most of the animals were scrawny. What feed he could scrape from the bottom of a bin he threw out for the chickens. The horse had to make do with some hay. If the sound wouldn't have shocked the woman, Barker would have put a bullet through the pig's head to put it out of its misery. There was no way the animal would live out the week.

"Come and get it," she called from the back door.

Barker walked slowly, his thoughts all jumbled up. He washed off his hands and let more of the cold water ginger up his mood a mite. Then he went inside, noticing how the woman only stepped back a half pace, so he had to crowd by her, his body brushing hers.

He sat at the head of the table and poked at the meager stew. He wondered what the meat was, then decided it didn't pay to ask. After a plate, he pushed back, took a long drink of water, then said, "That was mighty good after living on oatmeal and boiled coffee for so long."

Thoughts of Ruth's cooking made his belly grumble in protest at this poor woman's simple fare.

"It . . . it's gettin' dark out. You shouldn't be on the trail in the dark. There's Apaches all around and . . . and road agents. But you know that since you was after one."

"Reckon I can handle them. I was a scout for Colonel

Carson during the Navajo War, and finding road agents is my job." He tapped his deputy's badge.

"Didn't mean to say you couldn't handle all that, but . . . you can stay the night. If you want." Her hollow eyes showed dark desperation. He knew what she meant—what she wanted.

"Ma'am, I'm a married man and take my vows seriously."

"I didn't mean, I—" Tears welled in her eyes.

"It gets mighty lonely out here, doesn't it? After your man died?"

"Does," she said, sniffing.

"You need to get into the county seat and see about selling this place. You can't own the land—no woman can own real estate and that's the law, sorry as it is. But you can make a few dollars off the sale and use it to find a different life."

"Where?"

He thought for a moment, then said, "Santa Fe is a growing town. You might like Socorro. I don't advise Mesilla or El Paso del Norte or even Franklin since those are mighty tough border towns."

"You've seen so much of the world. Wh-where do you call home?"

"My wife's waiting for me," he said, standing. "I'll help with the dishes and—"

"No, no, you go on." The woman licked her lips, then said, "But you can stay. We don't have to do anything. I just need to feel a man holding me again."

"Take my advice about getting off this spread," he told her. "It'll kill you for certain sure if you stay overlong." He put his plate and fork into a pan, then said, "You're a generous woman. That will make a difference with the kind of man you deserve."

He left without looking back, although he knew she was standing in the doorway watching as he stepped up into the saddle and rode away. The stars lit the way for him, and a sliver of moon would rise before long.

As he crossed the desert on his way to the main road that would take him back to Mesilla, he knew he had done the right thing but did not understand why it felt so wrong.

9

MASON BARKER REACHED THE ROAD JUST BEFORE
midnight and turned east, but he had ridden hardly half a
mile when he saw campfires off to the south. If there had
been one fire, he would have kept riding, but the dozen
or so told him this wasn't even a bunch of drovers from
some big spread. The only reason so many fires would be
burning—and still stoked this late at night—had to be that
this was a military encampment, with at least two dozen
men. As he neared, he saw that he had underestimated the
number. An entire company bivouacked here.

"Don't come no closer," rang the challenge. "Who're
you?"

Barker gave his name but didn't add that he was a deputy marshal, just to see what happened. There'd be plenty
of time for that introduction later.

The soldier stepped closer, clutching his carbine. He
squinted up at Barker, then turned and spat.

"I know you. You and the lieutenant was all buddy-buddy a while back."

"Is Lieutenant Greenberg in camp? Or did your captain bring out this patrol?"

"Don't have a captain right now. He got hisself kicked in the head by his horse." The soldier didn't quite chuckle, but he came close enough for Barker to understand it was an unpopular captain with his head stove in and that this was something to laugh at, leastways among the sentries.

"From the sound of it, that might have improved his disposition."

This did get a guffaw out of the sentry—and it also brought an indistinct squat, powerful shape moving from the shadows.

"Private, you—"

"Well, if it isn't Sergeant Sturgeon," Barker said loudly enough to cut off the noncom's dressing-down of a noisy lookout. "Just the man I want to see, since you don't seem to have an officer in charge."

"The lieutenant's got some of the men, and he's rangin' mighty far to the south," Sturgeon said. He started to chew out the sentry again, but once more Barker cut him off. He felt a tad sorry for the lonely private and the way he had incited him to laugh out loud.

"You see anything of a vaquero all decked out in fancy duds with a sombrero out to here?" Barker held his arms wide to either side of his head.

"That 'bout describes 'em all, don't it?" the sergeant said. Then he laughed. He quickly stifled the mirth and said sternly to his private, "Get back on duty. Me and the marshal got matters to discuss."

"Marshal? You didn't say you was no marshal."

"You didn't ask the right questions, then," Sturgeon said

with an edge in his voice. If the private didn't learn to keep his yap shut, he would be walking sentry duty until the holes in his boot soles stretched all the way up to his flapping tongue.

Barker dismounted gingerly, not sure he was glad to have both feet on the ground. Standing still was mighty fine, but walking, even a little bit, sent jingles of pain down into his legs.

"You look to be in a bad way. You get yerse'f all shot up?"

"Nothing of the sort," Barker said. "Why, if I hadn't decided to ride for home without stopping, I could have been sleeping in a nice warm bed this very night."

"Ain't gonna find a soft bed here. Where's that bunk? I might get myself a bit of it."

Barker snorted and shook his head. "This big an expedition means trouble," he said. "The Apache go off the reservation again?"

"Some, maybe," said Sturgeon, "but they're not the ones we're after. Rustlers. There's not a cow safe anywhere in this part of New Mexico Territory."

"You were chasing after rustlers to the east of Mesilla. The same gang bring you this way?"

"Might be. Doesn't matter," Sergeant Sturgeon said. "We stop one gang and another springs up like weeds along a riverbank."

"I wonder if my vaquero might be part of your gang of rustlers," Barker said, more to himself than to the buffalo soldier. "He lit out for this part of the country mighty fast when he came to my attention back in Mesilla."

"These canyons are a wild, crazy maze, that's the truth," Sturgeon said.

"Might be we can throw in together. I've got a map showing where I lost him."

"You *lost* him? You tracked him but you *lost* him?"

"You make it sound nigh on impossible for such a thing to happen. He outrode me." Barker said nothing about the nameless vaquero outgunning him, too. His vanity was still a bit pricked over that. Any decent lawman would have captured the Mexican at the watering hole, not let him get off a few shots and ride away.

"Rumor has it you're the best tracker Kit Carson ever had serve with him. You could track a spring breeze through a tornado."

"Never heard that one," Barker allowed. Secretly, he was puffed up with pride at the sergeant's high praise. It didn't do much for him to remember he had lost his quarry in the blink of an eye.

"I got me a couple scouts who brag on finding every rock in this godforsaken part of the country. A map would help them—us—find our rustlers."

"Didn't see anyone else . . . " Barker's voice trailed off. He had seen another rider in the Peloncilla Mountains. The suspicious man who was sure he was being followed for some sexual peccadillo. Thinking of the lone pilgrim out in the mountains forced Barker to think on the woman all by herself on the ranch with the slowly dying animals. She had needed him and he had failed her.

But he hadn't failed his own marriage. But where was the line delineating who he was supposed to help and how?

"You lookin' sudden strange there, Marshal," Sturgeon said. "You feelin' all right? I know you got your back problems."

"That obvious?"

"A blind man can tell that. This is somethin' more." The sergeant looked at him intently, but Barker wasn't about to answer. The thoughts running through his mind—just for a moment—had been personal.

"This map of mine's not that much good since I'd have to be the one to point out the landmarks. I made it more for my own benefit than for anyone else to follow."

The buffalo soldier kept staring at him real hard, then said, "Come on into camp and get a cup of coffee. Looks as if you could use it."

"We have to be on our way. Otherwise, he'll be too far ahead of us," Barker said. But he was so tired he could hardly keep his eyes open. The coffee would help.

"No rush, 'less you want to have your horse step into a prairie dog hole in the dark."

"Not so many in the road."

"Never can tell. What's a cup of coffee gonna set you back? A half hour? You that all-fired hot to get back to Mesilla?"

"Truth is, I am, but my throat's so parched even your worthless cavalry brew might slip down all good and fine."

Sturgeon laughed and escorted him into the camp, after giving the sentry a final disparaging look.

When they were out of earshot, the sergeant said, "Most are like that boy. Can't keep their mind on soldiering longer'n a few minutes and for all the fightin' we've done, they's not been in a real fight yet."

"Mixing it up with rustlers isn't the kind of fight you generally get into," Barker said. He handed his mare's reins to a private, who led the horse to a crude rope corral. Barker sank down beside one of the many fires still burning brightly. "What's the reason you keep the fires stoked like this?"

"Well," Sturgeon said slowly, looking around, "it's like this. The lieutenant took both scouts with him, and I haven't heard from any of them in two days."

"So you wanted a beacon for them to find their way in the night?"

"Somethin' like that."

"Might be you'd give away your position to those rustlers, too."

"That's a consideration, but if I have to choose 'tween gettin' the lieutenant back and scarin' off those thieves . . ."

"Not often you see a newly minted officer with such promise," Barker said.

"He treats his men right. Not like most of them."

"Not like the captain who got his head kicked in?"

Sergeant Sturgeon thought on the answer for a spell, then said with a grin, "You can say that. I can't."

"You worried that Lieutenant Greenberg tangled with the rustlers and lost?"

"These are wild lands. Me and a lot of soldiers have chased Apache all over and never found them. Even with the scouts ridin' beside the lieutenant, ambush isn't out of the question."

Barker told of the man he had come across, jumpy about a husband finding out about his wayward wife and her lover.

"Don't recognize him from your description, but that don't mean much. All we ever done is see the varmints in the distance."

"Seems stealing beeves comes under my jurisdiction, too," Barker said, sipping coffee that wasn't half as bad as he'd feared it would be. "You get this from Dooley back in Mesilla?"

"Did."

This set off a new train of unwanted thoughts. He was glad to get the store owner and the lieutenant together for some mutually beneficial trade, but he wished Nate had taken the initiative and acted as the go-between. A profitable exchange between Hugh Dooley and several forts could have made them all a damn sight richer and given Nate something to be proud of.

Why'd he leave behind the meager pay as if he didn't need it?

"You think we can find this spot on your map, where you lost the vaquero?"

"Before noon," Barker said, turning the paper around to orient himself. "Might be hard to ride into the hills since the trail's hardly more'n a footpath. And there's no way to be sure he's one of the rustlers."

"But you think different," Sturgeon said.

"I think I found a man with a whale of a lot of money and no obvious way to have come by it legally." And the watch. He couldn't forget the watch the vaquero had sold to Nate. That implicated the Mexican in the stagecoach robbery, at least as far as taking stolen property, but if Barker had to lay a bet, it would be on a certain vaquero also being a bandito.

"Rest up, if you can after drinkin' that coffee. It's strong enough to bring the dead back to life."

But it wasn't strong enough to keep Barker from drifting off to sleep in a few minutes. With the dreams he had, he wished it had kept him awake.

"THAT'S THE SPOT WHERE I LOST HIM," BARKER SAID. "He rode on south, or so I reckon."

The sergeant stood in the stirrups and slowly studied the terrain.

"Wish I had the lieutenant's spyglass. My ole eyes aren't as good as they used to be, but I think I see a dust cloud in that direction way too big to belong to a single rider."

Sturgeon pointed due south. Barker pulled his hat brim down and squinted against the afternoon sun. The return was taking longer than he'd expected, and he'd be on the trail at least one more day before starting back to Mesilla. Might even be two days now that he made out dim figures riding inside the far dust cloud.

"Four men, I make it," he told the sergeant. "From how much dust they're kicking up, they have a small herd of cattle."

"Fifty?"

"Could be. I'm not an expert on such things, but it's not two or three beeves. It's got to be at least a couple dozen."

"Wrong time of year for a roundup," Sergeant Sturgeon said, turning about and signaling for his corporal to join him. They exchanged words for a few minutes, then the corporal trotted back and passed along the orders.

"If the whole column advances, we'll be spotted," Barker pointed out. "If it's just you and me and a handful of soldiers on fresh horses going after them, we might capture ourselves some outlaws."

"They'll have the herd between us and them," Sturgeon said. "Might be we can outflank them, split my squad into two elements, and—"

"You do what you want with the rest. Give me a couple men and let's ride. I think they might have spotted us."

Barker shielded his eyes with his hand and caught a sudden silver-and-gold flash that caused him to sit straighter in the saddle. He ignored the twinge when he recognized the source of the reflection. The vaquero he had been tracking rode along with at least three others, not the least bit concerned about the cloud of dust getting kicked up.

A sudden breeze swept some of that dust away.

"You called it, Sergeant. There's about fifty head of beeves."

"And gettin' their tenderloins stolen," Sturgeon said. He motioned, and two sections of his patrol split and went to cut off escape, leaving only the private who'd stood sentry duty the night before and one other. Both were scared but looked resolute. That was the best Barker could hope for. He rode down the sloping trail as fast as his mare could take the rocky path, the horse soldiers close behind.

When he came to a level stretch, he goaded his horse into a gallop. This was foolish, but he wanted to get out where he could spook the outlaws and force them into a mistake.

He quickly saw that he was the one who had misjudged. The four rustlers weren't giving up their stolen cattle easily. Two hung back while the other pair continued to move the herd southward. They were more than twenty miles from the border, but the closer they got, the better their chance of getting away scot-free—and with the stolen herd.

The vaquero was one of the pair who now faced a charging Mason Barker. His broad sombrero was tipped back so he could sight along the rifle. Barker hardly flinched as the bullet whined past. The vaquero got off another shot before his partner fired for the first time. The Mexican might fire more rapidly, but the other outlaw was something of a marksman.

The bullet tore through Barker's shirt, going between his arm and his rib cage. Somehow all that was carried away with the hunk of lead was a bit of his shirt. He remained unscathed, but the second outlaw proved the first shot was no fluke when he put a second round through Barker's hat. The floppy-brimmed hat flew up, caught the air, and flapped backward, the chin string almost strangling him. Flailing about a moment as it unbalanced him, he fought to stay in the saddle.

"We's a-comin'," came the cry from behind. Then lead tore past him, but in the other direction. Sergeant Sturgeon and his two soldiers opened fire with their carbines to distract the outlaws.

Barker swung around and bent low to keep the rustler from getting a better shot at him. The only worry he had was if the outlaw shot the horse from under him. A couple more shots whistled past, too high.

And then Barker felt his horse crouch and launch, jumping a narrow arroyo Barker hadn't even noticed in his fixation on the rustler. The horse landed with a bone-jarring thud and sent a lance of pain all the way up Barker's back. He gritted his teeth. He had come this close and wasn't about to give up. The two rustlers, the rifleman and the vaquero, swung around and prepared to run.

"Cut 'em off!" Barker's order was drowned out in a new thunder, deeper and more frightening. The herd had been turned and now rushed directly back toward him. The vaquero and his partner went to either side of the cattle, shouting and urging the frightened animals to stampede.

"Go to your right. Veer right!"

Barker looked over his shoulder and saw Sergeant Sturgeon waving wildly to him. He turned back, bent low, and saw that he would be trampled if he didn't go one way or the other. The sergeant had told him to go right, but what made him decide to gallop in that direction was the vaquero. The Mexican had taken that side of the herd to goad.

Using his knees and tugging on the reins, Barker convinced his horse to go over rockier ground than what lay straight ahead—and he missed the brunt of the charging cattle. A few head rushed past him, but the driven beeves were not in any position to run over him.

A momentary pang about the fate of the cattle passed when he saw his chance to follow the vaquero. The fleeing Mexican passed from sunlight to shadow and almost vanished. One instant Barker saw the reflection off the flashy silver-threaded jacket and then . . . nothing.

Barker kept riding and entered the shadow cast by the tall mountain peak, immediately spotting his quarry. The trail narrowed as it curled through rocks leading east, forcing the vaquero to squeeze between boulders. Judging from his frantic movements, the vaquero knew he was close to being taken into custody. Barker vowed to see the cattle thief locked up in his jail—or in an army stockade. If neither of those outcomes was likely, he wasn't above putting a bullet into the son of a bitch.

He wanted to take himself a prisoner, but good sense prevailed. He didn't ride through a particularly narrow gap in the rocks, because it felt wrong. His back might twinge on him, but now his gut was all knotted up and telling him he would regret being hasty.

Swinging down from the saddle, he pulled out his Winchester and advanced warily. Before he pressed through the vee in the rocks, he looked around for any telltale sign that his quarry waited ahead. He saw an indistinct shadow move against the rock to his left. The vaquero ought to have gone to the other side so he didn't have the sun at his back.

Maybe he didn't think about it—or maybe he did. If Barker surged through, would the sun blind him long enough to prevent an accurate shot?

Sounds behind him forced him to be sure he wasn't boxed in between two outlaws. Sturgeon came toward him on foot. Barker pantomimed the situation. The sergeant looked up and shook his head. There wasn't any way he could climb into the rocks to give a cross fire or even to distract the vaquero.

Barker motioned the soldier forward, then cocked his rifle and lunged.

A bullet tore past him on the way to the ground. Twisting, he brought his rifle up and fired wildly. He wanted to keep the vaquero distracted so the sergeant could take him out. But Sturgeon rushed up and fired—at nothing.

"He lit out," Sturgeon said.

"I want him. I'm gonna get him." Barker's resolve was stronger than his body. He couldn't even stand without the sergeant's help.

"He's gone. Long gone."

"He—" Barker bit off his determination to arrest the rustler. It had less to do with bringing a lawbreaker to justice than it did putting away a man who had taken advantage of his son. Nate had bought the stolen watch from the vaquero, then the vaquero had rubbed everyone's face in his guilt by ordering a fancy new watch for Nate, obviously paid for with stolen money.

Barker couldn't prove any of that, no matter how vexing it was to him, but if he caught the Mexican rustling cattle, they could put him in prison for a good, long time.

"We lost the others," Sturgeon said. "No reason to think we can nab this one, either."

"How'd he get into those rocks from this trail?" Barker walked a few yards and saw nothing but a rocky chute. It was as if the vaquero had flown to get to the perfect spot for an ambush.

"They know these here hills like a calf knows its mama's teat. That's why I wanted your map."

"Didn't do much good," Barker said glumly.

"Saved a few head of cattle for some rancher. The lieutenant will have somethin' good to report."

Barker said nothing. Lieutenant Greenberg might report victory, but returning to Mesilla without anything to show for his jaunt into the countryside would make Barker look mighty ineffectual. Maybe the mayor was right hiring a town marshal. Mason Barker couldn't even catch a rustler in the act of cattle thieving.

"You all right, Marshal?"

"Right as rain," Barker said, following the buffalo soldier back, but every step was burning hot misery. What he needed most was a good, long soak in a mineral bath to ease his back, but that wasn't likely to happen. He sucked up his resolve and tried not to show too much pain, so Sturgeon wouldn't worry about him so much.

10

THE SECOND SHOT OF WHISKEY WAS GOOD, BUT the fifth went down even better. Barker was long past being able to taste the vile liquor, but what it did to ease his pain was nothing less than a miracle.

"You better go easy on that popskull, Mase," the barkeep said.

"Gus, my good friend, this is the medicine the doctor ordered."

"Ain't got a sawbones in town right now, and if you're callin' me a doctor, then I'm doublin' the price. There ought to be something extra for my special skills."

Barker laughed. He felt better than he had in a couple days. Returning empty-handed, after leaving Mesilla as abruptly as he had, had set the tongues a-waggin'. Mostly, he ignored the gossip as it trickled back to him, but some of it hurt. The guilty fled when no man pursued. The preacher had said that in a sermon a month back, but the rumors of Barker having a woman out west of town rankled. He kept coming back to the poor widow woman and how hard she had it. All she'd needed from him was comfort, and he hadn't given it. But what was it about her that touched him so?

He had run with the worst of men since taking the job as deputy federal marshal, and none of their evil had rubbed off on him. He had always known who he was and what he stood for, but seeing her—he hadn't even heard her name—made him feel guilty. It drove home how little any man could do, whether arresting the outlaws or keeping good men from dying and leaving behind their women. He had done the right thing, but it still felt wrong. The preacher might have some words to comfort him, but he doubted it, since he and the minister didn't get along too well after the imbibing incident.

At least, that's the way Barker always thought of it. The preacher had been drunker than a skunk. Whether another lawman would have run him in or let him go, Barker couldn't say. He had stayed with the preacher, pouring hot coffee into him, until he sobered up. The man hadn't been the least bit grateful. If anything, it had made him angry, and he had become even angrier when Barker told him he wouldn't breathe a word of the bender to anyone else in town.

What had set the preacher off on a binge Barker couldn't say, but he had heard of drunks who would be on the wagon for years, then go out on a tear and have to climb back up to their pinnacle of sobriety. Might be what happened, but Barker couldn't say. If he had come right out and told everyone in town, he wasn't sure anyone would have believed him. He had hinted at the good deed he'd done, and even Ruth had scoffed at the notion of a man of the cloth being a common drunk. For all he knew, she might be right and one thing alone had gotten the preacher to knock back almost a half bottle of rye.

"Should have run him in. Then there wouldn't be any dispute," he said to himself.

"How's that, Marshal?"

Barker looked up and saw Gus Phillips staring at him.

"You takin' to conversin' with yourself?"

"Gets lonely out on the trail."

"Where'd you go off to? You didn't tell nobody in town."

"I was tracking cattle rustlers. Me and a company of buffalo soldiers almost caught them."

"Bet you had a shoot-out and almost got trampled, too," Gus said, smiling. The smile faded when Barker glared at him. "Just tryin' to be sociable. Didn't mean nothin' disrespectful."

Barker turned back to his shot glass and watched the patterns reflected in the amber fluid from the flickering gaslight above the bar. He sloshed around the whiskey a bit, then knocked it back so the liquor could join the rest in his belly. He felt a little tipsy and ought to go home, but it was a rare occasion when he felt this good. Ruth didn't appreciate him drinking. He had given up smoking because of her strident complaints, and that didn't bother him at all. Smoking was a way of killing time. Getting the fixings, rolling the cigarette, watching the lucifer flare, tucking everything away. The actual smoking wasn't as pleasurable as the building.

"You meet the new marshal yet?" Gus asked.

"Not had the pleasure. I got back late, spent yesterday filing reports and he was somewhere else."

"He had a squabble to settle out at the edge of town and

didn't get back till late. I heard all about it. Miz Percheck done took a fryin' pan to the top of Amos's head again."

"Amos isn't the sort to take kindly to that. The new marshal didn't try to arrest him, did he?" Barker saw the answer on Gus's face. This would be talked about for the next couple weeks. "Shots fired?"

"A lot of 'em. All by Amos, of course." Gus came closer and leaned both elbows on the bar so he could speak confidentially. "He holed up in his barn and 'fore Marshal Dravecky flushed him out, he'd shot two mules and that old spotted dog of his."

"Amos loved that dog. He must have been powerful pissed."

"He was powerful drunk, that's what he was. The marshal had to let him sober up 'fore he went in after him."

"Dravecky actually went in the barn after him? Now, that's either downright brave or the dumbest thing I've heard."

"Well, the marshal's new to town, so he doesn't know Amos's ways, and his missus wasn't 'bout to tell a newcomer 'bout her hubby. She wasn't talkin' to anybody by that time."

"Considering Mrs. Percheck's nature, she might have wanted Amos dead." This caused a pang that sent Barker's thoughts back west to the desolate ranch house and the woman in it. She would trade about anything for her husband not to be buried in the soft earth beside the dilapidated barn. Audrey Percheck would likely kill Amos herself one day.

"Who can say? She ain't too talkative, 'cept when she's bawlin' out Amos."

"So the marshal arrested him?"

"Throwed him in jail and set bail at a hundred dollars."

"That's mighty steep, especially when Amos had a headache from being beaned with a frying pan."

"That's so. The missus ain't pleased since she needs Amos to help out with the chores, and nobody in this town's got that much money for bail. It's causin' all sorts of ill will."

Barker shook his head and chuckled.

"I leave for a couple days and everything goes to hell in a handbasket."

"What's even better, Amos—" The barkeep stopped in mid-sentence and pushed to his full height to look over Barker's bent back.

"What's wrong?" Barker turned his head in the direction of the doorway, but nobody was there. Then he heard the quick movement of boots grinding down on the thick sawdust covering the floor, causing the planks to creak. He looked over his other shoulder and saw strutting in about the biggest man he had ever seen.

"Top of the morning to you, gents," the mountain of a man said, touching the brim of his expensive bowler. He settled down in a chair, took out a deck of cards, and began shuffling them, laying them out on the table and making them jump and turn to his bidding.

Barker looked at him curiously. It was going on nine at night. Then he decided this might just be the break of the workday for the gambler man, who'd probably slept away the daylight hours after a long night of cards.

"He just got to town yesterday," Gus said. "Tinhorn and a cheat. I know it, but I can't catch him at it."

"Throw him out of the Plugged Nickel. There are other saloons for him to cheat customers in," Barker said.

"You see him, Marshal. He's bigger 'n the pair of us

combined, and I ain't sure much of it is fat. He moves real easy, like a mountain lion, and he's quick."

"I can see that." Barker watched the gambler riffle through the cards, shuffle them, and then deal a perfect five-card-draw poker hand, faceup and where an opponent would be.

"What are the chances of a royal flush comin' off the deck like that?" Gus asked.

"Not so good."

"But he's good, Marshal. Look at his fingers. He's a big man, and his hands look like they belong to some fancy lady. Even that dancer over at the Monterrey Belle don't have graceful hands like his."

"Never looked at that particular lady's hands," Barker said. "Not the way she dresses."

"He took a half dozen customers fer a pretty penny last night," Gus said. "I don't want him hangin' around here."

"You're the owner. Tell him to leave."

"He weighs half again what he ought to because of the weapons he's a-carryin'. I seen the handles of two derringers pokin' from vest pockets, and I'm sure he's got a knife up his left sleeve."

"Might not be all he has up his sleeve." Barker watched the gambler shuffle and deal out four perfect poker hands, all faceup. It wasn't lost on anyone watching the display of card-handling skill that the gambler dealt the spade flush to himself.

"Interest you in a game?" the gambler said, seeing Barker's interest.

"You're too quick with the cards for me to want to lose my money," Barker said.

"Mase, please." Gus put his hand on Barker's arm. He shook it off.

"Gentlemen, join me for a friendly game of poker?" The gambler beckoned to a trio of cowboys who'd pushed into the saloon. "The first drink's on me."

The cowboys exchanged glances and made a beeline for the table.

"Bartender, a round for my friends. Whatever's best."

"Can you pay for it?" Gus demanded.

"I'll be able to soon enough," the gambler said, laughing heartily. The cowboys, dazzled by the offer of free booze, didn't understand what the man had said.

"What am I gonna do, Mase? I can't let them play with him. He'll steal their eyeteeth!"

"Keep them all happy for a spell, and I'll be back soon."

"But, Mase!"

Barker stepped out into the chilly evening air and looked up and down the street before heaving a deep sigh. He had thought of Mesilla as his town before the mayor hired a new marshal. Now he was nothing more than an itinerant lawman who just happened to make a home on the outskirts of town.

That didn't dampen his desire to help his friend, and Gus Phillips was that. As he walked along, feeling warm and good, he got to thinking about the rest of the citizens in Mesilla. He hadn't made that many friends here, not real friends. Ruth had her social group from church, but he was always on the trail and didn't much care to attend services, not after his run-in with the preacher.

He stopped in front of the hotel. There were a couple others in town, but he thought of this one as *the* hotel since it was the fanciest. Barker stepped through the doors with their beveled glass windows and worked his way around a chair at the edge of a rug to stand in front of the room clerk's counter.

The man—boy, really—looked up and smiled.

"Howdy, Marshal. Heard tell you got back to town. You met the new—"

"The gambler fellow. The big, tall one. Which is his room?"

"Mr. Antonio? He's a huge one, isn't he? Why, he carried a steamer trunk up the stairs under one arm and never broke a sweat."

"Which room did he take the trunk to?"

"Well, I reckon I ought to tell you he's not in. He left not twenty minutes back. Said he was going to find a gambling emporium and—"

"The room," Barker said. He wasn't feeling all that friendly toward small talk. "Can you give me the key or should I just kick in the door?"

"Oh, no, don't do that! Mr. Morrisey would take it out of my pay for the repairs, then he'd fire me. I need this job ever since that horse stepped on my foot." The clerk thrust out his injured foot for Barker to see.

"Sorry about that," Barker said, softening his tone. He usually judged when to be tough and when to soft-soap the people he talked with. "You need any help, you see that old woman north toward Las Cruces. She says she's a bruja, but she makes some of the best potions and ointments for what ails you."

"Thanks, I might do that. Since the doctor up and—" The young clerk reached behind him and pushed the key across the counter when he saw Barker's scowl. "Mr. Antonio's in Room 17."

"Thanks. And I won't so much as scratch the door frame."

Barker mounted a steep flight of stairs and found the room he wanted, then shoved the room key into the lock

and turned it slowly. The well-oiled mechanism opened
and let him into the dim room. He worked at getting a coal
oil lamp by the bed lit, then found the steamer trunk by the
wardrobe. He grunted as he pulled it across the room and
then heaved it onto the bed so he could examine it.

"He carried this under one arm? Damn," Barker muttered as he opened the lid. The gambler's clothing was
neatly packed away, as befitted a man for whom appear-
ances were everything. Barker didn't bother keeping in
order the frilly-fronted shirts or the pants with the gros-
grain ribbon running down the sides, especially when he
found the boxes in the bottom of the trunk.

He pulled them out and pushed back the lids to reveal
complicated mechanical gadgets. Some had a frail-looking
rod that ended in a clamp, while others were spring-powered
and looked strong enough to lift a card table. Barker was
at a loss to figure out what some of the gadgets did, but he
knew enough to see at least one thrust a card down a man's
sleeve and into his hand when properly aligned. Barker
triggered it a couple times, marveling at the workmanship,
the smoothness as it unfolded and shoved out card holders
and then snaked back into hiding.

Then he found a small bottle tucked away in a corner
of the trunk.

Holding it up, he slowly read the smeared label on the
brown glass. His eyes widened. His gambler carried a full
bottle of laudanum. He started to return it, then hesitated.
He wiped his lips with one hand while holding up the bottle with the other. This was a potent narcotic. It wasn't illegal to have, but nobody thought well of a person imbibing
it. Every whore he had ever heard of who killed herself had
done it with too much laudanum. Hand shaking slightly, he
thrust the bottle into his pocket. Then he patted the pocket

and traced the outline of the bottle, knowing it wasn't right to take another man's belongings. But this . . .

He dumped everything back in, slammed the lid, and dragged the trunk behind him. There was no way he could lift the trunk, much less carry it down the steep flight of stairs to the lobby. Step by step it clunked behind him until he reached the lobby.

"Where you going with Mr. Antonio's trunk?" the clerk asked.

"Has he paid up?"

"For the next week."

"He'll be leaving, but I don't expect him to ask for his money back." Barker grunted as he pulled the trunk across the floor and to the hotel's front porch where he left it in plain sight. A handful of curious people gathered, but he didn't even acknowledge them. He went directly back to the Plugged Nickel.

Gus waved to him, but he ignored the barkeep, stopping directly in front of the gambler.

"I found all your cheating doohickeys," he said. "You can leave Mesilla right now, and there won't be any trouble. You think to stay and cheat, well, we got a mighty small jail cell waiting for you."

"Cheat?" piped up a cowboy. "He's been cheatin'?"

"You can't go around spreading lies about me, Marshal," Antonio said, his eyes fixed on the silver badge pinned to Barker's coat lapel.

"Not a lie. I got you dead to rights. Want to show your arms? Pull back those sleeves and let these gents have a look at your skin."

"You can't call me a card cheat. This is my reputation you're maligning."

Barker moved so he had an easy reach to his six-shooter.

This move usually calmed men down and made them think what would happen if they threw down on a lawman. Antonio was different. He stood and kicked back his chair. The Plugged Nickel went deathly silent, and Barker knew there would be bloodshed unless he did something.

"You got more guns and knives on you than an entire regiment of horse soldiers," Barker said. "Let me show you something." Without taking his eyes off the gambler, he called to the barkeep, "Gus, set up three shot glasses."

"What do you mean, Marshal?"

"Put them one atop the other."

"In a pile?"

"Yeah." Barker saw Antonio's furrowed brow and knew he had caught the gambler's curiosity. Now he needed to instill a bit of fear.

"All set up, Marshal," Gus said.

"Move out from behind the glasses."

"No, Mase, you can't!"

Barker slid his pistol from its holster and fired three times. The first slug blasted the top shot glass to hell and gone. He might have missed with his second shot, but it didn't matter since the third took out the bottom glass and sent the second spinning out of sight.

He then spoke to Antonio.

"What'll it be? You clearing out of town right now—leaving that money on the table—or you and me going out into the street to settle this?"

"You're a good shot, that I'll grant," the gambler said. Barker saw the man's brain working fast and hard as he tried to come to a conclusion. He wanted the gambler to come to the right decision. "But are you fast?"

"Don't have to be," Barker said, lifting his pistol. "You so much as twitch an eyebrow and I'll blow it off. I still have three rounds left in this popgun, and chances are real good I won't miss with any of them. But even if I only hit you with one . . ." He let the implication settle in. From behind him he heard Gus muttering about broken glassware and sweeping up the debris.

"This isn't the most hospitable town I ever been in," Antonio said.

"But it just might be the most hospitable town you ever left behind," Barker said. He stepped away to give the huge gambler a way out. As Antonio reached the door, Barker called out, "Your gear's in front of the hotel. It's a beautiful night to be on the trail."

"For where?" Antonio sounded bitter. From the way his eyes flashed to the table and the money left there, Barker knew that rankled him more than being backed down by a hick marshal.

"For somewhere else."

Antonio grumbled and disappeared into the night.

"You goin' after him, Mase?" Gus looked uneasy. "Don't want him comin' back in to cause trouble."

"He'll be on his way. No more trouble. I've seen his kind before. He might look mean and be bigger than any two of us, but he's not hunting for trouble."

"I want him arrested, Marshal," demanded a mostly drunk cowboy at the card table. "He was cheatin' us!"

"Split the pot amongst yourselves and be glad he didn't clean you out."

"But he—"

Barker's cold stare silenced the man. A more sober player split the pile into a rough estimate of thirds and pushed two piles away, one to each of his partners. Barker suspected the biggest heap went into the man's own poke, but so what? It shut up the drunk and sidetracked more trouble.

"What's the ruckus? I heard gunshots."

Barker turned and realized he still held his six-shooter. He slowly returned it to his holster.

"No trouble, Marshal."

"You must be the deputy federal marshal," the man standing in the doorway said.

"And you're the new town marshal."

"Let's talk outside," Marshal Dravecky said. He let the doors swing behind him. Barker was slow to obey. His mouth was cottony, and his hands shook more than he liked in reaction to his run-in with Antonio. Walking deliberately, he stepped out into the cold desert night. A pale moon rose and cast its quicksilver light over the new marshal. Dravecky stood in the middle of the street, face hidden in shadow, his badge gleaming as bright as a star in the sky.

"I heard you were still out dealing with Amos and his wife."

"Word does get around," Dravecky said. He hooked his thumbs in his gun belt and faced Barker. "I don't depend on gossip for important things."

"You learn that down in Hell's Half Acre?"

"There and other places in Texas." He took a deep breath and continued. "There's only one lawman in Mesilla. I'm it."

"I got jurisdiction," Barker said, irritated, yet understanding what Dravecky meant. "My jurisdiction runs throughout all of southern New Mexico Territory."

"For federal crimes. For crimes the federal marshal thinks important enough to post rewards on."

"Marshal Armijo can't be everywhere all the time. He gives his deputies leeway."

"Not in Mesilla. In Mesilla I'm the one who enforces

the law. If you got a federal criminal to arrest, you clear it with me first. That understood?"

"We got off on a bad foot, Marshal . . ." Barker started. He didn't get any farther.

"Damn right we did." Without letting Barker offer a drink to smooth ruffled feathers, Dravecky whirled about and stalked off.

Some men were always touchy, Barker knew, and Dravecky wasn't comfortable enough in his position yet. That had to explain his attitude.

He turned to go back into the Plugged Nickel, then touched the brown bottle he had taken from the gambler's luggage. Laudanum. Powerful stuff. And the liquor he had swilled earlier was wearing off. Fingers curled around the bottle in his pocket, Barker began walking slowly toward the stables. It was time to go home to Ruth, if she'd have him, smelling of whiskey the way he still did.

11

THE SOUND OF GUNFIRE DISTURBED AN OTHERWISE
idyllic day. Mason Barker stood up in his stirrups and put
his hand to his eyes to shield them from the blazing sun.
Turning slowly, he tracked the direction of the shots. It
might be nothing, but why would anybody in their right
mind be hunting in the middle of the day, under the hot
sun? Rabbits were too smart to venture out in this heat, but
maybe a traveler had come across a snake and was taking
care of it.

The heat reminded Barker that no snake with a whit of
common sense would be out, either.

He turned his mare's head and gently tapped with the
reins. It didn't seem to be a matter where hurrying would
gain him anything, and by taking it slow and easy the past
week or so, he had found a contentment lost years back.
Not locking horns with the new marshal in Mesilla helped.
Keeping away from town allowed him to concentrate on

his federal duties. And since he had found that little brown bottle of medicine in the gambler's luggage and appropriated it, a drop or two of the laudanum had taken care of his backache—and a damn sight more.

Since he didn't have to drink to kill the pain, he wasn't coming home reeking of beer, or worse even—drunk. That pleased Ruth, and her disposition had mellowed considerably. The only thing that refused to go his way was Nate, but he hadn't heard anything bad about his boy, so he had to count that as good news. By moving out of the house the way he had, Nate would be forced to rely on himself. That'd put a little steel in his spine and might make him a tad more amenable when he finally got around to passing by.

It did a boy good to live in a man's world and find responsibilities. In this day and age, with things the way they were, getting by was hard work. That would straighten Nate right up.

Barker followed the base of a sand dune and came to a halt when he saw the main road leading from El Paso to Mesilla. He had been a few miles to the south serving process for a new judge over in El Paso and had not bothered to follow the sunbaked dirt track but rather had cut across country to save time. Even this had gone well for him. Not only had he not gotten lost, he had served the papers and earned himself the tidy sum of ten dollars for the duty.

But this? He heard more gunfire, sporadic and followed by the clank of chains and the creaking of leather harness. Then all hell broke loose. He might as well have been in the middle of one of those big battles the veterans of the war were always spinning yarns on. From the amount of lead that had to be flying, he imagined two vast armies crashing together at Gettysburg.

He pulled his rifle from the saddle sheath, levered in a round, and heaved a deep sigh. The day had been going way too good to end without some problem coming his way. Winchester clutched tight and pulled into his shoulder, he guided the horse onto the road and toward the ragged gunfire. At least the sounds were more like a dozen men firing instead of an entire regiment.

Trotting forward, he rounded a bend in the road and found the stagecoach mired in the soft sand of a dune. The driver had been forced off to the side and had foolishly tried to escape through the desert rather than staying with the road.

More than a misjudgment, the attempt to flee had cost him his life. Barker saw a man sprawled on the ground, a whip still clutched in his hand. Barker galloped forward, ready to fight. But there wasn't anyone to shoot at. The shotgun messenger was dead in the driver's box. Judging from the number of bullet wounds Barker could see with a casual glance, the man had to weigh five pounds more than he had when he left the depot—and all of the extra weight was lead embedded in his body.

"You the law?" A head poked up inside the compartment. A hand followed and a shaking finger pointed out into the desert. "Five of 'em. Road agents. They're only a few minutes ahead of you."

"Five?"

"All I saw 'fore I took cover."

Barker lowered his rifle. One against five killers was terrible odds, even if they didn't know he was after them. But he was the law, and it was his duty to bring the killers and thieves to justice. Damning himself as a fool, he kicked his horse to a gallop and struggled up a sandy slope so he could look out over the desert to the north.

A dust cloud was settling from their hurried departure, but now he saw the five outlaws. They were too far away to get a good look, but he knew one thing. The bandito riding lead wore a huge sombrero like the one worn by the Mexican he had chased down into the Bootheel. It had been too much to expect the vaquero to disappear into Sonora and never return. Barker lifted his rifle and sighted in, elevated the muzzle to account for the distance, and triggered a round. The rifle bucked and gave him a momentary twinge in his lower back, and then this discomfort faded. His bullet wasn't intended to bring down any of the outlaws, but rather to vent his own anger and to let them know they had an implacable tracker on their trail.

He wasn't sure they even noticed his bullet. The slug probably drove itself into the dunes to vanish for all time. The road agents wouldn't ever be scared of him at this distance, unless he got lucky and winged one of them. Even then, killing one of the murdering sons of bitches was out of the question.

Barker made his way back to the stagecoach, where the passenger had climbed out and now stared at the guard's body draped over the edge of the box.

"My God, they turned him to a bloody mess."

"Driver didn't fare much better. I'll recommend no photographs unless the undertaker can fix 'em both up. I'm not sure he's good enough to do that." Barker rode closer and knew that wasn't ever going to be possible for the guard. His face was unrecognizable. At least a dozen bullets had smashed into him, obliterating his identity. He might have been a handsome gent or the ugliest man alive. It didn't matter now because not even a loving wife could identify him.

"They hit us from both sides, left and right, just as we

rounded the bend in the road and those sand dunes rose on either side and one was ahead in the road to stop, but the guard, he, he, the guard he got shot from behind so there was one behind us—"

"Whoa, slow down and catch your breath, mister. There water on the stage? Get yourself some. Or if you got some whiskey, that'll go a bit farther in settling your nerves."

"Y-you see this kind of thing all the time, Marshal?"

"Not often enough to get used to it, but often enough to learn to hate the men responsible. What can you tell me about them?"

"They didn't even shout to the driver to stop. J-just opened fire."

A coldness settled in Barker's belly. That meant the gang found as much pleasure in wanton killing as they did in spending the money they stole. That was bad and would only get worse. When simple killing didn't carry the thrill it once did, they would go on to more elaborate ways of murdering. From the look of the guard, they were well along that bloody road. A simple bullet to the head would have killed him, but so many additional slugs to his face showed that pure mean drove the road agents, not necessity.

"You the only passenger?"

"The only one. I'm on my way to Tombstone. I . . . I got a job on the newspaper there." The haggard passenger looked at Barker and asked, "Is it like this in Tombstone, too?"

"Well, sir, let me put it this way. You won't have any trouble filling the front page with news, and there's a reason they call the paper there the *Epitaph*."

"I don't know if I want to continue."

"Getting you into Mesilla is easy enough. What you do

from there is up to you." Barker rode around the stage and saw that the strongbox was gone. Where it had been bolted in the boot only ripped wood remained. The outlaws had yanked it plumb off the stage.

"Why didn't they kill me, too?"

Barker eyed the reporter and shook his head.

"Might be you weren't good enough to waste a bullet on," he said. Then a thought struck him. "You tell them you were a reporter?"

"I . . . I don't remember. When the driver veered off the road, I was shouting out the window. Then they were shooting, and I don't remember much after that." He wiped sweat from his forehead, then replaced a dusty, battered bowler hat to cover the thinning hair. "I might have. I must have."

"There's your answer. They want you to tell the world about what killers they are. You get a look at any of them?"

"Not after I ducked down inside the compartment. I saw one. Got a good look at him. He . . . he wore a huge sombrero."

"Did he have a fancy embroidered jacket, too?"

"No, he wore a serape slung over his shoulder. A hole cut in the middle and it was draped. It was so many colors I can't describe it."

"No need," Barker said, trying to stem the flood of words before he drowned in them. "Identifying a man from the cut of his serape's not gonna hold up in court. You see the face under that sombrero?"

The reporter shook his head.

Barker circled the stagecoach again, getting a better idea of how difficult it would be to right it and drive it back to Mesilla.

"You up for a bit of work?"

Barker didn't much care if the reporter was. They got dried branches and fresh greasewood and creosote brush and put it all under the stagecoach's wheels. Barker scooped away what sand he could to give some purchase, then climbed into the driver's box. His nose wrinkled. The flies were already working on the guard's body, and the hot sun had turned it downright noxious.

"You want me to push? When you get the horses pulling?"

"You wouldn't budge this stage an inch. Put more limbs under the wheels if it looks like they're gaining purchase." Barker wiped his sweaty hands on his jeans, took the reins, and got the team pulling, slowly at first, then with more power. He let out an earsplitting "yeehaw!" and snapped the reins just right to make the team bolt. The wheels turned, the reporter did as he had been told, and the stage pulled free to rattle onto the road.

"Wait, wait for me. Don't leave me!" The reporter ran behind, fearful of being stranded.

It took Barker a few seconds to slow the team and finally bring them to a halt.

"Not going to leave you for the buzzards." He looked back and saw the carrion eaters working on the driver's body. Dumping the guard's body was a powerful urge, but Barker finally upended the corpse and let it crash to the ground, then fastened the reins around the brake, climbed down, and dragged the body to the boot.

"Help me get him up," Barker said.

The reporter did the best he could, which meant Barker did most of the disagreeable work. Then he led his horse back to the driver, looped his rope around the dead man's boots, and dragged him to the stagecoach. The short trip tore him up something fierce, but he was dead enough not to care and the buzzards had already begun their work on him. If nothing else, both driver and guard would get a decent burial outside town. That was better than letting the birds, bugs, and coyotes dine on them.

"C-can I ride up there with you, Marshal?" The reporter made tentative stabs with his finger to indicate the driver's box. Barker reckoned he didn't want to be alone in the compartment. Or maybe the driver's box was as far from the bodies as he could get.

"Come on up, but you have to promise me one thing."

"Anything."

"Keep quiet and don't throw up."

"That's two things."

Barker glared at him, then smiled. The reporter grinned weakly but kept quiet. That was a good sign. He didn't say two words all the way back to town.

"YOU HAVE A WAY OF TURNING UP LIKE A BAD PENNY," Marshal Dravecky said to Barker. "How'd you just happen to be on that road?"

"Wasn't. I had just served process for a vacate order when I heard gunfire."

The reporter piped up. "They attacked from all sides, Marshal." Barker had seen how every foot of the trip back to Mesilla had built pressure in the man until he had wanted to explode and tell all he knew over and over. The threat of walking—or riding in the compartment just ahead of the two bodies—had kept him dammed up until they stopped in front of the marshal's office.

Now he wanted to spill everything he had seen, like a mountain freshet striving for the thirsty desert below.

"I'll get to you in a minute," Dravecky said.

"He's a reporter." Barker wasn't above throwing a little kerosene into the fire. "Might make for a good witness."

"Not at a trial!" The reporter turned white under the brown mask he had accumulated from road dust caking onto his sweaty skin. "I mean, I saw them, but I can't identify them. Not at a trial."

"Marshal," Dravecky started, but Barker put up his hands in a gesture of surrender.

"It's your problem," Barker said. He started to go.

"Like hell it is. The robbery took place out on the road, beyond town limits. I keep the law inside Mesilla, not out there in the desert. This is your crime to solve."

"Your bodies to bury," Barker said, taking an inordinate pleasure in dropping the problem into Dravecky's lap. "If the stationmaster wants to put up a reward, let me know. And if your reporter here can sketch a wanted poster, I'll be glad to carry that around and post it along the road."

"You know who they are, don't you?"

Barker hesitated. He had a good idea who was responsible but didn't even have a name for the vaquero. If he crossed the man's path again, there was sure to be gunplay. He couldn't imagine the Mexican not wanting to put the same number of bullets in him that he had the guard— plus one for good measure. The vaquero might even want to indulge in a bit of torture. With the Apaches on and off the reservation all the time, one might have thrown in with the robbers. Expertise in the ways of pain was a specialty with them, especially the Mescaleros fighting their sworn enemies.

Right about now, that might be any white man or soldier in the Tenth Cavalry.

"Well, give me some names," Dravecky said.

"Don't know 'em, Marshal. Sorry. But you keep alert,

since they probably know you." This time Barker did turn to leave.

"They know you, too, Barker. They know you, too!"

Barker didn't reply, but the marshal's parting shot hit the bull's-eye. Barker was certain the road agents knew him and would take an evil delight in killing him. He needed to contact Marshal Armijo and find out if there had been any sightings of the gang elsewhere throughout the area. Maybe he could get in touch with Lieutenant Greenberg and find out what the cavalry had learned as they patrolled the entire region. The more he knew, the less he had to worry about one of the gang back-shooting him.

He swung into the saddle and started from town. He had earned his keep this day. He had money due him for serving the eviction notice and had brought in a survivor from a stage robbery. Hell, he had even taken a shot at the escaping robbers, even if they hadn't noticed him.

This turned him a bit morose. It was one thing to have the owlhoots hunting him down because he was a danger to them, but what if they considered him less than a horsefly? He was buzzing around, but did they notice or even care? He had been ineffectual doing more than . . .

His mare dug in her heels and tried to rear because he yanked back so hard on the reins. He settled his horse and stared hard into the Lucky Lew Saloon. Inside, his back to the door, the serape-sheathed vaquero was making sweeping gestures and laughing loudly.

He wore the sombrero.

Barker hit the ground hard and let his horse go, not even bothering to whip the reins around the iron ring at the side of the saloon. He dragged out his six-shooter and cocked it as he went into the Lucky Lew. Marshal Dravecky ought to have been there to make the arrest, but Barker couldn't identify the vaquero except by the sombrero. This way he could spirit the Mexican out of town and get him locked up someplace where the federal marshal's jurisdiction was unquestioned. One of the forts would be a good choice.

As he walked into the smoky barroom, Barker lifted his six-gun and pointed it straight at the vaquero's back.

"You're under arrest for the murder of the Halliday Stage Company's driver and guard and then robbing said coach. Get your damned hands up."

Barker caught his breath and his heart ran away in his chest. Only force of will kept his hand from shaking as he clutched the six-shooter a little tighter. He expected the vaquero to make a fight of it. The man was going to be hanged for two murders and probably should swing for more than that. He wasn't likely to give up easily.

Yet he did. He raised his hands high and muttered, "Don't go shootin' me in the back."

"Turn around real slow."

The world moved as if it were dipped in molasses. The man pivoted, pushed his sombrero back, and faced Barker's leveled pistol.

The name escaped Barker's lips like the soul leaving a dying man.

"Nate!"

12

BARKER HEARD NOTHING BUT THE POUNDING OF HIS heart in his ears. In spite of his resolve, his gun hand wavered, then slowly sank so his son wasn't in his sights.

"Nate, what are you doing here?"

"It might come as a shock, Pa, but I like to take a nip now and then." Nate laughed. From the sound Barker knew he had been drinking for some time and was more drunk than sober. "When I ain't round you and Ma, I fall in with bad company. If you call all my friends here bad company!" He threw back his head and laughed. The echoes in the silent saloon mocked Barker.

He slowly raised the six-shooter again.

"You're wearing a serape."

"It keeps the dust off when I'm out on the trail, and it's a damned sight cooler than a canvas duster." Nate pounded on it and produced clouds of choking dust.

"The sombrero. Why are you wearing it?"

Nate stopped laughing, looked hard at him, then shook his head. He looked around at the others in the saloon and addressed them. "Has my old man been out in the sun too long? Why am I wearing a sombrero? To keep the sun off my head!"

"That sombrero, that particular one," Barker said, the pistol almost too heavy for him to hold anymore.

"I bought it. I was caught out in the desert and a dust devil took my hat. Whipped it clean off my head and carried it away. It was an old hat and not worth chasin'."

"The sombrero," Barker said.

"You're gettin' mighty impatient, old man," Nate said, a nasty tone edging his words. "Might be you know your time's near and you want to rush everybody?"

Barker said nothing. He lowered the hammer on his six-shooter and slid the Colt back into his holster. Nate wasn't sporting a sidearm, but Barker saw the shiny patch on his right hip where a holster had been riding. For whatever reason, he had left his six-gun somewhere else while he had come to town to drink.

Barker didn't like his son drinking or carrying a six-shooter, but at least he had the good sense to get drunk without his weapon. More than one man had misjudged his sobriety—and skill—with a gun.

"You want to know where I got this sombrero? From the same gent what sold me the watch. I happened into him out on the trail not an hour back and I needed a hat. He offered me his."

"What was he going to use for a hat?"

"How the hell should I know? Might be he needed my money more than he did this fine sombrero."

"Where is he?"

Nate flared. "Out in the desert cookin' his damn brains out, for all I know."

Barker tried to sort it all out and couldn't. He had seen the vaquero wearing this sombrero. He was sure of that. But why would the vaquero sell his hat to Nate? After the robbery, a few dollars was the last thing the road agent needed. From what Barker could tell, the road agents had gotten away with a considerable amount of money and maybe a U.S. Mail bag, too. More than one soldier received money in the mail from wherever he called home.

"How much?"

"What?" Nate stopped his tirade and just stared at him. "How much?" The confusion on his face mirrored Barker's own.

"What'd you pay for the hat?" He was even more confused by the play of emotions on his son's face. There was panic and disbelief and finally relief. All that was pushed down as contempt curled Nate's lip.

"A dollar. I paid him a whole dollar. That satisfy you?"

Before Barker could say another word, the rhythmic clop of horses—lots of horses—filled the street. He glanced over his shoulder and saw Sergeant Sturgeon riding just in front of his guidon bearer.

"You better go get liquored up with your friends, Pa," Nate said. The disdain was more than Barker could explain—or tolerate. He saw that the cavalry sergeant led only a squad, not the full platoon. Not sure what that meant, he wanted to find out.

"You stay here. I want to talk to you later."

"Whatever the deputy federal marshal says."

Barker started to argue, then swung around and left. He found his horse down the street, captured the reins, and led the mare back to the marshal's office that had once been his. This was something else he needed to talk to Marshal Armijo about. A federal marshal, even a deputy federal marshal, needed an office. Sharing with Marshal Dravecky wasn't in the cards, but maybe he could convince Armijo to pay him a stipend and he could call his own house his office. The extra money would come in mighty handy.

"Sergeant," he called as Sturgeon dismounted. "What brings you to town?"

"Good to see you here, Marshal," the sergeant said. "I need to have a word with you and the new marshal . . ." Sturgeon struggled to find the right name.

"Dravecky," Barker supplied. The sergeant's grin of relief was at such odds with the way Nate had faced him that Barker wondered what was wrong in the world when he felt closer ties to a buffalo soldier than he did to his own flesh and blood.

"The lieutenant's out on patrol and wanted me to spread the word about this gang that's preyin' on purty near every ranch in the area."

Barker quickly told the sergeant about the stagecoach robbery. Sturgeon's expression hardened.

"They're gettin' way more vicious in how they commit their crimes," he said.

"I'd come to the same conclusion. It won't be long before the killing's not enough."

"What do you reckon they'll go and do then?" Sturgeon asked.

Barker could only shake his head. He had seen terrible cruelty in his day, and yet he couldn't begin to understand the mind of a killer for whom the act of murder was a thing of joy.

"'Fraid you'd agree with the lieutenant," Sturgeon said.

"Smart man, your lieutenant."

"Seems to be. Better'n we had for a while." The sergeant took a deep breath and stared at Barker. The intent was obvious.

"I can't go traipsing off with you to find them," Barker said.

"You're the best tracker we got."

"What happened to the pair that went off with Lieutenant Greenberg before?" He was less interested in that than he was in avoiding going by the widow woman's ranch again. He had done the right thing, and it had hurt her. He wasn't sure he could do the right thing twice. He wasn't a man who gave in to temptation easily, but there was something about that woman that touched his heart. He had a desire to help and knew what was riding high in his mind wasn't the way to do it, no matter what she wanted.

"One got killed. Accident. He fell off his horse and tumbled down into a canyon. Took a full day to fetch his body off the rocks and bring it to a spot where it could get buried."

"The other one?"

"He decided he'd had enough of army life and just rode away. Might be he had other reasons since he was half-Apache. The notion of tracking down his own people kept him in the field 'cuz he hated 'em so, but chasing Mexican banditos wasn't what he wanted."

"You suppose?"

"That's just a guess."

"A good one."

"What are you really thinkin', Marshal? I can tell when a man's thoughts are on something else."

"How long would we be gone?"

"How long would it take you to track them cayuses to

their lair? We got reason to think they are holed up in those canyons."

"Skeleton Canyon," Barker said. "I lost the vaquero near there. Nasty place to go hunting. You can be within ten feet of a man and never see him."

"And there're dozens of places where he could ambush us."

"Not dozens," Barker said, shaking his head. "Hundreds. That whole place was made for outlaws to hide in. Or Indians. If you don't ever want to be found, you lose yourself there."

"You know the country better'n the two scouts we lost."

"There might be a reward for the outlaws."

"Me and my boys're army. We can't take no reward."

Barker's mind slipped and slid in odd directions again. A hundred dollars wasn't out of the question for a gang of buzzards intent on feasting on the Halliday stagecoaches.

That much money could change lives. Any place where that woman didn't have to see her husband's grave every time she went to feed the starving animals was a better place. A hundred dollars could give her that. Or it might give Nate a start on a different life. Then again, with such a reward Barker might hire a handyman to help out at his own place so Ruth didn't have repairs and chores.

"I'll send word to my wife that I need to be gone for another week." He touched the ten silver dollars pressed into his vest pocket, which he'd received for this day's work. "I need to send her that message and give her something."

"You want one of my men to take the message?"

"My son's over at the saloon yonder," Barker said, making a vague gesture in the direction of the Lucky Lew.

"Good to have family you can depend on."

Barker looked sharply at Sturgeon, wondering if the

man was mocking him. He saw nothing but a guileless black face sheened by sweat from the day's heat.

"Be back in a few minutes."

"It'll take a spell for my men to get provisions, water their horses, and convince themselves to get back on the trail."

Barker left the squad and walked back to the saloon, vowing this time to find out more about his son's connection with the nameless vaquero. If nothing else, he wanted the Mexican's name. It wouldn't be much, but it might spark someone's memory out nearer the Peloncilla Mountains. There was no way in hell Nate's benefactor and the murderous leader of the outlaw gang weren't one and the same.

He stepped into the dim interior of the bar and looked around. Several men played cards at the rear. Beyond them, making a botch of it, two drunks shoved pool cues at ivory balls and laughed whenever they got near. There seemed to be some bet involved, since in the span of a few seconds, Barker saw each man miss and both of them knock back shots of whiskey.

"Where'd he go?" Barker called to the barkeep.

"Your boy? He left right after you did."

Barker touched the coins in his pocket. He'd have to send the money to Ruth some other way.

"He say where he was going?"

"Not a word, but he looked to be in quite a hurry. You musta lit a fire under his ass to get him movin' that quick, Marshal."

Barker took one last, long look at the men in the saloon and decided none of them knew more than what the bartender had passed along. He stepped back out into the heat. He'd have to take Sturgeon up on the offer of messengering the money to Ruth. He didn't have to like it, but he saw no way around it.

In a half hour, Barker and Sturgeon rode from Mesilla at the head of the squad, heading due west for the New Mexico Bootheel country.

Barker couldn't help thinking the area had been misnamed, no matter what it looked like on a map. It wasn't a bootheel, it was a boot hell. And he had agreed to lead a handful of men into the burning heart of it.

13

"DON'T KNOW NUTHIN' 'BOUT THE GANG 'CEPT THE name of their leader," Sergeant Sturgeon said as they worked to pitch camp. It had been a long day's ride and Barker had gotten the twinges, but he wasn't going to be seen dipping into the bottle of laudanum to ease his saddle pain. Whenever a man let another know his weakness, it always got used against him. He trusted Sturgeon and the rest of his squad, but one of them might inadvertently mention seeing him use the drug. Whoever might be within hearing of that could do Barker considerable harm. Marshal Armijo wasn't one for his deputies to be using such potent drugs for any reason.

Barker had to admit the tincture of opium eased the pain, but it also made his hand a trifle shaky at times. The more laudanum he used, the worse the tremors became. While he was at home, that hardly mattered. Ruth thought he was only having the delirium tremens from not imbibing. Sometimes he wished he didn't read as much as he did. The symptoms were detailed in the book he had gotten on Italy and the Roman emperors.

He was slow to understand what the sergeant had just said. When it penetrated the fog swaddling his brain, he dropped his gear, turned, and demanded, "You got a name? What is it? Who is that son of a bitch?"

"Thought you'd have heard it by now." Sturgeon finished spreading his bedroll. Somehow he managed to lay out the army blanket without so much as a wrinkle.

"I've seen him but don't have a name to hang on that peg."

"Don't actually have a name," the sergeant admitted. "His gang calls him the Sonora Kid. A youngster, from the sound of him."

"He's the one that wears the big sombrero? And the serape?"

"That's the Sonora Kid. Rumor has it his men are scared of him because he is so wild and free with his bullets."

"From what I saw at the stagecoach robbery, they can keep up with him shot for shot." Barker mulled over the name. "Where in Sonora is he supposed to hail from?"

"What's the difference? He snuck over the border to do harm. The ranchers claim as many as five hundred head of cattle have been rustled since he came north."

"That's a fair number, but we saved fifty head. Or is he working up to stealing an entire herd of beeves? A real herd?"

"Wouldn't put it past him to kill four or five cowboys and take an entire herd when it gets closer to time to drive 'em to market," Sturgeon said, considering a crime of that magnitude. "If he upped and did that, he'd take their horses, too. That could make a man rich in Mexico."

"That'd make a man rich in *New* Mexico, too," Barker said. "But we decided. This Sonora Kid isn't plying his trade out of need. He enjoys the killing. The notion he is thumbing his nose at the law makes the stealing worthwhile."

Barker settled down on his blanket and leaned back, fingers under his head as he stared up into the twilight sky. The times he had run afoul of the vaquero confirmed his suspicion. The Mexican was toying with him, giving Nate the watch and then selling him the sombrero. It was the bandito's way of taunting him. Barker began to wonder if he was only a convenient target or if the vaquero had something personal against him.

That caused a cold lump to form in his belly. If the Sonora Kid had declared his own private war, Ruth and Nate might be in danger. Nate especially, since he and the Sonora Kid had crossed trails twice before. Barker corrected that. *At least* twice. Nate was turning into a wild stallion. There was no way of telling who he ran with now, after quitting his job at Dooley's store and leaving home.

"I hope to hell he isn't," he said softly.

"How's that, Marshal?"

"Nothing, Sergeant, nothing at all. I was just thinking out loud how best to track down the Sonora Kid."

"You have any ideas?"

"I do, but we'll have to try them out in the morning to see if they're any good."

The rest of the camp slowly drifted off to sleep. In the distance a coyote howled, and the crunch of the sentry's boots on the sand came closer every few minutes. Barker's nose twitched at the smoke from the dying fire, and he knew he ought to sleep. Tomorrow would be another hard day in the saddle.

But sleep evaded him. There wasn't any torture too extreme if the Sonora Kid harmed so much as a hair on his wife's or son's head.

"USED TO BE MINING THROUGHOUT THE AREA," Barker said, looking down the middle of Skeleton Canyon. "Most all the silver chloride ore played out. What didn't get dug up was too dangerous to work."

"Silver?"

"Never found much gold that I recall," Barker said.

Sergeant Sturgeon handed a pair of field glasses to him. Barker peered through them, not sure they improved his vision. Although parts of the rocky walls were magnified, the amount he could see at any instant proved too limited. He preferred to see a large expanse of land, hunting for movement that shouldn't be there. More often than not, that movement wasn't a running buck or a wolf but a man.

He scanned slowly, getting dizzy at the speed at which the land rushed past.

"Keep movin' real slow or you'll go cross-eyed," Sturgeon warned.

"Noticed that." Barker kept looking, finally finding an abandoned mine halfway up the canyon wall on the far side, maybe a mile distant. He found the real use for the binoculars. The mouth of the mine jumped up sharp and clear and big enough for him to see if anything moved just inside. If the Sonora Kid or any of his gang hid out there, he would see them.

"Don't see any trace of a fire or that anyone's been to the mine in a month of Sundays."

"What was chipped out of the rock?" Sturgeon asked again.

"Silver, like I said. Some gold, but not enough to make it worth hiring a small army to protect the mining operations. This part of the mountains funnels Indians escaping from their reservations down into Mexico, too. That makes it doubly dangerous."

"Thieves and Indians," Sturgeon said. "Not what you'd want to deal with if you were a hard-rock miner."

"Most of the prospectors found their strike, sold out, and moved on. The men who burrowed into the hills were a different lot, greedier and less likely to be run off—if there was a buck to be made here."

"Gettin' planted in the ground doesn't match the reward, no matter how much gold or silver you take out."

Barker didn't answer. He had slowly panned down the side of the canyon to the floor, where a small stream meandered along. He had been in Skeleton Canyon a time or two and knew that much of the water was alkali. The stream ran clean enough in the early spring, but that was a month and more behind. As the stream and its feeders dried up, they left only sluggishly flowing water that sucked up the bitter minerals from the ground left as tailings from the mines. After so many years of mining, there was plenty of dross to poison even a stream at full flood.

"Somebody's riding along the stream," Barker said. He handed back the field glasses and pointed out the section of the canyon floor where he had seen movement.

"You got good eyes, Marshal," Sturgeon said. "I mighta missed that."

Barker doubted it. Sergeant Sturgeon was a wily veteran trooper. One day he'd have to ask him where he had served during the war. Then again, maybe he didn't want to know. The black companies weren't sent to the easy battles. Fort Pillow was only a hint of the blood that had been spilled.

"We can't get down there quick enough. If we ride on along the rim, is there a way to get ahead of that varmint?"

"Better to go down here," Barker decided. "I don't know of a better trail. If we got on one of the sections that've broken off, we'd have to backtrack and we'd never run that rider to ground."

Sturgeon took his advice without comment, getting his squad started down the steep trail amid some grumbling. As the troopers passed him, Sturgeon either dressed them down or uttered words of encouragement. Barker liked seeing how the sergeant dealt with his men in different ways, giving each what was needed to bring out his best.

"We'll be on the canyon floor in an hour."

"I got a spot in sight where the rider'll be then, unless he stops."

"No reason to stop if he sees us," Sturgeon said.

"Might not have a choice. He's walking his horse, tellin' me he's either looking for something or his horse is pulling up lame."

The last of the horse soldiers started down the steep incline. Sturgeon snapped his reins and followed. Barker waited until they got a ways down the trail before starting himself. There was no rush. There was no reason for their quarry to be looking for anything. He rode a horse in need of some liniment and a bit of bandage around a sore leg.

By the time he reached the bottom of the canyon and hadn't been made into a target, Barker was feeling better. The outlaw—if it was one of the gang—hadn't spotted them. Even better, none of the others in the gang had, either. So far they had managed to get mighty close to their quarry without being seen.

He looked at the steep walls festooned with crevices and wind-driven holes. The Apaches loved this area because it afforded them the best ambush sites west of Dog Canyon. The sluggish stream in the middle of the canyon carried silt and a whitish current that made Barker loath to get closer for fear his mare would try to drink. The minerals in this water would likely kill a horse or a man within minutes.

"What do you see, Marshal?"

Barker knew he had to dismount to answer the sergeant's question. He felt a bit twitchy down low in his back, but nothing he couldn't tolerate for a few minutes. He swung his leg over and dropped to the ground, walking along the streambed. The rider had ventured close to the stream only once, then veered away, obviously aware of the poison running in the water.

"He must know of better water," Barker said. "He's keeping his distance."

"Might not be that at all."

"Is," Barker insisted. "If he thought we were on his trail, he'd ride in the water to cover his tracks. He's making a point of keeping away." He walked from the solitary hoof-print and found broken twigs and other evidence the rider had come this way. More prints showed up in a section of a game trail. Barker pointed. "He's following this patch of soft earth and not caring if anyone finds his tracks."

"We're gonna get him," Sturgeon said with some determination. "I been after them for a month and this is the closest I've got—'cept for that run-in with the stolen herd a while back."

"I was there," Barker said dryly. He kept walking, not bothering to mount. Swinging up into the saddle might hurt more than it was worth. Besides, he'd found ample evidence that the rider wasn't the only horseman using this path. At least two others rode horses with distinctive shoes. One horseshoe had a deep notch cut into it and another was coming loose. If that horse broke into a gallop, it would lose the shoe and leave its rider behind for an easy capture.

"How many you see? I make out at least one other."

"Two, possibly a third went this way several hours before our rider." He dropped to one knee and ran his fingers around the print, then measured the length of the stride. He looked up to the sergeant. "He's not going to stay on this horse longer than another mile. Not the way the horse is pulling up lame. It started hobbling bad a dozen yards back and by the time it reached this point, any rider, even if he was dead drunk, would know he had a problem. I was right up on the canyon rim when I said I saw him walking his horse."

Sergeant Sturgeon rode back down the path to tell his troopers to be cautious, that the outlaw was afoot and not too far ahead. Barker watched the sergeant's broad back for a moment, then reached into his coat pocket and took out the laudanum. A couple drops, bitter without water, caused him to make a face. He swallowed hard, took a swig from his canteen, and presented a poker face by the time the soldier returned.

"What do you think?" Sturgeon asked.

"If I wanted to hide out here, if I were them, I'd say we're not more than a mile from their camp." Barker looked at the towering red rock walls on either side. The walls narrowed ahead, then spread out and probably branched into two or more canyons. "They'll be at the narrows."

"So they can fight off attack from either direction."

"And have a way to escape if they can't outfight their attackers," Barker finished.

"No way I can get half my men to the other side of their camp, then," Sturgeon said, sucking on his teeth. He frowned as he tried to come up with a way of catching the outlaws in a pincers attack.

"There's no way to get around. Even if you've got Apache scouts, they're not likely to get past to plug up the escape route on the far side of the camp," Barker said. "We got to attack from this side and make sure it's quick."

"Think we can sneak close enough?"

"I'm not sure I can scout that close without warning them," Barker said. "I can track, but when it comes to being sneaky . . ."

"None of my soldiers is worth beans doin' that either," Sturgeon said. He looked up as the sun disappeared behind a high white cloud. "We get close, then attack at sundown, while they're eating."

Barker considered how quickly the sun set in the high-walled canyon. It would be dark within an hour, and he wasn't positive the outlaw camp was ahead. If he wanted to camp here, that's where he'd camp, but even if they found somebody there, he wasn't sure it would be the outlaws. And if it proved his guess was right, would the outlaws be eating as the sun went down or waiting until a later time?

He had too many distracting thoughts to concentrate. The image of the fancy watch Nate had been sold kept coming back to him. The Sonora Kid had twice shown his fondness for watches, once selling a stolen one to Nate and another time buying a watch for Nate to taunt Barker.

"We can't move in for a spell," Barker said to Sturgeon, forcing himself to ignore whatever bothered him about the watches. The owlhoots ahead demanded his full attention. "They'll eat later, long after dark."

"Gets dark early, don't it?" Sturgeon judged the height of the walls. "Should we hang back and risk being seen?"

"I'm not much of a scout, but I'm likely the best you've

got. Let me see to the camp. If I'm not back in a half hour or there's gunfire, come right on in." Barker doubted his own abilities, but too many questions had cropped up. He had to be sure this was the Sonora Kid's gang. If they shot up a bunch of cowboys that had come into the canyons to hunt for strays, they'd never hear the end of it, either from the army commanders or Marshal Armijo.

Sturgeon's impassive face betrayed not a whit of emotion. He finally nodded once, knowing what Barker meant. The marshal handed over the reins to his horse, hitched up his gun belt, and set off through the underbrush, trying not to make too much noise. It would be just as bad to be shot because they thought he was a rabbit as it would be if they knew a lawman had found their trail. Dead was dead, after all, no matter the reason they'd shot at him.

Moving slowly, carefully, he made his way through the thicket to an open area where scrub oak and juniper grew in profusion. Barker crouched and waited, looking hard into the stand of trees for any movement. He doubted the sentry for this gang would be wily enough to lure him out into the clearing for a better shot. More likely, the air would be filled with bullets right away.

As he crouched, he thought hard on what he had seen and how they had followed this trail. Anyone in Skeleton Canyon was likely to be up to no good, but he hadn't definitely identified the rider as being one of the Sonora Kid's gang. Truth was, he couldn't identify any of them other than the Kid himself. The buffalo soldiers might be after an innocent man and he might be wasting his time skulking around the outskirts of a camp. He didn't know for sure that more than one man was camped ahead. The other horses might have continued deeper into the maze of canyons, with only the solitary rider waiting ahead.

He pressed against the bole of a pine tree and got sap on his coat when he heard horses nickering. Barker moved like molasses flowing uphill on a cold day, not wanting to catch any lookout's eye. He saw two men come to the far edge of the clearing. They spoke low, but he knew it was Spanish, and couldn't catch more than a word or two as the pair relieved themselves. When they'd finished, they ducked back into the woods. Barker heard the horses again.

The camp wasn't far—just beyond the trees. Since the two had come this way, he figured there wasn't a guard watching this part of the wooded area. If there was a guard at all, he had been posted on the road.

Casting a long shadow to his left, Barker made his way across the clearing and slipped quietly into the cool woods. The horses were corralled not far away. Barker skirted them, not wanting their neighing to alert those in camp.

He moved like a ghost, closer until he heard the men arguing. From behind a tree, he caught sight of the reason for the disagreement. The man he had spotted from the canyon rim held the front leg of his horse and pointed.

One drew his pistol and made to shoot the horse, but the owner batted the gun away and scuffled with his partner for wanting to put the horse down.

Barker rested his hand on his own six-shooter when he saw a man sitting on a log, facing away. The huge sombrero was identical to the one Nate had worn in town. Barker's six-gun slid from the holster and he lifted the pistol to get off a shot. His hand trembled too much for a decent shot, whether from anticipation or too much laudanum he didn't dare say. Barker spun about, his back to the tree and the camp, and fumbled out the brown bottle to take a few more drops. Holding out his hand, he waited for the shaking to stop.

It must be the opium that caused him to shake like an aspen leaf in the wind.

He looked back and saw the five men gathered in a tight circle, the Sonora Kid using a stick to draw in the dirt.

Barker had to think again on what he intended. Shooting the outlaw from ambush didn't seem much different than shooting a rabid dog; he had never shot a man in the back before and wasn't going to start now. Good sense nudged at the sinful thinking of violating his oath as a lawman and pushed his planning in another direction. He could get off a shot or two and kill the gang leader, but he would be an easy target for the others. Shock might hold them in check for a moment, but they were hardened outlaws. Getting shot at wasn't likely to panic them the way it would five law-abiding cowboys.

And he had never killed a man before, much less shot one in the back.

A quick look over his shoulder showed the men still intent on the dirt sketch. The only way of catching or killing the entire gang was to alert Sturgeon and his soldiers.

Barker was too intent on getting away to pay attention to where he stepped. His weight came down on a dried tree limb. It cracked with a sound like a gunshot.

Then there was actual gunfire—all the slugs directed toward him, from the direction of the outlaw camp.

14

THE BULLET TORE PAST AND KICKED UP A LONG FUR-
row of earth beside him. Barker dodged in the other direction, not even realizing he had made a decision that might
have cost him his life. If one slug had gone to his right, a
dozen came at him when he dived left. He scrambled, fell
to his knees, got his feet back under him, and tried to sprint
away. A bullet hit him in the heel and knocked him flat.

This saved his life. More gunfire crisscrossed through
the space he had just vacated.

Barker rolled, flopped flat onto his belly, and leveled his
gun. He didn't have a decent target, but when he spotted
the long orange tongue of flame from a six-shooter, he fired
toward it. He heard his bullet splintering wood. He had hit
a tree trunk rather than an outlaw intent on ventilating him.
He fired again and again, knowing he was out in the open
and fast running short of ammunition.

The road agents shouted curses in Spanish and spread

out to advance in a fan sure to catch him in their cross fire. He kicked, dug his toes into the ground, and scrambled along, driving his stomach into the rocky ground in his frantic attempt to find refuge. When he saw it, he rolled fast, got to hands and knees, and dived. He screamed in agony, as much from the bullet that finally found his leg as from the pain in his back. He crashed to the ground behind a fallen log barely tall enough to shield him from the outlaws.

Ignoring the stabbing pain in his leg and back, he craned around, poked his pistol over the top of the log, and fired his last rounds. No answering screams of rage reached him. He had missed with every single round. He dropped back behind the dubious protection afforded by the log and fumbled to reload. His hands shook, but this time he knew it was from the intensity of the fight and not from the laudanum. Finally reloaded, he poked back up over the log and saw a dark figure coming toward him. He fired four times and was rewarded with answering fire from three directions that drove him back behind the log.

He got off the remaining two rounds and again worked to reload. There was no way he could wait for the twilight to deepen and hide his escape. The gang was circling him, waiting for him to make a run for it. He clicked the gate on his six-shooter closed, took a deep breath, and got his knees under him. With a surge, he came to his feet, stepped over the log, and let out a screech like a banshee as he ran forward toward his attackers.

Rather than burn through his six rounds as fast as he could, he fired with measured speed, each discharge like a peal of doom. His aim wasn't any better, but the unexpected frontal assault caused the gang to hesitate—that would reward him a few seconds more of life, and that was all he could hope for.

Then the air filled with more whistling bullets than he could track. It took Barker a second to realize these were not heavy lead pellets coming to kill him but carbine fire from behind.

Sturgeon and his buffalo soldiers had heard the gunfire and moved in for the attack.

This buoyed him but did not turn him cautious. He kept running and firing. A distant grunt hinted that someone had been hit in the gang's camp, but Barker ignored this small victory. Step after step carried him closer to the edge of the woods. He heard the road agents running away ahead of him and the pounding of horses' hooves behind.

"Get down, you fool. Take cover. We'll get 'em!"

Sergeant Sturgeon thundered past on his horse, his men flanking him in a precise battle line that quickly fell into disarray when they reached the edge of the woods. Barker slowed to a walk, reloading as he went and realizing he was out of bullets. What he had in the cylinder was it. Six rounds. He had to make them count.

It was as if he existed in a curious bubble separated from his surroundings. He heard the soldiers cursing as they had to dismount to advance through the woods. They were on either side of him—and the sergeant somehow led them forward to the camp. But Sturgeon's commands came as if from a distance. The fusillade from the outlaws was nothing more than the whine of annoying insects. Barker strode forward, invincible now that he had survived their first attack.

"They're gettin' away, Sarge!"

"Stop them. Shoot the horses out from under them. Block the road!"

Barker kept walking and emerged from the woods where the Sonora Kid had drawn his plans in the dirt while the rest watched. Barker's six-gun came up and fired. A horse squealed like a stepped-on piglet. He fired again, but no reaction reached him. Sturgeon pressed close to his right side, and a corporal came up from his left.

"All the horses are gone. Ever' last one of 'em hightailed it, Sarge."

"Forward, fire by the numbers, odd, even!"

Barker was aware of every other soldier firing, then the next rank advancing to fire. They provided cover this way for their comrades in arms.

This worked for a dozen yards. Then the withering fire from rocks forced the soldiers to take cover.

Barker would have kept walking and firing if Sturgeon hadn't yanked him hard and swung him around behind a rock. As he sat heavily, a rifle slug ricocheted off the top of the rock.

"You been eatin' locoweed?" Sturgeon demanded. "They're killers! They'll kill you if you stick your honkin' big nose out there like that."

"I need more bullets," Barker said, aware that he had used the last of his ammunition.

"All we got's for our carbines. You stay down and let us catch them rustlers."

"Rustlers," Barker said, still in his curious world where danger hardly existed and he was invincible. "They're killers and stagecoach robbers and—"

He spoke to an empty air. Sturgeon had ducked low and run to get his men re-formed to renew attack.

Barker heard horses in the distance and knew the outlaws were escaping. He shoved his useless six-shooter into his holster, then began a wide arc that would bring him around to outflank the gang. As he worked his way up to higher ground, he stumbled and went to one knee. Whatever he had fallen over moaned. He reached down and found a soldier staring up at him.

"Marshal, done been hit. Feels bad."

"Take some of this," Barker said, fumbling out the laudanum from his pocket. "It'll make the pain go away."

"Can't fight no mo'."

He made sure the soldier had swallowed the opiate, then carefully replaced the bottle in his pocket. Somehow, it seemed more precious than life itself.

Barker snatched up the soldier's carbine and continued on the arc to go against the gang's right flank. He scrambled through the rocks, wiggled like a snake atop a rock still warm from the day's sun, and peered over the top down into deep shadow. Unable to tell where any of the outlaws were, he sighted along the short barrel and waited.

When one road agent fired, Barker immediately squeezed the trigger. He was rewarded with a moan. The outlaw turned and looked up toward him but couldn't see him. He fired again, hitting the man a second time. Then the soldiers rushed forward, rifles blazing.

"Hold your fire, don't shoot no more!" Sergeant Sturgeon ordered.

The sudden silence was as frightening as the constant barrage. Barker lay belly down on the rock for a few seconds, then called out, "I'm above you, Sergeant. I'm standing up. Don't shoot."

Barker got to his feet and for the first time realized how weak he was. He slipped, hit the rock, and skidded down the curving surface to land in a heap a few feet from the soldiers.

The buffalo soldiers snickered. Even Sturgeon's sharp order didn't stop the smirking, and Barker noticed the sergeant worked to hide his own amusement. Forcing himself to sit up, Barker checked to be sure nothing had broken. The only aches and pains he had were old, remembered ones, with the exception of the bullet hole in his leg. Using the carbine as a crutch, he levered himself to his feet.

"How many did we get?"

"You winged this one, but the corporal stopped him when he tried to sneak away. Can't rightly say we got any of the others."

"Don't go chasing them in the dark. You'll get ambushed. Wait till morning. We can track them," Barker said. He felt the same pull that the sergeant did to go after the outlaws. To be this close and have them escape seemed so wrong, but they had other responsibilities.

"Sergeant," Barker said, "you've got a wounded man on the other side of this rock. I used his carbine. Hope that doesn't violate army regulations."

"Don't know that it does, you bein' a federal lawman, Marshal. Otherwise, I'd have to take you into custody for misappropriatin' government property." Sturgeon laughed at his small joke, then motioned to a pair of soldiers to see to the wounded man. "You be all right, Marshal? I want to see what's in the camp."

"Don't go messing up the map in the dirt. I want a look at it. When I get there." Barker put one foot in front of the other and found that his strength returned quickly enough if he kept walking. Only when he slowed or stopped did he find himself in trouble if he tried moving another inch. The bullet wound in his leg was minor, bloodier than it was serious. He was just overall weaker than he wanted to be.

"Won't do more'n we have to." With that the sergeant trotted off.

Barker started to follow the soldier, then slowed and stopped in spite of the aches he then felt in both knees.

Something tugged at the edge of his hearing, his sight, his sense of smell. Rather than go back to the camp, he explored farther south, in the direction taken by the fleeing road agents.

He wended his way along the twisting game trail, increasingly wary because of the deepening shadows. It was hardly six o'clock and the canyon bottom was darker than midnight. Barker swung the carbine to his shoulder when he saw two figures ahead. A horse stood just off the trail, nervously pawing at the ground. But it wasn't the horse that held his attention. A man knelt with another standing beside him. For a few seconds, Barker couldn't make out the meaning of the dark blobs. Then he did.

The kneeling man wore a sombrero.

He lifted his rifle, but something gave him away. The standing outlaw snapped off four quick shots. The sudden blaze from the muzzle blinded Barker. He jerked to one side, lost his balance, and fell heavily when his wounded leg gave way under him. He rolled over, brought the rifle up so he could fire in a prone position, and saw only the kneeling man. Where the other road agent had gone he couldn't tell. Then he realized that the horse had disappeared, too.

"Throw up your hands! You're under arrest!"

The outlaw didn't stir. Barker's finger drew back on the trigger, but he didn't fire. Something wasn't right.

"What's goin' on, Marshal? You needin' some help?"

"Over here, Sergeant," he called. Barker got to his feet and kept the carbine trained on the sombrero-wearing man. "There's a second one around somewhere."

"We'll sweep the area." Sturgeon gave the orders, and four soldiers crowded past, then galloped away. Barker edged closer.

"Don't try going for a gun. I'll shoot you where you are." Barker was ready to fire at the slightest twitch. Nothing. No movement.

Sturgeon rode past, hit the ground, and ran a couple paces. He clutched his pistol as he got his footing. Between the buffalo soldier and the marshal, they had the outlaw dead to rights. If he so much as sneezed, they'd shoot him down in their cross fire.

"Don't see anybody else, Sergeant," the corporal reported, returning from a quick ride down the trail deeper into the canyon.

"That's all right. We got ourselves one of them," Sturgeon said.

"Do we?" Barker closed the distance and used the rifle muzzle to knock the sombrero off the man's head. The hat went flying, but the man toppled to the ground, unmoving.

Sturgeon came up and used his boot to prod the man in the chest. No movement. The soldier bent and rolled the man over, then looked up at Barker.

"He's dead. You done killed him."

"I never even shot at him."

"Somebody did." Sturgeon pointed to a bullet hole in the back of the man's neck.

Barker considered the angle of the wound and the possibility a stray army bullet might have ended the man's life. He shook his head.

"The other man shot his partner. He stood over him, aimed down like this"—he made a gun out of his fingers like a small boy might—"and killed him."

"Why? Doesn't look like he was too injured to ride. No other wound on him."

"Might be the killer wanted his horse."

Sturgeon snorted in disgust.

"Troopers don't leave their comrades behind. If I had any inclination before, I surely don't want to sign up for this outfit now, though there's not much left of it. We done too good a job wipin' 'em out and runnin' 'em off."

"We didn't get but two of them," Barker said. "And counting this as ours is pushing the truth till it squeaks."

"You don't know him? Look at the sombrero."

Barker stepped closer, then reached into his pocket, found a lucifer, and struck it. The match flared, then settled down to a guttering flame that illuminated the dead man's face.

"The vaquero I've been chasing," he said in a dull voice.

"That's got to be the Sonora Kid. Their leader's dead."

"Would one of the gang kill his own leader like this?" In his imagination, Barker watched ghostly figures going through the assassination.

"If his own worthless life hung in the balance, friendship'd go out the window," Sturgeon said. "Get caught by us or kill the Sonora Kid? One of the gang didn't have a problem makin' that decision."

Barker went through the vaquero's pockets, hunting for something. He didn't know what he sought, but he didn't find it. No money, no watch, nothing. He straightened and looked at the body.

"It doesn't make any sense."

"You've got too strong a moral sense, Marshal," Sturgeon said. "These men, they don't have any moral anchor. What they want to do, they just do."

"He didn't have a watch."

"How's that?"

"I expected more, I reckon," Barker said. "This is the vaquero I've been trailing. No question about that."

"And the Sonora Kid wore that sombrero. We stopped

the Sonora Kid, Marshal. And tomorrow we'll catch the rest of them. How far can they run in the dark?"

Barker wasn't sure, but he thought it might be all the way back to Sonora. That meant the whole of southern New Mexico Territory would settle down and be more law-abiding. He wasn't sure what he felt about that.

Except that it didn't seem right.

15

MASON BARKER SHIFTED THE SADDLE, LIFTED A
mite, and rubbed his sore behind. Sergeant Sturgeon
laughed at him, as he had about every day during the past
week as they went deeper into the Peloncilla Mountains
hunting for the road agents who had escaped. After an
entire week Barker still couldn't tell how many men they
were chasing. It might have been one or it could have been
three.

What he did know was that his butt hurt something
fierce from being in the saddle this long. The days were
hot and deadly if he didn't swill enough water. Just finding
decent watering holes took about all the skill he had as a
tracker. At times he wished he was part Apache. They always tracked water like a bee goes after a flower.

But the buffalo soldiers rode stolidly, never complain-
ing, enduring more hardship than he did since they shared
their water with him when he wasn't able to find anything

but alkali holes. He wondered if they had iron plates stitched into their britches. It was the only explanation.

"I'm ready to get back to the fort and tell the colonel that we done run them back into the heart of Mexico," Sturgeon said. He wiped the sweat from his face, squeezed out his scarf, and knotted it back around his neck. At one time the cloth had been bright yellow, but the sun and wind had faded it until it was almost white.

"I'm ready to go back and die," Barker said. "But I won't tell your commander that we ran them bastards off. More likely, they led us a merry chase, staying just beyond our reach, watching us and laughing their damn fool heads off."

"You're a good scout, Marshal. I understand why Colonel Carson kept you on. You must have given the Navajos hell."

"More like it was mutual. The only ones I ever saw who could outride a Navajo are the Apaches. And I'm saying that because as I get older, what they do on horseback looks all the more miraculous to me." Barker heaved a sigh and leaned forward in the saddle to take some of the pressure off his hindquarters. "The trail was never good, and it got confused more than once. All we can claim is two dead outlaws."

"We can claim the Sonora Kid," Sturgeon said.

Barker stayed silent on this point. They had argued, friendly-like, about the vaquero's identity. The sergeant was sure this was the gang's leader, but Barker worried about what had happened. The least palatable notion was that the Sonora Kid had actually killed the vaquero and made it look as if they had stopped the top bandito. Still, Barker couldn't deny he was glad to see the vaquero dead and buried. Whether he was the Sonora Kid or not, he had been one mean son of a gun. Keeping him out of Mesilla and preventing him from robbing stagecoaches and rustling cattle was sure to improve the entire southern reach of New Mexico Territory.

But was he the Sonora Kid?

"He was," Sturgeon said, reading Barker's thoughtful expression perfectly. "Don't care if you back me up on that. I'm reporting that the leader of that gang's dead and gone."

"You could be right," Barker allowed.

"I'll see that any reward goes to you."

"That's mighty thoughtful of you," Barker said. "I doubt there's any reward, but it would surely do me a world of good." He stretched and winced. He had been riding without taking any laudanum to save what little remained in the bottle. He looked over his shoulder at the soldier who had been wounded in the fight with the outlaws. He had taken three bullets and had been in terrible bad pain when Barker gave him some of the tincture, and now he rode as hard and as long as any of his fellow troopers.

Barker kept down the unworthy thought that this just wasn't right. He needed more and more of the opium just to stay in the saddle, and here this soldier was almost healed after a week, the laudanum having done nothing more than take the edge off his pain when he was first shot.

"Your leg troublin' you some?"

"Not too much," Barker said truthfully. He pointed to the east. "That the road we were hunting for?"

"Looks to be large enough for heavy wagons. It runs north. Your skill's better'n any of ours, Marshal. You found us the road home."

The road home. The words rang like a bell in his head. It had been almost two weeks since he had slept in his own bed, Ruth alongside him. Hell, it had been that long since he'd had a bath. Fleas gnawed on his tough hide, and every time he moved, caked dirt cracked and fell off his coat and face.

The road home. The road to heaven on earth.

"You and your men deserve a rest."

"If the lieutenant's back, we'll get it."

"But not if the colonel has any say in the matter?"

"Oh, Colonel Tomasson has all the say in the world 'bout it. He's the post commander, but Lieutenant Greenberg can argue with the best of 'em and can get us furlough or even extra rations. Sometimes."

Two of the soldiers riding directly behind began arguing whether it was better to get a three-day pass or extra victuals. Barker appreciated the contention since he wasn't sure how he'd answer after having his belly rub up against his spine from lack of decent food for so long. Ruth's cooking would put the weight back on him, but it would take longer than three days.

Even though he had been hard at work chasing the outlaws from the territory, he doubted Marshal Armijo would give him more than a few days off. Barker wondered if he might make out that the bullet wound in his leg was worse than it was, but he quickly discarded that notion. He wasn't being paid to malinger. He'd just have to make do with whatever time away from the job he could take to be with Ruth.

"Here we are, Marshal, on the road back to the fort. Thank you kindly for your help." Sturgeon thrust out his huge hand. Barker's was engulfed in the firm handshake.

"Any time, Sergeant, any time."

"We'd have this country cleaned slick as a whistle if'n there were more like you." With that, Sergeant Sturgeon bellowed for the squad to advance, and the troopers trotted away, leaving Barker alone on the dusty road.

East lay home.

He snapped the reins and got his mare stepping along at a fast walk toward the Organ Mountains and home.

"HE OUGHT TO BE WITH US," RUTH SAID. "IT'S NOT right."

"I can't go hunting for him." Barker tried to keep the anger and hurt from his voice.

"You can ask around. Those soldiers you're always going on about, how good they are and how they cover every square inch of the territory. Have them look for him. He hasn't gone far."

"I'll do that, but asking the army to spy on Nate isn't right."

"It's not spying. I just want to know where he's got off to. It's been weeks, and he never so much as said goodbye. I want to know if he's all right."

"I'm sure he is," Barker said, but he knew that he lied. That wasn't the proper thing to do ever, and less so since he and Ruth were fixing to go to church services.

"I want to know." She faced him and looked hard up into his eyes. Then she smiled. Just a little. "It's good that you're not drinking like you were. I cannot abide a man smelling like a brewery."

Barker instinctively touched the brown bottle in his pocket. The laudanum was almost gone, and it was the reason he hadn't needed a shot or two of whiskey since he'd been home. The opium kept away the pain and let him move about easily. Being with Ruth made taking the drug even more important, but he had to shove his hand into his pocket to hide the shaking. He needed a few drops right now, but it seemed a weakness he didn't want his wife to see if he took them. She would neither understand nor approve.

"You're sweating, Mase."

"It's hot, in case you didn't notice."

"Not so much inside. And you're pale. You sure that gunshot wound in the leg didn't get infected?"

"It's healin' up just fine. Come on or we'll be late for church."

"Now I know you're sick. The Mason Barker I know would ride twenty miles out of his way to be certain he was late. The preacher can be a long-winded cuss, especially on days this hot."

He grunted and held out his arm for her to take. She looped hers through his and they left the house. Barker was almost staggered by the heat, although it was still early morning. He wasn't sick, but the drug did this to him. He got cold sweats and his mouth turned to cotton wool. Worst of all, his visits to the outhouse were getting to be few and painful. But the laudanum eased his pain. There was no gain without some drawback. To move and ride and be with Ruth without his back stopping him was worth a bit of sweating and having shaky hands.

He helped her into the buggy, then climbed up and took the reins. Driving, it didn't matter if his hands trembled. If anything, that helped keep the balky, swaybacked horse moving along, unwillingly so.

"We won't have to stay long," Ruth said, answering a question he hadn't asked.

He nodded and kept his eyes focused on the road ahead. The horse pulled slowly, but that didn't keep every rock and pothole in the road from sending shocks up into his back. Barker considered another drop or two but wouldn't do it while Ruth watched him like a hawk.

"I'm glad you've given up drinking. That means your back is feeling better, doesn't it?"

"Still gives me twinges," he admitted. He saw no reason to lie about it since he knew she saw how he winced now and again. Sitting up a little straighter did nothing to ease the pain.

"You ought to go to a doctor over in El Paso and see to it. Or there's talk of a good doctor up at Fort Bayard."

"He's a vet."

"So? There's no difference between the human animal and the four-legged variety."

"You've gone to too many of these sermons without me," Barker said, grinning. Ruth stared at him for a moment, then laughed.

"You must be feeling better. You sound more like your old self, joshing like that."

Barker continued to guide the horse onto the smoothest portion of the road, but there was hardly any patch without hills and valleys as big as those in the Peloncillas. Gratitude for finally arriving at the church flooded him as he parked under a cottonwood in the shade.

"Not much of a turnout today," Ruth said. "There's Miz Warner. I'll need to speak to her about that recipe she promised."

"For cobbler?"

"Apple pie," Ruth said. "Now I know you're feeling chipper to ask after dessert."

He helped her down and watched her bustle over to where Mrs. Warner held court with three other wives. Ruth and Mrs. Warner quickly excluded the others, fast friends swapping recipes. Barker started toward the church, where it had to be cooler inside. If he was first in, he might find a pew near a window where a breeze could keep him awake.

"Marshal, a word with you."

He heaved a sigh of resignation.

"Morning, Mr. Mayor. Out to rustle up some votes?"

Mayor Pendleton sidled closer, took his arm, and steered him back into the shade. Barker was glad for that. Otherwise, he would have had to shoot him to get out of the sun. Pendleton was a leather-lunged politician who never fell silent if even one person who might vote remained within earshot. Then Barker remembered he had left his six-shooter at home. This was Sunday, after all, and besides, there wasn't likely to be much call to shoot the mayor.

"What are you doing about the crime that grips our town?"

"You hired a town marshal. He told me in no uncertain terms my presence in town wasn't appreciated."

"Did he, now? I'll have a word with Marshal Dravecky. It can't hurt to have two lawmen on patrol up and down our streets."

"What crime are you talking about, Mayor? My wife didn't mention any in Mesilla." Ruth would have berated the new marshal if there had been reason to do so. As much as she liked him being home, at least a little more, she would have told him if Dravecky wasn't doing his job.

"Well, not so much in town," Pendleton said reluctantly. "Dravecky keeps most of the fighting and drunkenness under control, but there is trouble collecting fines from the, uh, the Cyprians."

"So he's not extorting your ladies of the evening enough to suit you?"

"I'm not implying anything, just that, he, well, that's not the real concern. The outlying regions, all around Mesilla, there's complaints."

"About?" Barker wiped sweat from his forehead with the clean linen handkerchief Ruth had tucked into his pocket. He tried to keep his hands from shaking. And he had to watch what he said. His mouth was dryer than the desert outside Mesilla, and focusing on the mayor was a mite more difficult than it should have been. But Barker thought that might only be lack of interest in what Pendleton had to say.

"Horse thieves. Rustlers. Nothing much. A horse here, a couple head of cattle there, but reports are increasing."

"I got a telegram from Marshal Armijo," Barker said. "He thinks it's a band of Warm Springs Apaches off the reservation in Arizona. The cavalry has been notified. Corralling Indians is their concern."

"The reports I get don't mention redskins," Pendleton said.

"I'll contact Armijo and see what he wants me to do."

"There's more . . . petty thieving."

"How's that?"

"It's hard to point at any given theft, but taken together, well, Mr. Dooley said there's been shoplifting lately. More than a kid stealing penny candy."

Barker said nothing about this. More than once he had seen Pendleton swipe a peppermint from the jar when Dooley wasn't looking. If anything, Dooley was smart enough to leave the candy where it was easily swiped to keep the kids—and politicians—from taking more valuable merchandise.

"What does your new marshal have to say about that?"

"He thinks it's Mexicans."

"He's probably right," Barker said dryly. "There's nobody else in Mesilla who would ever think to steal anything from the general store."

"I know you killed the leader of that gang, that Sonora Kid."

"The cavalry laid claim to that," Barker said. He was glad to pass along whatever praise there was for the shooting to Sergeant Sturgeon and his troopers. Still, the vaquero's death had been strange, and the rest of the gang, the ones not killed in the gunfight, were probably deep inside Mexico by now.

"If I have to use political pull with the governor, I will."

"To do what?"

"Why, to force you to do your duty, Marshal. What do you think we've been talking about? Stop all the rustling and petty pilfering before it turns serious!"

"I'll round up all the Mexicans," he said. His sarcasm was lost on the mayor.

"See to it. Ah, the minister is ready to begin the sermon. I'm glad we had this talk. I'm sure you will perform your duties from now on, Marshal."

It took all Barker's willpower not to take a swing at Pendleton. That wouldn't have been the proper thing to do in the sight of the preacher and God on the Sabbath, but Barker would have been willing to argue his case with St. Peter at the Pearly Gates when he finally passed, just for the pleasure of it now.

He tightened his fingers into a fist, to see what it might feel like. He took a slow swing at empty air since Pendleton was already shaking hands with the minister. As his arm swung around, he lost his footing, stumbled, and the world turned red with pain. He caught the rough trunk of the cottonwood and pulled himself upright. The pain refused to abate.

Hands shaking, he got the brown bottle from his pocket and took a swig from it. The bitter tincture burned his tongue but began affording some relief in less than a minute.

"Mase, come along now. The sermon's 'bout to start." Ruth waved to him from the church steps. He returned the wave, then started for the door to join her. The sermon had better be a powerful one, because he had nothing but desolation in his soul.

The bottle of laudanum was empty.

16

"I'M GONNA BE SICK," THE STATION AGENT FROM ME-
silla said, turning away. Mason Barker had to swallow his
own bile at the sight of the overturned stagecoach and the
dead bodies.

Four passengers, the driver, and the shotgun messenger,
all dead and left in the hot New Mexico sun to decay. He
rubbed his nose as he walked closer, and his eyes watered
from the rising stench. They hadn't been dead longer than
a few hours—more than long enough to begin to stink to
high heaven. The day was too hot for the coyotes to come in
to pick at the bodies, and the way the dead passengers were
trapped inside the compartment had discouraged the buzzards. Both guard and driver were pinned under the stage.

He started counting bullet holes in the wood sides and
then gave up. He couldn't count that high. It looked as if the
stagecoach had driven through the stream of bullets coming out of a Gatling gun.

"You know who these folks are?" he called back to the station agent.

"No," came the weak answer. "Just told they was on the stage."

Barker shook his head. The people were as riddled with bullets as the stage. Figured. They'd been inside when somebody opened fire. He couldn't even guess how many men had been responsible, but from his examination, it seemed the road agents hadn't bothered to fire a warning shot to get the driver to stop. They'd just opened up. Nowhere could he see any evidence that the driver had whipped the horses in an attempt to escape or had put on the brake to stop.

"Not likely to find who they are, then," Barker said. "They've been robbed." He strained, reached down through the window, and flipped back a torn vest pocket where one man's watch had been ripped out. The watch chain and fob had left distinctive marks, too. He imagined it clearly—a dirty hand grabbing the chain and then yanking it free.

A slow circuit of the turned-over stage showed that the passengers' luggage had been rifled. The contents had been strewn out and then the desert wind had finished the scattering to all points of the compass. Barker tugged a frilly-fronted shirt off a mesquite bush and held it up. It had belonged to a gambler. Nobody else would wear such foppery.

"What am I gonna tell the home office?" The station agent rode to Barker, making a point of looking away from the carnage.

"That you lost a stage to outlaws," Barker said. "No sense tossing in a spoonful of sugar to make it sound any different."

He turned back to the stage and frowned.

"How is it you thought to fetch me? The stage couldn't have been more'n a couple hours late." Barker looked up and saw how pale the man had turned.

The agent swallowed hard, started to speak, then swallowed again after pouring some water into his mouth and over his head to calm himself. Barker waited patiently for the answer. The corpses weren't going anywhere, and he needed as much information as he could gather to track down the sons of bitches who had murdered six men just like . . .

. . . just like the Sonora Kid had done a month earlier.

"Marshal Barker, I thought it was a joke, but my clerk said it was real blood."

"What was real blood?" Barker's patience began to fray. Remembering the Sonora Kid hadn't done a thing to ease his suspicions about the death in the Peloncilla Mountains.

"The n-note. It was writ in blood. Said the s-stage had been robbed out here on the road."

"You still got the note?"

"It's back with my clerk. I fetched you as soon as I convinced myself it was for real."

Barker didn't ask what had been the deciding factor. He peered back into the compartment, then pushed back and faced the station agent.

"The note was written in blood and there was a writin' instrument with it?"

"It was wr-rapped inside. The man's finger!"

Barker had guessed as much. A second look had shown a passenger's index finger had been sawed off. He circled the stage again, thinking hard on why outlaws would want to alert the station agent of their crime and to do so in such a gruesome fashion. Their robbery wouldn't have been discovered until the next day, after the stagecoach had failed to arrive. Maybe a rider would have come across the turned-over stage and done his civic duty by reporting it. From the bullets and blood, it seemed that anyone finding the scene of this crime would have been inclined to ride along a little faster and not get caught up in it.

On his second circuit, studying the rock-hard ground, Barker's eye was struck by a dazzling point of light coming from something in the dust. He bent and almost toppled over. The pain in his back had gotten worse since he finished the laudanum that Sunday at church. He had stayed out on the trail with his flask of whiskey, which hadn't been hard after the telegram he got from Marshal Armijo. The mayor had lit a fire under the governor, and the governor had seen to it that the federal marshal sent his deputies out after all the petty thieves.

Barker had been on the trail most of the time and had been able to do more than take a nip or two of whiskey to dull the pain. But it wasn't anywhere as good as the opium. He was thinking of riding to El Paso to see if he could find more. Or over to Tombstone. Rumor had it the Chinee in Hoptown got opium directly from the Celestial Kingdom.

He wished there was a doctor in Mesilla or even Las Cruces. Going to the vet at Fort Bayard was hardly the way to get another bottle of the potent narcotic. Why use painkillers on a horse? If its condition was that bad, it was put out of its misery.

He rubbed his back, wondering if he ought to be put out of his misery.

"What you got, Marshal?"

His fingers flipped over the silver concha, and he managed to straighten up without venting a groan. Barker held it high, let the sunlight reflect off the Mexican ornament, then tucked it into his pocket.

"Might not be anything, but my guess is that it fell off a sombrero belonging to one of the banditos."

"They was Mexicans? You can tell that?"

"I'll want to see the note. Don't go tossin' it to the dogs."

"It was writ in good enough English."

Barker kept his opinion of *that* to himself.

"There any ranches nearby?" he asked, more to get the station agent's mind roving in other directions than for real information. He knew that the Bar K land was not five miles north of the road. Many's the time drivers had complained about the Bar K cattle on the road, slowing them down. A steer used to grazing out in this sparse land didn't much care if it found sustenance along a road or up in the foothills of the Organ Mountains.

He listened with half an ear as the agent rattled on nervously about whose spread was closest.

"Why don't you get on back to Mesilla and round up some men to fix your stage so you can get it to town?"

"The bodies . . ."

"You know how pleased the undertaker'll be to have six burials in the offing. Why, Digger O'Dell might actually crack a smile he'll be so happy."

"The main office'll offer a big reward for this, Marshal. A hunnerd dollars, maybe. We can't lose coaches like this. Why, Little Tom even upped and quit us, takin' a job over in El Paso. Replacin' him's gonna be hard. He—"

"Passengers would get a mite edgy, too, thinking they'd be killed," Barker said.

"Oh, yeah, them, too. Who'd want to ride a Halliday Stage if they'd end up like . . . like this." The station agent stared at the wreckage and quickly turned away, ready to puke.

"I'll see if any of the hands on the Bar K have seen

riders crossing their land recently." Barker knew he was more likely to get a reply asking after rustlers. If the Sonora Kid's gang had returned, it was likely they'd camped nearby and needed food. Taking down a cow or two would make for some mighty fine eating. Anyone who'd murder six men the way these banditos had would probably think on celebrating.

"When you be back in town, Marshal?"

"I'm not sure. You tell Dravecky to keep an eye out for a Mexican wearing a sombrero missing a silver concha."

"You want him to arrest him?"

Unworthy thoughts rattled through Barker's head. He finally said, "I just want to know what they do and where they head when they ride out of town."

"I'll let him know."

"You tell him not to tangle with them. Not without a dozen men armed with shotguns backing him up. Whoever's wearing that sombrero is likely the architect of this here massacre."

"I . . . Do what you have to, Marshal, to stop these . . . these animals!" The station agent sawed at his horse's reins and galloped back toward Mesilla. In this heat the horse would collapse under him before he'd ridden a mile. Barker sighed. The horse would have enough sense to slow down, no matter what its rider wanted.

He made a more careful study of the stagecoach and its dead occupants but found nothing more. The silver concha might have been left in the dust at any time, but he didn't think so. The weather, the sun, the constant scraping of sand blowing over it would have dulled its finish if it had been in the road very long.

Then there was the sombrero the Sonora Kid had worn. It had conchas like this one. He pulled it from his pocket, squinted hard, and examined it. It had come from Mexico. Nowhere could you find better silversmiths, even among the Navajo. He was no expert, but he thought it might have been made down in Taxco. There had been a comb he saw over in El Paso that he had wanted to get for Ruth, finely wrought and too expensive to buy, that had been made down in the southern Mexico province with a design similar to what he held.

Barker went to his horse, fumbled in the saddlebags, and got out his pint bottle. He sloshed around the amber contents, took out the cork, and stared at it for a moment. When the twinges hit him, Barker upended the bottle and drained a half inch. It burned like the sun all the way to his belly, but it would take twenty minutes to dull his pain.

He stashed the recorked bottle back in his saddlebags and mounted, not bothering to stifle the moan. There had to be more he could do to ease the backache.

Turning north, he rode until the sun cooked the left side of his body. He knew he was on Bar K land because the scrawny cattle hunting for grass or anything else to eat all carried that brand on their hindquarters.

Just before sundown, he drew rein, took off his hat, and slapped it a couple times against his leg to get the trail dust off, then settled it back. No reason he shouldn't look all purty for company. Barker rode on down into the cavalry camp, the sentry coming out to challenge him, a private he remembered from the foray into the Peloncillas.

"Howdy, Marshal Barker," the soldier greeted. "The sarge, he didn't say nuthin' 'bout you comin' by."

"You out after rustlers?"

"Yes, suh, we surely are."

By now their voices had carried to the nearest campfire, bringing Sergeant Sturgeon.

"You're like a bad penny, Marshal. Can't get rid of you no matter how I try."

"I'm the only one who'd drink your vile coffee and lie to you 'bout how good it was."

"If you're anglin' for some coffee, come on in." Sturgeon motioned him to ride on past the guard, who hoisted his rifle back to his shoulder and slowly returned to pacing his duty post.

"Pull up a rock. You got your own cup?"

Barker was already fishing around for it. He hesitated as his fingers slipped over the slick glass of the whiskey bottle. He left it where it was, though another nip or two would have set well with him. He knew how awful the coffee these soldiers boiled could be.

"Where's your lieutenant?" he asked.

"The colonel called him back to the post. Reckon you're out here for the same reason we are."

"Not rustlers," Barker said. He told of the stagecoach robbery—slaughter—and concluded by saying, "I know that vaquero was killed, but I'm doubting it was the Sonora Kid."

"You thinkin' he killed his partner, put the sombrero on him to make us think he was dead, then hightailed it into Mexico?"

"I've seen savagery in my day but nothing like this. Not before the Sonora Kid blew up out of Mexico."

"It does look like history is repeatin'," Sturgeon said. "The cattle thievin's like before, too."

"So the Kid and his gang—or a new one—hid out for a month and then returned?" Barker shook his head. He had doubts that the vaquero had been the Sonora Kid, but when the inhuman killings had stopped, there had been a reason to believe it was over and done.

"This isn't the only stagecoach that's been shot up. One I came on a week back, farther north, was lucky."

Barker perked up. "I hadn't heard about another robbery."

"No robbery. The stage line laid a trap. Inside the coach were four riflemen. The first sign of an ambush, they all popped up and returned fire. Whoever'd tried to bushwhack them didn't have the stomach for the fight and rode away."

"Too bad they didn't have a posse with them to run them to ground. Where was this?"

"Near Mineral Springs, a week ago Tuesday."

Barker couldn't remember what day it was now, and it hardly mattered.

"They have a description of the outlaws?"

"Not a good one. The driver thought he saw the leader wearing a sombrero but couldn't say more. In this weather, a sombrero makes good sense." Sturgeon held out his arms to show what area a sombrero might shade.

"Reckon I ought to go to Mineral Springs and ask around 'bout that trap and see if any of them can give a better description."

"Ride with us, Marshal. We're headed east into the foothills."

Barker looked at the purple-clad Organ Mountains, sharply rising from the desert floor. Hidden away in canyons and valleys were decent rangeland and more than one ranch.

"You just fishin' or you have a nibble?" Barker asked.

"Bait is a herd of cattle just waitin' to be stolen," Sturgeon told him. "Not that the outlaws seem to be doing more than eating a couple steers."

"In celebration of killing," Barker said softly. Louder, "I'll ride with you. No telling what trouble we can find."

Sergeant Sturgeon smiled, his white teeth almost glowing in the twilight.

THE CATTLE LOWED, ALERTING BARKER. HE PERKED up. He had been lost in thought about the stagecoach massacre and the chance that the Sonora Kid wasn't dead, after all. In his gut he knew the Mexican still lived and was responsible, even if Sergeant Sturgeon had declared the dead vaquero to be the gang's leader.

"Someone's ridin' this way," Sturgeon whispered.

"They can't hear us. They're across the valley," Barker said, but he kept his voice low, too.

"I'm not takin' any chance, no sir."

Sturgeon raised his gloved hand and passed a silent signal along to his squad. They stirred, then mounted. The sound of the horses came louder than the soldiers' voices as they grumbled at being disturbed from their catnapping.

Barker turned his head up and studied the stars above. Thin wisps of clouds moved across the sky, but the moon wasn't likely to rise for some time yet. When it did, the entire valley would be as bright as day. He wondered if that would benefit them catching the rustlers or would work against them. Sturgeon had positioned his men to deal with cattle thieves coming from either up in the valley or off the desert.

Already his planning had failed, since it seemed as if the rustlers had come off the valley rim from higher country.

"You see 'em?" Barker asked.

"I can smell them," Sturgeon said.

"There." Barker pointed at shadows drifting along, moving toward the tight knot of cattle. The rustlers approached the cattle like ghosts, not riding directly toward the target but sidling along, keeping in shadow.

"Get ready," Sturgeon told his corporal. "When I give the order, have the bugler sound charge."

"That's not the Mexican gang," Barker said, too late. Sturgeon had given the signal. The clarion sound of the bugle echoed across the valley.

The shadows stopped moving. The soldiers charged forward, but Barker chose a different technique. He fixed on a dark splotch, the last place he had seen movement, and rode directly for it. When he got halfway to the darkness melting into the deeper black of junipers and pine, he dragged out his rifle and fired. A flurry of motion ahead showed he had flushed out his quarry.

And it wasn't a Mexican bandito intent on rustling. The Apache let out a war whoop and attacked, riding directly for Barker. The sight of a brave swinging a hatchet that caught faint glints of starlight momentarily unnerved him. Then he levered in another round and fired as his mare galloped forward. Barker was luckier than he was skillful in knocking the brave off his horse.

In a flash, he surged past the Apache struggling to get to his feet. The fall had knocked the wind from him.

Barker could have gone back and taken a prisoner, but he found himself engaged with two more Indians. He fired, dazzling himself each time. He missed both of the Apaches but drove them off.

As he reached the spot where they had hidden, he wheeled about and readied for a new attack. There was no need. The soldiers had captured the Apache brave he had knocked from his horse and were in pursuit of the other two. Sergeant Sturgeon bellowed orders to his other troopers to secure the prisoners they had already taken.

The buffalo soldier trotted to Barker and said, "We've had one real good night. Caught four and are chasing down two more."

"Your men won't catch them, not in the dark."

"Doesn't matter. Colonel Tomasson will be pleased to have some rustlers to show off."

"That matters," Barker agreed, knowing he ought to do a better job blowing his own horn. Chief deputy marshal would be his if he worried more about keeping the good he did under Armijo's nose.

"Come on back to the post with us. You can ride on to Mineral Springs afterward."

Barker considered this, then agreed. The lure of the hot springs to ease his back drew him powerfully. There might even be a pharmacy in Mineral Springs where he could buy more laudanum without anyone in Mesilla finding out. More than this, if the colonel put in a good word for him with Marshal Armijo, that promotion to chief deputy might just come his way after all.

"You have a scout to lead the way or do you want me to find the trail?" he asked.

17

MASON BARKER FROWNED AS HE WATCHED THE POST commander step out of his office. Colonel Tomasson returned Sergeant Sturgeon's salute as the squad rode past, then he called out.

"You're the marshal?"

Barker peeled away from the squad and let Sturgeon take his prisoners to the stockade. With a quick move, he slid from the saddle, landed hard and endured the jolt, then walked forward to meet the post commander.

"Name's Mason Barker, federal deputy marshal. Pleased to meet you, Colonel." He stared hard at the officer, trying to place him.

"I know you," the man said, his concentration on the matter as intense as Barker's. "But how's that? You've never been to the post since I've been commanding, have you? No, I don't think so. I don't forget a face."

"You were on General Carleton's staff," Barker said, finally remembering.

"I was."

"I never met you, but Colonel Carson and I went to a staff meeting in Santa Fe where you were in attendance."

"During the Navajo War! Yes, I remember you now. You were Carson's chief scout." Tomasson beamed that he had finally put a job to the face in front of him.

"Not chief scout. Just scout. I was one of a dozen who went into Canyon de Chelly ahead of the troops."

"A nasty scout, that. Those winding canyons were treacherous. I remember trying to trace them out on a map that General Carleton used for his overall strategic planning."

That was about how Barker remembered the colonel. A staff officer who never strayed from a safe bivouac and three squares a day. Since the man remembered him, it made him wary to come to a conclusion about Tomasson that might not set well with the present reality. Barker hadn't said a word in that meeting. For all that, Colonel Carson had said damned little, listening to James Carleton spew his wild-ass plans for the war. Barker continued to be amazed that the strategy had worked, except the part about Bosque Redondo that had been doomed from the day the first Navajo stumbled into the reservation, no matter that it had been well intentioned.

"If it hadn't been for the Apache scouts with us, it would have been more dangerous. Navajoland wasn't an easy conquest."

"As I know, as we all know." Tomasson chuckled as he remembered what seemed to be better days for him. He hadn't commanded a post of buffalo soldiers then nor was he plagued with rustlers who could simply disappear across the border, where he dared not go to capture them.

"Sergeant Sturgeon's squad captured some Apaches off the Warm Springs Reservation, from the look of them. You've got a good man there."

"Where is Lieutenant Greenberg?"

Barker shrugged. "Can't rightly say. I was after a gang of Mexican banditos that've been causing considerable trouble, when I came across the sergeant. For a while we thought the banditos were also rustling the cattle. Turned out that wasn't the case."

"You must join me for dinner, Marshal. We can discuss combining forces to bring a semblance of law to this god-forsaken country. It will be good working again with a man of your tracking ability."

"Much obliged," Barker said. He was thinking about telling the colonel how duty called and he had to ride on to Mineral Springs, but Sturgeon interrupted with his report.

Barker stood to one side as the sergeant gave the salient points of the patrol.

"Good work, Sergeant. What happened to Lieutenant Greenberg? Why didn't he return with his command?"

Sturgeon stared directly ahead, braced as if he stood on the parade ground waiting for inspection. Barker saw the quick play of emotions as the noncom worked on a possible answer, then said briskly, "Sir, he was after the same band of rustlers, but he took a different trail. We became separated."

"When can I expect his report on my desk? But then, you wouldn't be able to answer that. You're only an enlisted man." Tomasson grew even angrier at his missing lieutenant. Barker started to come to the man's defense since Greenberg wasn't present to speak for himself, but Sturgeon did it first.

"I've never served under a better officer, sir. If the lieutenant is still in the field, it's because he is after other Apaches off their reservation. Ones that I neglected to capture. Sir."

"Yes, well . . ." Tomasson scowled. "Good work, Sergeant. Dismissed." He returned Sturgeon's crisp salute and turned to his office. Barker wasn't sure what to do when Tomasson closed his office door without saying another word.

It took him a few seconds to gather the reins on his mare and go after Sturgeon.

"Wait a minute, Sergeant, I got a question."

"What is it, Marshal?"

"Where'd the lieutenant really go?"

"He didn't confide in me, but he took a half dozen men and rode north from where we caught the Apaches. He's been on his own for close to a day."

"Could he have heard some rumor and gone to investigate?"

"Could be. The ranchers talk to him and not me. What I hear comes from the cowboys, not the ranch owners, 'cept when they're griping about rustlers taking their cows."

Barker knew the heart of this problem. The ranchers might hire black ranch hands, but dealing with black soldiers was a different matter. Greenberg was likely to have been told something by one of the ranchers that would never trickle down to the buffalo soldiers. Barker glanced over his shoulder at Tomasson's closed office door. Tomasson didn't seem too pleased with his command, either. Unlike some officers, of Ben Grierson's stature, the colonel considered this command a demotion or possibly even a punishment.

Barker was glad not all officers were like Custer and Tomasson.

"You talk to the post sutler to find if anybody's seen Mexicans wearing a sombrero without a concha?" he asked.

Sturgeon turned and stared at him, then laughed.

"That's the stupidest question you could ever ask a merchant," the sergeant said. "They don't notice Mexicans, much less if they are missing a bit of silver decoration on their hats. The only way this post sutler would notice is if he traded for that concha. And even then, he wouldn't pay no never mind to the man with it. His eyes would be on the silver and nothing more."

Barker had to laugh at this. His eagerness to track down the gang—whether it was the Sonora Kid's or another, newer one—had consumed him and made him stupid. Or maybe it was simply being in the saddle all day long. He needed some laudanum for the way he hurt, the way his hands shook, and the way he was acting like a damned fool.

"I don't rightly know if the colonel expects me to stay for dinner. He invited me, but that was before he got all pissy."

"Stay. If he don't feed you, I'll see that the cook slops up a plate of beans for you." Sturgeon looked around, then grinned. "He owes you something for making the deal with Dooley. We've been gettin' almost decent food."

"That was a deal between him and your lieutenant," Barker reminded him. He saw that this turned Sturgeon morose again. In the field, the sergeant was alert, but when he rode past the sentry at the low wall surrounding the fort, he became a different man. Barker suspected most of that attitude change came from the commanding officer.

"Can I stable my horse? She won't eat much, and if I have to, I can sleep in the stall tonight and be on my way tomorrow morning 'fore reveille."

"One more horse isn't going to upset nobody in the stables. I'll see to that."

Barker spent the rest of the afternoon tending his horse and talking with the soldiers, most of them veterans of the chase through the Peloncillas after the Sonora Kid. He wasn't sure what he wanted to learn, but one of them might have seen or heard something that he had missed.

"No, suh," the corporal said. "I didn't follow nobody from where we shot it out. But I seen a single rider headin' off. Took that trail to the southeast."

Barker pictured the land in his head and nodded. That trail curved around awhile, then went straight south into Mexico. Anyone escaping the cavalry and wanting to hide out for a spell would go that way. The other trail was equally winding, but it curved out and spit any rider following it into Arizona.

"You see his face?"

"Only the back of his head. And then not so much," the corporal said.

"What kind of hat was he wearing?"

"No hat. Bare head. Dark brown hair or maybe it was just dirty and some other color. He was bent almost double like he was carryin' one o' our slugs in him. Or might be he just rode that way."

Barker thought more on this. If the escaping bandito had been shot, it explained why there hadn't been any stagecoach robberies or much in the way of thievery in the territory for close to a month. The outlaw had been recuperating. But now he was healed and back.

From the brutality of the murders in the stagecoach

holdup, Barker had to believe it was the Sonora Kid who had escaped and had finally returned like a bad penny. If it wasn't the leader of the gang, it was someone who had learned brutality firsthand and enjoyed the bloodletting. From a practical standpoint, it didn't matter if the vaquero had been the Sonora Kid and was dead with his partner back and acting in the same murderous way, or if it had been the Sonora Kid himself who had escaped.

Dead was dead when lead started flying, no matter whose finger pulled the trigger.

"You tell me any more about—" Barker clamped his mouth shut when a private ran up, breathless.

"You the marshal the colonel's goin' on about?" The private looked at the corporal with a hint of defiance. Interrupting like this wasn't done unless on higher orders.

"Colonel Tomasson want to see me?" Barker heaved to his feet. He had asked about moonshine on the post and been told that it didn't exist. Sturgeon and three other sergeants were too vigilant to allow it. He wished he could take a swig before seeing the colonel again, but he had done harder things in his life.

"Right away, suh. You need me to show you the way?"

Barker looked past the private. The colonel's office was across the parade ground, where a tall mast from a sailing ship held the unit banner. The extra rigging kept the pole from snapping in the high winds that often whipped across the post. Barker wondered how many flags had been lost until somebody—a former navy officer?—suggested the pole.

"I can find it."

Relief on the private's face showed that none of the soldiers enjoyed the colonel's company all that much. Barker said his goodbyes to the corporal and the private and sauntered to the office, where he rapped sharply and waited.

"Come!"

Barker pushed open the door and stepped into the close, small office. It would have been better to leave the door open, but the vagrant desert breeze might have scattered papers on the desk all over the floor.

"Marshal! I'm glad my striker found you. I was afraid you'd left." Tomasson leaned back in his chair, hands on the edge of his desk. "I hate paperwork, and that's all there seems to be these days. Not like when we were hunting down the Navajos."

"Why not let your adjutant do this for you?"

"My adjutant got kicked in the head and isn't doing so well. My other three officers, a major and two lieutenants, are in the field."

"That's all your officer corps?" Barker felt a small bit of sympathy for the commander.

"You're not privy to military rumors anymore, Marshal. Fort Selden is likely to be decommissioned when the Southern Pacific comes through and connects down into Texas."

"Heard tell of the railroad coming through but didn't pay much mind to it." Barker knew better than to worry over such things. The railroad might mean easier transportation and the eventual death of the stagecoach, but considering how the Mexican outlaws had been devastating the stage road traffic, that would be a good thing. Dealing with train robbers was likely to be easier than the road agents holding up the stage.

"Not sure where the tracks will be laid, but somebody in Mesilla is holding out for a considerable sum of money for the right-of-way."

"Sounds 'bout right," Barker said.

"You might consider moving to Doña Ana if the railroad goes through there. Mesilla will dry up and blow away without the railroad."

"They offering a better price for the land?"

"Free."

"Free?" Barker snorted at this.

"They're looking to the future, not the present. Give the railroad the land and their town will flourish at the expense of Mesilla and others all around."

"But we're a stage depot on the route to . . ." Barker's voice trailed off. He had just reasoned that the railroad would kill the stagecoach companies. Why rattle your teeth and eat grit by the pound when you could ride in comfort at twice the speed in a railcar?

"You're not a dull fellow, I see," Tomasson said. "But if you are like me, you are also a hungry one. I have ordered dinner set up in my quarters. It would be my pleasure if you'd join me."

"You're wrong there, Colonel," Barker said. "It's *my* pleasure to join *you*."

Tomasson beamed, and Barker knew he had struck the right note. The colonel put a few rocks atop the piles of papers, then exited the office.

As Barker joined him, the colonel asked, "We might ruin dinner with this question, so I'll put it right out there. I need a scout. I know your skill from the days you rode for Colonel Carson and . . ."

"Colonel, Colonel!" A rider galloped up, then stopped his horse so fast the dug-in hooves sprayed dust all over the officer and Barker.

"What's the meaning of this unseemly interruption, Private?" Tomasson brushed off the dirt from his natty uniform. "I'll have you on report unless . . ."

"They was ambushed, suh. All of 'em are dead."

"Who? What are you talking about, man? Spit it out!"

"The supply train from Fort Union. They was ambushed and they was all killed. And—"

"And what?" Tomasson's face had drained of color. Barker ignored the officer and watched the messenger closely. Whatever else he had to say, he wasn't inclined to spit it out.

"Who else was killed?" Barker asked, his tone gentler than the colonel's but no less insistent.

"Suh, it was the lieutenant. Lieutenant Greenberg. Him and his men was all slaughtered, too. They's all dead!"

18

"THE JOURNEY OF DEATH," MASON BARKER MUT-
tered as he rode beside Colonel Tomasson. The Rio Grande
was not far to the east and provided a clear, if never easy,
marker to the north. *Jornado del Muerto,* the early Spanish
explorers had called this trail, and it never failed to live up
to its name. In the summer, the river was mostly dry and
water had to be found elsewhere. Such a task was never
easy in such hard desert. Spring brought raging currents
thanks to runoff from the high mountains in the northern
part of New Mexico and made crossing the river nigh on
impossible. During the winter it was often possible to ride
across the dry riverbed.

And water or the lack of it was not all that menaced
a traveler; Indians, road agents and the hammering sun
added to the danger.

"That's what they call it," Tomasson said glumly. "I
cannot imagine losing another officer like this."

"You all right, leaving the post without an officer in charge?"

"The quartermaster is capable enough. He was a captain during the war."

"Demoted because there weren't enough officer's positions?"

"Yes," Tomasson said. "He stayed in the army, though he ought to have found himself a town in need of a general store and settled down. Something about the military holds him."

Barker wondered if Tomasson might not have been a general at the end of the war, then thought not. James Carleton had only been a one-star general. He might have worked his way up to major general, but mostly Barker hadn't cared enough to follow the man's career. When decent officers like Grierson couldn't get a star, it was no wonder that Tomasson remained a colonel—and was probably lucky to keep the gold chickens on his shoulder epaulets.

"What was in the supply train?"

"I didn't think to check the equipment request, but there was a considerable amount of ammunition to be sent this month. I always order five times as much as I need and get barely enough to send out armed patrols."

"That's the way it is with the army," Barker acknowledged. He had seen it work against Colonel Carson, who never quite got the hang of proper military ordering. But then Carson could not read or write anything but his own name. Barker had heard of a clever quartermaster at one of Carson's posts after the war requisitioning more whiskey than flour for the soldiers. The fort hadn't been properly prepared to defend itself, but there wasn't a soldier on the post who wasn't appreciative of an illiterate commander and a conniving quartermaster.

"How much farther, Private?"

The messenger rode a few yards to the colonel's right, obviously not wanting to eavesdrop on his commanding officer and yet fearful he would be called upon and not hear.

"Up ahead, not a half mile. You know the spot in the road where it dips down toward the river? The wagons have to slow and—"

"I don't know this spot," Tomasson said harshly. "A half mile, you say?"

"No more'n that, suh."

"Lieutenant Greenberg must have gotten wind of the ambush and ridden to warn the freighters," Barker said.

"He should have sent a messenger back to the post. I could have had a company out to protect the supply train."

"Might not have been time," Barker said, but he knew the colonel was right. Whatever Greenberg's reason for personally leading a handful of soldiers to meet the supply train had been, he had not shown good sense. It was hard to believe Greenberg's inexperience might have done him in, though Barker thought that was likely the case. He had liked the young officer, and that colored his thinking when it came to deciding what Greenberg would or wouldn't do. It wasn't beyond the pale that Greenberg wanted to save the supply train and win a medal.

"We'll never know," Tomasson said, standing in his stirrups and peering ahead. The site of the massacre had proven to be closer to a quarter mile.

Strewn across the road and toward the river were opened crates that had contained rifles. Kegs of black powder and what Barker took to be boxes of cartridges for the troopers' carbines had been cracked open and the contents spilled out.

He frowned at the sight. If Indians had attacked, there wouldn't have been a single brass cartridge anywhere. The Apaches would have picked up even a single round, knowing that could mean the difference between life and death for them later. What he saw made no sense. The contents of two wagons had been spilled, not stolen.

"Who'd do this?" Tomasson asked.

For a moment, Barker thought the colonel meant scattering powder and ammunition, then he saw the colonel staring at four soldiers. The morning sunlight glinted off their brass buttons as they lay head to toe to head beside the wagon. Their attackers had gone to great trouble arranging the bodies. Barker sucked in his breath when he saw how many rounds had been used to kill the men. Their heavy blue wool jackets had absorbed most of the blood, but he counted dozens of bullet holes in each of the men.

"I've never seen such mercilessness," Tomasson said.

"I have." The words were hardly audible as they escaped Barker's lips. Louder, he said, "The stagecoach robbery I told you about? This could be its twin the way—the victims were cut down and then repeatedly shot long after they died."

"Men can be sorely wounded and live on. I saw a man hit nineteen times in battle and he survived. Perhaps . . ."

"No, Colonel, that's not what happened. The banditos I'm chasing did this. Their ruthlessness knows no bounds."

Behind him he heard a soldier trying not to vomit and failing. They had just found the rest of the soldiers in the wagon train, including Lieutenant Greenberg. He and the three men with him had received special attention from the butchers responsible.

Barker left the colonel to shouting out orders to retrieve

what had been tossed onto the ground and then get an inventory. Barker rode in a wide circle, studying the ground, getting a feel for what had happened. As with the stagecoach ambush, there had been no subtlety to this attack. At least six men had opened fire on the soldiers, catching them in a withering cross fire. While unspent cartridges had been tossed from the army supply wagons, Barker found three spots with piles of spent brass where the outlaws had waited and then opened fire.

He tried to estimate how many rounds had been fired. He quit counting at one hundred. The outlaws hadn't tried to cover their tracks either to or from the ambush site. They had ridden in from the east, crossing the river and waiting for at least a couple hours. Barker found the places where the road agents had relieved themselves, discarded whiskey bottles, and otherwise left their imprint.

And after the slaughter they had taken one wagon and ridden south-southwest. He shuddered. That road bypassed Mesilla and went toward the Peloncilla Mountains. This reinforced his belief that the Sonora Kid was back and deadlier than ever.

"That way, Colonel," Barker said as the officer rode up. "One wagon and something else, a smaller wagon maybe."

"A caisson."

Barker looked at the colonel.

"Why'd they want to take that, unless . . ." His voice trailed off when he saw the officer's grim expression.

"They stole a mountain howitzer, shot for it, and enough black powder to wage a small war."

"They're going into the Peloncillas," Barker said. "With a cannon. If they find the right spot in those hills, they can hold off a company of your troopers."

"I can only hope that's what they want with the howitzer," Tomasson said. "If they set it up for a defensive position, its loss is irritating but not critical."

"What else could the Sonora Kid want with it?" Barker said more to himself than to Tomasson.

"They can cause immense destruction with even a small field piece. They can blow open the strongest bank vault. If they go far enough west, they can lob a round or two at a steam engine and inflict serious damage on the railroad laying tracks into the territory."

Barker's thoughts turned in other directions. The Sonora Kid had shown he had a taste for blood. If he pulled that field piece into a town like Mesilla, he could kill dozens of people with only a few rounds.

"How hard will it be to learn to use it properly?" Barker asked. "I remember how difficult it was for Colonel Carson's unit to deploy artillery."

"If all he wants to do is kill, it's not hard. Just start firing and let the shells fall where they might. Load the barrel with links of chain or nails and there's no need to be accurate. Just figuring out how to load and discharge is all that's needed."

Barker shuddered in spite of the heat. The mental image he had of chain shot and solid cannonballs ripping through a town's populace frightened him, and he didn't scare easily. The gang had shown less inclination to steal than to kill. This was an unstoppable killing machine.

"I'll post a guard over the wagons," Tomasson said, "until new teams from the post can be brought out. I'll see that the wheelwright comes, too. Those axles look in mighty bad shape."

"You know how many men were with the supply train?" Barker asked.

The colonel didn't.

Barker put his finger to his ear, then turned in the direction of a soft moan. He pointed into the bosque lining the river. He urged his horse forward as he slipped his pistol from its holster. Such caution wasn't necessary because he found the source of the pitiful sounds immediately.

"You said you'd seen a man shot up nineteen times and he still lived. You can add another to your story, Colonel."

Lying in the underbrush, a private writhed in pain. The back of his blue coat showed a half dozen holes. Barker dismounted and knelt beside the fallen man. Many of the slugs had cut into his coat and not penetrated more than a fraction of an inch. Whether the coat had saved him or the loads used by the outlaws shooting him were punk didn't matter. He had caught a lot of lead and survived.

"We'll get you to Fort Selden and take care of you there," Barker assured the man. The private's eyes flickered open. He recoiled when he finally focused on Barker. "Easy now. You're safe. Colonel Tomasson is here."

"The outlaws. It was the Sonora Kid!"

"Now how would you know a thing like that?" Barker asked gently.

"Heard one Mexican call him that. You . . . you—"

"At ease, Private," Tomasson said. "There's no call to exert yourself. We'll have you up and in the saddle again in no time." Tomasson looked at Barker and added, "This is a guard from Fort Union."

"Guessed as much," Barker said since the wounded soldier was white.

"We can't go after the gang without mustering more troops," Tomasson said. To the wounded soldier he asked, "When did this happen?"

"Don't know. Yesterday?"

"That's probably right," Barker said. "The tracks are a day old, if not more. They have quite a head start."

"I'll put two companies into the field, if I can get my other units to return."

Tomasson went to a soldier and spoke rapidly. The soldier saluted, vaulted into the saddle, and galloped off in the direction of Fort Selden. Barker reckoned the colonel had sent word back to prepare for the worst. Before the colonel returned to the post, messengers would be dispatched, ordering the return of all patrols and alerting other nearby forts. Concentrating on finding the outlaws and the stolen howitzer took precedence over cattle rustlers and even Indians who had sneaked off the reservation.

Barker had to agree with the officer. This wasn't any run-of-the-mill outlaw they were after. It was the Sonora Kid.

"HE DIED," SERGEANT STURGEON TOLD BARKER. "About halfway to the post, he died from the wounds."

"They looked shallow," Barker said.

"He lost a whale of a lot of blood, Marshal. Might have been better to leave him be and try to nurse him back there in the woods, but the colonel, well, the colonel wanted none of that."

"I can understand," Barker said, and he did. Tomasson wanted as many of his command as possible in the field chasing down the Sonora Kid. Leaving one to nursemaid the wounded soldier from Fort Union removed a carbine from the fray. Still, it was a sorry end to the soldier's life.

But he had delivered one fact that Barker had felt in his gut but lacked proof of. The Sonora Kid had returned to bedevil the whole of southern New Mexico Territory.

"I'll see if Marshal Armijo won't post a big reward on the Kid's head," Barker said.

"That might be real dangerous," Sergeant Sturgeon said. "If the reward's too small, nobody'll care. If it's too big, you might be floodin' the territory with bounty hunters. Some are tough hombres, but they won't believe they're up against a killer like the Kid."

"Can't let it go unmentioned," Barker said glumly. "I need to know if anyone sees him or his gang."

"But a big reward might lure 'em into thinkin' they can bag him like a snipe."

"If we don't locate him, more'n a man or two's going to get killed," Barker said. The horrific power of the mountain howitzer would be trained on unsuspecting towns just for the Sonora Kid's sick pleasure. He had to be stopped. Fast.

"You talk to that federal marshal of yours, but there has to be something more to convince ever'one how dangerous the Kid is."

"You're right." Barker looked at the flagpole that had once been the main mast of a sailing ship. The cross members were about the right height. Going to his horse, Barker unlooped the rope and sat on the boardwalk, using his knife and chewing his tongue in concentration to fashion what he wanted to be the symbol of this outlaw.

More than one soldier stopped to watch in puzzlement. Barker refused to answer their questions about what he was making until he finally cut off the end of the rope and stood. When he mounted and rode to the flagpole, he could reach up and touch the cross member. With a quick toss, he looped the rope over the beam and let the hangman's noose drop down.

"This isn't just any noose," Barker called to the soldiers now assembled. Across the parade ground, Colonel Tomasson came from his office to see what the fuss was about. "This isn't a simple noose. It's the Sonora noose and it's made special for the Sonora Kid!"

The soldiers muttered for a moment, but Sergeant Sturgeon's bull-throated roar cut through the sounds.

"Long may the soldier-killin' son of a bitch swing!"

Barker smiled grimly. This time there was a roar of approval. He'd see the noose filled. With the neck of the Sonora Kid.

19

HE COULDN'T STOP THE SHAKES. BARKER LOOKED UP
from his comfortable spot in the shade next to his barn, to
make certain his wife was nowhere to be seen. Ruth had
been feeding the chickens, but the poultry had ducked back
into their shed to avoid the increasing August heat. His
nose dripped and his eyes blurred, but he managed to pull
out the new bottle of laudanum he had bought in Mineral
Springs.

After leaving Fort Selden, he had ridden north again,
ignoring the Sonora Kid's trail into the southwestern
mountains to tend his own needs. An apothecary in Mineral Springs had sold him the drug, more on the basis of
him wearing his badge where everyone could see than for
any other reason. The chemist had eyed him strangely, but
Barker had muttered something about using it as bait for
a crook. The opium wasn't illegal, not exactly, but Barker

didn't want anyone in Mesilla knowing he needed it so badly.

If anyone in Mesilla found out, his wife would know, too. Ruth had strong feelings about opium and even drinking. She tolerated him smelling of whiskey now and then, but things had been smoother between them since he had begun using the laudanum. But if she found out . . .

He took the small bottle out and stared at it. The pain faded away when he took a few drops. He fumbled to get the cork out, almost dropping the bottle. His heart seized up at the fear of spilling the precious fluid. He captured the bottle with both hands and held it until he calmed. Only then did he trust himself to drop a bit of its contents onto his tongue. The bitter taste no longer made him recoil, because he knew the relief it would give later.

But that "later" was coming much later all the time, unless he took more, using the precious drug faster. He put a few more drops on his tongue. He thought it would burn a hole through, but he ignored the tiny pinpricks of pain where each drop landed.

He heaved a deep sigh and leaned back in the shade, trying to get his thoughts in line like one of Sergeant Sturgeon's squads. All neat and never out of place and . . .

"Mase!"

It took him a second to realize Ruth was calling. He sat straighter. The pain had gone. Scrambling to his feet, he went to the house.

"What is it?" Barker saw the youngster and his lathered horse and knew trouble wasn't brewing—it had already been brewed.

"This is Joey. His pa works at the bookstore."

Barker said nothing. He remembered the boy as being

a troublemaker, but whatever had happened to bring him racing from town was more than using a slingshot to knock out a neighbor's plate glass window or tying lighted firecrackers to a dog's tail.

"Go on, Joey. Tell him what you told me." Ruth sounded stern, which made Barker even more alert. She didn't use that tone unless she was angry and trying to look outwardly calm.

"Marshal, they came into town. Three of 'em."

"Who?"

"Now, Mase, don't badger the boy. Let him tell you in his own way."

"The gang. The Sonora Kid's gang. And the Kid was with them and he's got Marshal Dravecky holed up in the jail."

"Who's helping the marshal?" Barker knew the answer to that one. Nobody. He pushed past Ruth and grabbed his gun belt hanging on a peg just inside the door.

"Mase, get help. Don't take these horrible men on all by yourself," Ruth said, grabbing his arm. He shook her off.

"There might be more to this than you know," he said. Visions haunted him of the Sonora Kid wheeling the stolen mountain howitzer up to the jailhouse and firing it straight through the front door. That would kill the marshal and any prisoners inside. Judging from the way the outlaws had slaughtered so many other victims, they wouldn't stop with blowing the marshal to hell and gone. The howitzer would be spun around and turned down Calle de Guadalupe. An efficient team could load and fire twice or even three times in a minute.

Mesilla could be in flames, with dozens dead. A couple more rounds of cannonade would destroy the entire town.

There wasn't much in the bank, but this, too, would be open to easy theft.

"Joey," he said. "Go on to Fort Selden and let the post commander know what's happening."

"Fort Selden?" the boy said dubiously. "That's a mighty long way off."

"If you run into an army patrol 'fore you get there, tell them what you've told me."

"I don't know if my pa would want me to—"

"Do it or your pa and everybody else in town are likely to end up dead!" Barker lost his temper and didn't care.

The boy jumped and looked frightened. Good. That would keep him going until he alerted the cavalry to the danger.

"You're not telling me something, Mason Barker. What aren't you telling me?" Ruth followed him to the barn, haranguing him as he went.

He wiped his dripping nose on his coat sleeve and tried to control the shaking in his hands. But his vision had cleared and the pain had disappeared. The marshal paused, wondering if the laudanum was affecting his good sense. Then he decided it didn't matter. The federal government paid him to enforce the law, and the Sonora Kid had become his personal bugaboo.

"This'll all work out, Ruth," he told her as he cinched the saddle strap down tight around the horse. He stepped up and rode out, ducking as he passed through the door. She was shouting at him as he snapped the reins and broke into a gallop. There might not be much time left. The people in Mesilla would never know what they faced until the Sonora Kid yanked on the lanyard that sent a howitzer shell through their town.

As he neared the edge of town, Barker heard sporadic

gunfire. Reaching down, he pulled his rifle from its saddle sheath. He tried to remember if he had loaded the Winchester. The fuzzy edges around his brain refused to let that information come to him. He cocked the rifle and kept riding, not sure how many rounds he could rely on.

And then it was too late to slow down, take the time to check the magazine, and proceed. He saw two men with serapes draped over their shoulders and huge-brimmed sombreros pulled down, walking down the middle of the street, shooting at anybody who dared poke a nose out.

The two outlaws laughed uproariously. One tossed aside an empty whiskey bottle, then took three shots at it. Drunk though the bandito might be, his first shot shattered the bottle and the next two sent the fragments flying. After he had destroyed the empty bottle, he returned to shattering windows and putting rounds into walls and doors.

Barker heard a loud shriek of pain as a bullet penetrated a thin wood door and hit an occupant of the bakery.

The two outlaws laughed, turned their six-shooters toward the sound of agony, and reduced the door to splinters. Barker pulled his rifle up to his shoulder and squeezed off the best shot he could at a dead gallop.

He was more lucky than skillful. His bullet cut a hole in the brim of one man's sombrero and lodged in a hidden shoulder. The outlaw groaned, dropped to his knees, and clutched at his shoulder. Barker got off three more rounds. All missed.

And then he rode down the still-standing bandito, swinging his rifle to smash the barrel into his face. The outlaw fell back and crashed to the street.

"*Hijo de puta*," grated out the wounded outlaw. He lifted his six-gun and awkwardly fired. It was his turn to get lucky, since his wounded shoulder didn't allow him to raise his arm very high.

Barker felt sudden sharp pain in his leg. He looked at his right leg and saw blood oozing out of the hole just above the top of his boot. There wasn't any pain, so he reckoned it wasn't too badly wounded. His horse dug in her heels and kicked up a dust cloud, giving him time to twist about and point his rifle behind him at the outlaw who had shot him. The hammer fell with a dull click. He had run out of rounds in the magazine.

His horse recovered, wheeled about, and let him stare at the wounded Mexican, who fought to get to his feet. The one he had clubbed remained flat on his back in the street.

A dozen scenes played out in Barker's head, and none of them favored him. He laid the rifle across the saddle in front of him and struggled to draw his six-shooter. The outlaw fired first. And missed. Barker's aim was no better, but he put his heels to the horse's flanks and rocketed forward. He fired again and missed. Then he raced past, swinging his pistol. Luck was frowning on him again; he knocked the sombrero off but did not touch the bandito.

He left the outlaw in the dust behind. Rather than trying for a third pass, Barker kept his head down and kept galloping away until he reached a cross street. Leaning hard, he guided his mare down the road and out of range. By the time he had brought his horse back under control, he had shoved his six-gun into his holster and reached behind into his saddlebags for ammo for his rifle.

"Marshal, what's happenin'?" A woman fearfully looked out into the street but ducked back when a bullet tore away a chunk of adobe above her head. Inside the thick-walled building, she would be safe—but Barker wasn't safe any longer out in the street.

He slammed the last cartridge into his rifle and trained it on the outlaw standing at the intersection of the streets. The Mexican had lost his sombrero, but the brightly colored serape made for a good target. Barker leveled his rifle and squeezed off a shot. The outlaw jerked, then began firing. Barker's second shot spun the man around, but he came back, still sending lead flying in all directions. None of the rounds came near Barker, making him think the outlaw was close to dead. Another round brought down the wildly shooting road agent.

Barker's ears rang from the firing, but through the buzz came more distinct shots. Somewhere else in town a gunfight still raged.

"You need any help?" A youngster hardly old enough to shave came out, holding a thumb-breaker in both hands. If he tried firing that ancient six-gun, he would be more a danger to himself than to whomever he shot at.

"Get back inside," Barker said, working to reload. He had learned his lesson. When he tangled with the rest of the Sonora Kid's gang, he'd know how many rounds he had. When his rifle was loaded, he replaced the rounds in his six-shooter.

"I wanna help!"

"You see the men shootin' up the town?" Barker called. He listened to the answer with half an ear.

"No, but—"

"You got a horse?"

"I can git one. You want me to ride with you?"

"I want you to head north to Fort Selden and fetch the soldiers." Barker knew Joey was already on his way to alert Tomasson, but it never hurt to have a second messenger. He had learned that during the fight against the Navajos, when the Indians picked off single messengers with disturbing regularity. More than this, sending the young man out of town took him out of danger.

The image of the Sonora Kid firing a cannon came back to bedevil Barker, but he shook himself free of the notion. If the Mexican had brought the howitzer into Mesilla, he would have fired it already. Such a shiny, deadly toy would have been the first thing he played with, rather than shooting up the town and treeing Marshal Dravecky.

Barker's horse shied as he tried to get closer to the gunfire. The skittish animal finally reared and almost sent Barker tumbling to the ground. Realizing he wouldn't do the marshal any good if he was laid out cold, Barker dismounted and made sure the mare was securely tethered. He heaved a deep sigh, gripped the stock of his rifle, and then made his way cautiously down the street toward the jailhouse, where the bullets sang in deadly flight.

If Dravecky was holed up inside, he was the one sighting down the barrel of the rifle shoved through the narrow window looking out onto the street. Barker followed the barrel away to a spot fifty feet off. A two-story hotel had been shot to hell and gone. The windows were all shattered and the front door hung by one hinge. But it wasn't downstairs where Dravecky pointed his rifle. It was up to the second-floor balcony.

Without realizing it, Barker snugged the stock to his shoulder and fired in one smooth movement when he saw the flash of sunlight off a silver ornament. His shot missed, but he succeeded in driving the man wearing the sombrero with the fancy silver conchas back into a room and away from the balcony where he could fire down into the jailhouse.

"Who's out there?" The voice came faintly from the jail.

"You all right, Dravecky?"

"That you, Barker?"

"Me and the entire Ninth Cavalry." Barker waited to see if this got a response from the Sonora Kid. If he could flush him, he would shoot the bandito down like the mad dog that he was.

But nothing stirred in the hotel.

"You see him? Somewhere up in the hotel."

The marshal was still alive and kicking. He might be wounded, but his voice was strong and angry. He didn't need help and would likely feel a damn sight better if somebody plugged the Sonora Kid.

Digging his toes in, Barker ran across the street, momentarily exposed. He waited for the Mexican to open fire. He hoped that Dravecky had a good enough shot to take out the outlaw, but no shots came from either the hotel or the jailhouse.

He reached the hotel's covered porch and slammed hard into the wall, panting harshly. A quick glance inside showed only the empty lobby. The steep staircase on the far side of the room led to certain death if he tried to mount it. All a killer would have to do was wait at the head of the stairs and shoot whoever's head appeared. Barker made sure his six-gun was ready, gripped his rifle, and started into the hotel, only to slip and fall. The weakness in his leg saved him. From the top of the stairs came withering fire that tore away a hole as large as his head in the wall beside him.

Barker swung his rifle up and fired as fast as he could. Lying on his belly and shooting accurately up the stairs was almost impossible. All he wanted was to keep the Sonora Kid from taking aim.

"You clumsy oaf," came a gravelly voice behind him. More lead danced upward with his. A strong hand grabbed him by the collar and dragged him back onto the hotel porch.

"Howdy, Dravecky," Barker said. "Good to see you're still in one piece."

"What happened? You always go floppin' onto your face?"

"Leg gave way," Barker said, sitting up and pulling off his boot. He poured out the blood that had pooled inside.

"Land of Goshen," Dravecky said, staring at the stream of blood staining the boardwalk. "How'd you even stand?"

Barker knew his wound was more serious than he'd thought, but the laudanum he'd taken earlier had dulled the pain and let him keep moving. He pulled the blood-soaked boot back on and got to his feet.

"We've got an outlaw to arrest," he said.

"He and his men rode into town and opened fire on anybody on the street. I don't know how many they killed, but Dooley went down and it sure as hell didn't look like he was gonna get up again."

"I took care of a couple of them," Barker said. "How many more are there?"

"Just the Sonora Kid."

"You're sure it's him?" Barker wanted reassurance that he wasn't chasing phantasms as he had been when the vaquero was killed.

"If he ain't, then the real Sonora Kid's gonna be real pissed." Dravecky jerked his thumb upward and said, "He was yellin' at the top of his lungs who he was and how this whole town was gonna be his."

"What's his quarrel with this town?" Barker wondered.

"Don't know, don't care. How are we gonna get him?"

"Catch him between us," Barker decided. "I'll go around and up the back stairs. You wait here and plug him if you see him. Just don't get so excited you shoot me if I show up."

"I'm the town marshal. I ought to—"

But Barker had already begun to walk away, slipping around the corner of the hotel and heading toward the rear, where the back stairs led to the second floor. It took only an instant to know he didn't have to go up into the hotel. Drops of blood dotted the steps. Judging from the way it looked, the Sonora Kid had been wounded. Not badly by Barker's estimation, but enough to make him hightail it rather than shoot it out with the pair of lawmen.

Barker knew Mesilla like the back of his hand. He laid out the town in his mind and knew where the Kid must have left his horse. Hobbling, Barker started after him. He should tell Dravecky their quarry had escaped, but resolve hardened inside him. Everything the Sonora Kid did was an affront to him personally. The slaughter, the taunts.

As dedicated as Barker was to catching the outlaw, every step sent a lance of pain up into his hip. He looked over his shoulder to see if Dravecky or anyone else was looking, then took out the laudanum and knocked back a sizable amount; he needed this much to deaden the pain.

He tucked the bottle back into his coat pocket, dragged his leg a little, and finally, when the pain faded, walked with more confidence. The occasional drops of blood in the dry dust were as easy a trail to follow as if he saw the Kid ahead waving a flag.

People slowly, meekly looked out from behind curtains and past slightly opened doors. They saw Barker and vanished. He couldn't expect any help—and he didn't want any. This was his arrest.

But he knew the Sonora Kid wasn't going to surrender. When they met, it would be a fight to the death.

He slowed when he saw a sombrero in the middle of the street. Looking around, wary of an ambush, he reached down and picked up the hat. He turned it slowly until he came to the spot on the hatband where a concha was missing. Barker fished in his pocket and took out the one he had found at the stagecoach slaughter. It matched the others.

He tossed down the sombrero and looked around. The only place the Sonora Kid could have gone was down an alley. Barker made sure a shell rested in the rifle chamber, then started after him. At the far end of the alley, a man with a serape tossed over his shoulder struggled to get onto a horse. Judging from the way his right leg refused to move normally, he had been shot just as Barker had.

"Halt!" Barker yelled. "I've got you covered. I swear, I'll shoot you down if you go for that six-gun." He didn't have a good shot since the bandito was partially hidden in deep shadow.

The man brushed back the serape to free the butt of the six-shooter holstered at his hip. Barker prepared to shoot. He wasn't much for shooting a man in the back, but for the Sonora Kid he would make an exception.

"I'm reaching for the sky." The Sonora Kid's hands went high above his head. He turned slowly, still cloaked in shadow. "There's no need to shoot. Unless you want to."

"I swear," Barker said bitterly, "you tempt me sorely. You do, you filthy murderer." He sidled closer, knowing he wasn't going to make the arrest this easily. Not after the Sonora Kid had left such a bloody trail behind him.

The outlaw stepped forward and the hot sun lit his face.

Barker felt as if he had been punched in the belly. He lowered the rifle from his shoulder and stared.

The outlaw went for his six-shooter, drew, and fired before Barker could squeeze the trigger. Hot lead ripped through his left arm, forcing him to drop his rifle. He went for his six-shooter but fumbled.

This was all the time it took for the outlaw to flop belly down over the saddle and ride off.

Mason Barker held his six-shooter in nerveless fingers as he watched his son ride away.

20

A BULLET RIPPED PAST HIS HEAD FROM BEHIND, forcing Barker to slam himself against the nearest wall and use it as a pivot to turn around. He saw a furious Ed Dravecky coming toward him, smoking six-shooter in one hand and the discarded sombrero in the other.

"You had him. Why didn't you shoot?" The lawman's anger knew no bounds. He slammed the butt of his six-gun against an adobe wall so hard he knocked a powdery hole in it. He never noticed the cascade of dust onto his gun and hand. "You had a clean shot. You better have good reason you didn't shoot, Barker."

"He was surrendering," Barker said, his mind numbed and his mouth filled with marbles. Not only couldn't he think, the sounds that crept from between his lips sounded harsh and alien to him, as if someone else was speaking.

All that burned in his mind was the image of his own son trying to mount.

"He'd been hit. In the leg." Barker looked down at his right leg. "Like me. 'Bout the same spot."

"What the hell difference does that matter? It slowed him down, but it shouldna slowed *you*!" Dravecky slammed his pistol into the wall again, this time with less force and far less damage done to the adobe.

"That's the sombrero the Sonora Kid wore," Barker said. It felt as if his thoughts were on ice, and every time he stepped out, everything crashed to the slick surface. "Did anyone see the Kid?" Sudden hope flared within him. He had seen his son wearing a serape. That meant Nate was one of the gang, but the Sonora Kid might have escaped, using Nate as a diversion. It was something the slippery son of a bitch would do. Hadn't he killed the vaquero to make it look as if he had died and to throw off pursuit?

"They saw the kid," Dravecky said. "You followed him down this alleyway, and you could have stopped him and didn't."

Barker got his feet under him and went to the end of the alley, where Nate had mounted his horse. He walked in a spiral, moving out until he saw where a second horse had been tethered. His heart almost jumped from his chest, and he didn't care one whit that his hands shook as he pointed.

"Another horse. There were two here. If the Sonora Kid came down ahead of . . . of the other outlaw, he rode off before I got the owlhoot in my sights."

"In your sights," grumbled Dravecky. He frowned, examined the obvious evidence that someone had left a horse here long enough to drop a good-sized pile of manure but not so long ago that it had hardened in the sun.

"We ought to form a posse," Barker said. The words caught in his throat. If they were successful, his son would be caught or killed. But if they weren't, the Sonora Kid would continue his rampage across all of southern New Mexico.

"I'll ask Pendleton if we kin pay 'em. This is gonna be dangerous work, so they ought to get at least a dollar a day."

"Tell them about the reward for the Kid," Barker said. "Colonel Tomasson was talking about posting one for a hundred dollars. Split among them, that might make it easier to swallow a few days on the trail."

"A hunnerd, eh?" Dravecky rubbed his chin and looked thoughtful, as if he was weighing his chances of capturing the road agents by his lonesome. "All right, then. I'll let everyone know. Even if we get a hunnerd men ridin' with us, that'd be an extra dollar."

"We won't get that many," Barker said, looking at the settling dust where Nate had disappeared in a gallop. It had been a shock seeing his own son, but at least he wasn't the Sonora Kid. He couldn't be. He was wild and dangerous, but nothing like the bloodthirsty Mexican bandito. Nothing at all like him.

THE POSSE OF EIGHT RODE FROM TOWN AN HOUR later.

"This don't look so good, Barker," said Marshal Dravecky. "The trail's goin' straight into the mountains. Finding 'em once they get into those windy canyons is gonna be nigh on impossible. I might be new to this part of the country, but my eyes don't deceive me. That's a twist of canyons made for ambushing."

"I've tracked them here before," Barker said. "I had a troop of buffalo soldiers with me, though."

"Well, then if they can do it, so can we. Isn't that right, boys?"

A ragged cheer went up from the six riding behind them. Barker had never seen a more reluctant posse. Usually a shot or two of Dutch courage was all it took to get men lined up, albeit unsteadily, to ride in support of the law. With the added incentive of a hundred-dollar reward, he'd expected more enthusiasm. In any town, and Mesilla was no different, he figured on at least a dozen bravos who were handier with their mouths than they were with their brains. They always had something to prove and sometimes had enough deadly skill with a six-shooter to walk away from a fight alive. But these six were sullen.

Barker knew why, too. They had seen what the Sonora Kid and his gang could do. Even if they hadn't heard the incredible battle that had raged on their doorstep, rumors of the stagecoach massacre had to be common in all the saloons. Worse, some bluecoat might have let it out that the Sonora Kid's gang had slaughtered an army supply train, killing all the soldiers. If the outlaw notched his six-shooter handle as some gunmen reportedly did, the Sonora Kid would have sawed off the butt by now.

One posse member piped up. "We cain't go on much longer, Marshal. We, uh, we got other business back in town."

"You're a day into the hunt. What's another couple days in the saddle going to mean?" Dravecky said.

"We didn't sign up forever."

"Go now and lose your money," Barker said. "You've all earned a dollar on the trail and will pick up another going home, but if you ride off now, you've wasted your time and won't have two nickels to show for it."

The posse whispered among themselves. Finally the spokesman said, "One more day, Deputy. That's all. You hear that, Marshal Dravecky? Only one more day!"

Barker snapped his reins and started walking his horse down the trail leading into the foothills. The gang had had a hideout in Skeleton Canyon before—and with good reason. An alert lookout on either rim could spot pursuit an hour off. The terrain favored whoever was dug in and able to shoot from higher ground. And if the fight got too intense, several branching canyons afforded quick escape, some leading directly into the heart of Mexico, where a deputy U.S. marshal couldn't pursue.

Not legally.

Barker rode with his eyes fixed ahead on the rugged mountains, wondering what he would do if it came to pursuit south of the border. Wild flights of fancy rampaged through his mind. He could catch Nate and straighten him out so he wouldn't have to go to prison. Just riding with a butcher like the Sonora Kid would send up any of his gang to Yuma Penitentiary for a score of years. And if Colonel Tomasson caught him, it might be the Detroit Penitentiary since that was where most federal prisoners were sent. Barker swallowed hard and tried to spit, only to find that his mouth had turned to parched desert.

A swig from his canteen barely wet his whistle. And the dull, aching pain in his back was returning. He needed some laudanum, but he couldn't drag it out of his pocket without Dravecky and the rest of the townsmen from Mesilla seeing him. He might lie and say it was medicine he'd gotten from a doctor. In El Paso? He hadn't been in that direction in quite a while. Besides, Dravecky had shown how good he was at picking up a lie. That was a trait good lawmen had. His time in Fort Worth's Hell's Half Acre stood him in good stead.

Barker found he could push away the pain by thinking about the fight ahead. The Sonora Kid wasn't going to surrender easily. It would be a hell of a fight. A quick look behind him, both left and right, showed him three of the posse who weren't likely to share in any reward. They were more like rabbits than wolves. And the other three were hardly the steely-eyed killers he needed.

For two cents he ought to call off the hunt, wait for Sergeant Sturgeon and a platoon of buffalo soldiers to get here, and then go after the Sonora Kid.

But he knew that wasn't likely to happen. Fort Selden was miles away, and he had no way of telling if either of the young boys he had sent with messages had ever reached the post, much less delivered what he'd told them to tell Colonel Tomasson. From what he had seen of the colonel, the man wasn't likely to believe much of anything he hadn't seen with his own eyes.

"See that?" Barker said, attention suddenly back on the trail. "Riders cut off and went into that canyon." He felt uneasy. One thing he had learned over the years was human behavior. If the outlaws had holed up once in Skeleton Canyon, they were likely to do so again. Their reconnaissance would have given them several places to hide other than the one where Sturgeon and his squad had attacked before.

This wasn't Skeleton Canyon. From what Barker remembered of the area, it was a narrow, winding canyon that opened out miles away deeper in the Peloncillas. Once anybody entered, they either kept going to the far end or retreated. Climbing the canyon walls wasn't going to be easy—in fact it might be impossible even if there weren't outlaws waiting to pick off anyone making their way to the rim along a steep, narrow path.

"That's a shooting gallery, Barker," Dravecky said in a low voice. He inclined his head in the direction of the canyon mouth so he and Barker could speak in private.

"I know what you're thinking," Barker said, beating him to the punch. "A simple ambush in there and we're dead. We ride past a couple outlaws and they have us bottled up good and proper."

"I'm the town marshal, not a federal deputy like you," Dravecky said.

"I won't think less of you if you go back to Mesilla," Barker said, knowing it was a lie. He would. And Dravecky knew it, too. The marshal wiped his face with his bandanna and looked from the obvious trap to the six men clustered behind them on the trail.

"They're not the ones I'd've picked to guard my back," Dravecky said after a long spell.

"Me, neither," Barker said.

"If we all go back, you're still headin' in after the Kid?"

Barker saw no reason to answer. It was more than the most vicious outlaw he had ever run across in that canyon. The trail had been left so there wouldn't be any doubt where the gang had ridden. It didn't take a deep thinker to know this was bait and that he would be riding squarely into the trap.

Besides the Sonora Kid, he had Nate to think about. If he had to arrest his own son, he would, but he hoped it wouldn't come to that. Going in alone would force him to use different tactics. He'd sneak in, try to find Nate, and get him out of the outlaw camp in the dead of night—praying that that wasn't all that was dead in the night. He would rather be captured by Apache raiders than the Sonora Kid.

"You live in Mesilla very long, Marshal?" Dravecky asked unexpectedly.

"A few years."

"That makes you a citizen of the town, don't it?"

"As much as anybody. Me and the wife have done well by the people in town."

"Then it's my duty to protect a citizen of the town. You ride in and you got me at your side."

Barker thrust out his hand. It wasn't trembling hardly at all as he took Dravecky's hand and shook.

"You're a good man, no matter what the others say," Barker said.

"Others? What others? You mean the mayor. What's Pendleton have to—" Dravecky stopped, then laughed, startling the rest of the posse. "You mangy ole prairie dog. You had me runnin' there for a minute."

"It's getting close to sundown," Barker said. "We can either go in or wait for morning."

"In," Dravecky said without hesitation. "We can't afford to give them that much of a head start on us."

"Men," Barker called. "You make sure your six-shooters are loaded and ready. Your rifles, too. Everybody got spare ammo, like I asked you to bring?"

Two men hadn't brought any beyond what they carried in their six-guns. Barker and Dravecky split what extra they had among the men. There was no telling who would need it the most if they had to fight.

When they had to fight.

They entered the canyon, its walls rising like the jaws of a vise on either side of them.

"Marshal, the trail's too narrow for us to spread out. We'll be sittin' ducks if they's up in the rocks already."

"You can ride a ways off the trail, down near the stream'll be easier going," Barker said. The canyon was hardly a hundred feet wide in places. "Just don't stray too far and keep as many of the posse in sight as you can."

"They'll pick us off if we scatter," Dravecky said. He

spun the cylinder in his Colt, then jammed it into his holster. "What are we waitin' for? I got a hot meal promised me back in town."

"You're not married," Barker said.

"That cute little waitress at the restaurant? You know the one?"

"Griselda?"

"She's the one. Up from New Braunfels, she is. Doesn't speak English so good and thinks I can help her."

"You don't speak a word of German," Barker said.

"Might be, after a good meal, we can find things that don't need words."

"Some words might be the same," Barker agreed. And then all hell broke loose.

He heard the explosion followed by a whistling sound that deafened him. An artillery shell crashed into a rock not twenty feet away, lifting Barker off his horse and casually tossing him aside. Landing hard, he had the wind knocked out of his lungs. Pain shot through his chest as he struggled to breathe. He propped himself up on one elbow and saw distant flashes from the canyon walls behind them.

The worst possible thing had happened. They had ridden past the secreted outlaws and now had to get through withering fire to retreat.

There was no way they could ride into the mouth of that mountain howitzer.

"Can't get outta here," Dravecky said. He dived, arms cradling his head as a second shell whined through the twilight and exploded closer to the river.

"They're losing the range," Barker said. He realized he was shouting and toned down his words. The ringing in his ears deafened him.

"They got two of us. Henry and the Ellison boy went to water their horses. Shell hit 'bout where they were."

A third attack came. Barker looked up and saw the shell glowing orange-hot in the night. He made a quick appraisal of where it would come to earth and found cover an instant before it caused an eruption of dirt and rock on the trail in front of them.

"We have to get out of here," he told the marshal. "Retreat. Get whoever's left and get out. Watch for the snipers."

"What are you going to do? You can't attack them single-handedly."

"I'll cover your retreat."

"We won't make it even with your covering fire—with us, Barker, with us!"

He hesitated. The Sonora Kid—and Nate—were deeper in the canyon. He had spotted the ledge where the howitzer was being fired. If he started shooting for that spot, he might persuade them to give up using the cannon.

"Four of us, Barker. That's all that's left. You, me, two others. It'll take at least four rifles to shoot our way out."

Barker judged that the gang had only one sniper on each wall. The four of them against two outlaws. But even still, those were bad odds due to tactical position. They lacked the high ground, although the gathering darkness provided them with some cover. If they didn't fire unless it was a clean shot, they could retreat.

The howitzer spat another round that arced above them to blast a crater in the trail.

"Back. We'll all go back." Barker quickly explained his plan, such as it was. Ride fast, stay low, don't give themselves away with unnecessary firing.

It wasn't much of a plan, but it had to be better than galloping into the bore of a howitzer.

"What's the matter? You all givin' up? I didn't think you had the sand to fight! Hell, I _knew_ you didn't!"

"That's the Sonora Kid," Dravecky said. "I recognize his voice from when he was yellin' at me whilst I was pinned down in the jailhouse."

The ringing in Barker's ears refused to die down. He heard the words but only barely.

"Stand an' fight. Stand an' die!"

"Let's ride," Barker said, swinging into the saddle and clinging to his mare's neck. She shied, but he held her on the almost invisible trail. The shell exploded only a few feet from where they had been stopped. If Barker hadn't ordered them to retreat, they would have been blown to smithereens. As it was, he had only the sniper rounds and his own humiliation at turning tail and running to contend with.

The two outlaws fired constantly, even if they had scant targets. Barker saw one of the posse throw up his arms and fall backward from the saddle. Barker had to herd Dravecky ahead of him to keep the marshal from returning.

"He's gone. Dead. No hope," Barker rasped out.

Then came a screaming that ended with another explosion just behind him. Mason Barker felt himself lifted up and thrown ahead of his horse by the exploding artillery shell. He lay on the ground staring up at the cloud-veiled stars and then they slowly faded into utter blackness.

21

"NEVER THOUGHT I'D BE SEEING ANOTHER SUN-
rise," Barker gasped out. Every bone in his body ached. He
was familiar with pain, but this went to new heights and
then soared.

"Not the sun. It's a campfire."

"Fire? The outlaws can see us!" Barker tried to sit
up, but nothing worked. His arms and legs twitched but
flopped about independently of what he wanted.

"Don't get your dander up," Dravecky said. "I had to
boil water to clean your wounds."

"Wounds?"

"You were punctured three times. That doesn't count
the bullet in your leg from back in Mesilla."

"Shrapnel," he said, leaning back. He was stretched out
on cold ground with a rock or two poking into him, but that
hardly seemed to matter when he isolated the pain in his

left arm and up and down his right leg. "That leg of mine's going to end up in a butcher shop as sausage."

"No self-respecting butcher would touch that leg," the marshal said. "If a doctor had been here, he'd have given it one look and then lopped it off. Good thing for you I'm not a doctor."

"You patched me up pretty good," Barker said.

"You owe me." Dravecky heaved a sigh. "I sent Cullen to fetch the cavalry boys. Don't know if he'll find them or just keep ridin'. Don't much blame him if he decides Denver's better for his health than these parts."

"If Tomasson is on post, he's going to get mighty tired of me sending urgent messages to him. I'd already sent two young'uns."

"Third time's the charm."

"Hope it is. No way three of us could have taken charge in that canyon, not with a howitzer blowing us into tiny pieces."

"Where'd that field piece come from?"

"Thought you'd've heard about the supply train from Fort Union being massacred," Barker said. He gingerly tensed and relaxed different muscles, taking an inventory of what caused pain and what didn't. He succeeded in sitting up. "That wasn't as hard as I thought it'd be."

"That's 'cuz I gave you a healthy—maybe unhealthy— dose of that laudanum in your pocket. You always carry that?"

"Never can tell when a body might need it," Barker said cautiously.

"Nasty stuff. I see men hooked on it, then end up in opium dens chasing the dragon, slaves to it." Dravecky spat into the small fire. "Seen women ruined by it, too. Mostly whores, mind you, but some not of that persuasion."

Barker couldn't meet the marshal's gaze. The opiate killed the pain that filled him. What was wrong with that? He could stop taking it whenever the pain died away. He held out his hands and watched as they shook.

"Got any water?"

Dravecky silently handed over a canteen. Even a couple mouthfuls didn't cut the dryness in his mouth. Barker knew it went beyond needing water, all the way to needing the laudanum.

"Think they'll hightail it into Mexico?" Barker asked, trying to change the subject.

"Don't matter what I think. What do *you* think they're up to?"

Barker didn't have an easy answer for that. The Sonora Kid had lured them into a trap. Barker had known something like that might happen, and yet he had led men to their deaths in his eagerness to capture the Kid.

"I was surprised he didn't bring the cannon into town," Barker said. "That would have given him bloodshed enough to dream on for a month. Or maybe not. He's got quite a taste for killing now."

"I think we ought to leave them be. Let the cavalry handle it. That's what they're paid for."

"That's what *I'm* paid for," Barker reminded him.

"Mason, don't take this the wrong way, but you're all used up. This isn't your fight no more. You left me a real good town in Mesilla, hardly any crime, friendly enough folks, though they are takin' a while to warm up to me. But they're honest and the worst that happens is a fight in a saloon. Even that don't happen often. And all that's thanks to you. But you're at the end of your trail, drinkin' that laudanum like it was mother's milk."

"Don't tell anybody 'bout that," Barker said, his voice harsh.

"Won't," Dravecky said. "But you need to get out of the saddle, if that's what's hurtin' your back. I see it. Ever'body does."

"Everybody?"

"Ever'body 'cept you, Marshal. Find yourself a town like Mesilla. Maybe go up to Doña Ana. Rumor has it the railroad will go through there and they'll need somebody with your talent to keep the peace."

"If the railroad goes up north, Mesilla will become a ghost town."

"After spendin' time in Fort Worth, a ghost town'd be fine with me. Mesilla won't die out, not entirely. And if you're marshal up north a ways, you won't have to kill yourself ridin' a hundred miles in a couple days to track outlaws."

"I could ride the train, if what you're saying is true," Barker said. "How hard could it be, sittin' down all day in a fancy railcar, working as a railroad dick?"

"You're gettin' the idea. Now come on. I'll help you into the saddle, and we can be back in Mesilla by—"

"I'm not leaving here." Barker drew his rifle close, planted the butt end in the ground, and used it to push himself to his feet. He was a little wobbly but didn't fall over.

"There's nothin' I can do to convince you to give this up? The Sonora Kid and his gang are 'bout the worst I've ever seen." Dravecky paused, then went on. "I can see you're too bullheaded to give up. What do you think your job is here now, if you're all alone?"

"Watching. Waiting. Making certain they don't come back this way."

"All by your lonesome, you're gonna do that?"

"It works both ways. We were caught because of the sheer cliffs on either side. It'll be like them to try and escape from a bottle by wiggling through the neck. I can take a few of them out if they try."

"Might be they'd like that. From what I heard the last time you chased 'em into Skeleton Canyon, the Kid murdered one of his men to throw you off the trail. He's likely to order a full-scale attack just to kill you and get out of the trap he put himself in."

"There's something more he wants."

"There's something more you want, Marshal, and I'll be damned if I know what it is." Dravecky rolled up his gear and lashed it behind his saddle. "I'm leavin' you as much food as I can spare. I don't need to eat so much anyway." He patted his bulging belly. "Griselda is feedin' me right good."

Barker felt a pang at the mention of women feeding their men. What would Ruth say if she found out their son rode with the Sonora Kid?

"I'll see to that cavalry detachment, too, if none of the others have gotten through to that boneheaded commander at Fort Selden." Dravecky swung up into the saddle and looked down at Barker. "There's somethin' else here, isn't there? Somethin' personal?"

Barker jumped as if the marshal had stuck him with a pin.

"All that killing. I decided to make it personal."

"Back in town. You didn't shoot when you had the chance. Does you stayin' here like a clay pigeon have anything to do with not pullin' the trigger when you should have?"

"I'll see you in town, Marshal. Keep a couple cells ready for the Sonora Kid and his gang."

Dravecky snorted and shook his head. He used the ends of his reins to whip his horse to a canter as he started back to Mesilla. Barker watched until the lawman disappeared, and felt a terrible loss. He ought to have confided in Dravecky. He was a good man and would understand.

"Nate," Barker said softly. "What have you gotten yourself mixed up in this time?"

Barker wasn't sure what he would do when it came time to arrest the gang. If Sergeant Sturgeon was in the field, Barker was sure he could convince him to look the other way and let Nate go. He had to be a dupe, sowing his wild oats and falling in with the wrong men.

But what if he had joined in the massacre of the stagecoach passengers and the army supply train? Lieutenant Greenberg was a decent man, a good officer, and he had been filled with lead. A single bullet or two might have killed him, but there was no call to pump in twenty or more rounds. Dead was dead.

That kind of brutality was done for reasons that had nothing to do with robbery. Killing for the pleasure of it was wrong.

Barker began walking slowly around his tiny camp, getting the lay of the land and figuring how best to bottle up the gang if they tried to ride back this way.

Dravecky had taken him too far from the canyon mouth to be effective. The outlaws could slip either left or right and get away without passing by. It cost him some painful moments, but Barker kicked out the fire, then led his horse closer to the canyon and up a low hill where he could command the mouth better. He unlimbered his rifle, flopped belly down on the ground, and watched for movement.

All he saw was the occasional branch stirring from the

pitifully weak, hot wind, and brush shivering as a rabbit or other small animal crept about.

The day lengthened into afternoon and the heat wore on him. He fought to keep his eyes open and finally succumbed to sleep, only to be awakened by a strange sound. He grabbed for his rifle. His rifle was gone. So was his six-shooter.

"You were sleeping so sound, Pa, I didn't have the heart to wake you. I didn't want you firin' a gun in your sleep, either."

"Nate, you got away. You—"

"Got away? Are you drunk, old man? What do you think I got away from?"

"The gang. The Sonora Kid. I know there was another gunman with you in town. He made you go."

"You found the sombrero in the middle of the street. I saw you lookin' at it."

Barker started to roll over to face his son. Nate was behind him somewhere. A boot pressed down into the small of his back just hard enough to make him gasp in pain.

"Your yellow streak hurtin' you, Pa? You still boastin' 'bout how you never killed a man with your six-gun? Does that get them to buy you drinks at the Plugged Nickel? To hear your tall tales?"

"Nate, don't do this. We—"

"We? There's no 'we,' Pa. I think you've been out in the sun too much. Or maybe this has addled your brains."

The laudanum bottle dropped into the sand beside him. As he reached for it, Nate stepped down harder on his back, until the pain became excruciating.

"I saw you matchin' up the concha. Where'd I lose it? Where I held up the stagecoach?"

"Nate, please."

"Yeah, right." The pressure lessened, but the pain lingered. "I saw you comparin' the silver. You know who wore that sombrero. Then and there you knew I wore that sombrero."

"The Sonora Kid did. It was his signature."

"Signature. I don't write too good, but you're right. It was my signature. Men saw me wearing that sombrero and they stepped away. Never looked at my face, didn't have to. They became real respectful. You wear a badge to get respect like that, but they talk behind your back. They see me in the sombrero and they don't dare say nothin' except 'yes, sir' and 'no, sir.'"

"The Sonora Kid wore it," Barker gasped out.

"Old man, you are loco from too much sun if you don't understand by now. I'm the Sonora Kid. That's my gang in there and they do what I say. Anything I say."

"You slaughtered all those men? The soldiers?"

The ugly laugh answered better than words ever could.

"What went wrong with you, Nate?"

"I finally got some *cojones*. I let you and everyone else push me around too long. Then I found out how easy it was to just take what I want."

"You're alibiing for the Kid, claiming to be him when you're just riding with him."

"Crazy and a fool," the Sonora Kid said. "I killed the hombre who started the gang, so it's *my* gang now."

Barker screamed in agony as the boot smashed hard into his spine. Then he passed out.

22

MASON BARKER SAT IN THE HOT SUN AND SHOOK
as if he had the ague. His hands quivered and his guts
churned and there wasn't a thing he could do to stop them.
Worst of all, the same thought turned over and over in his
head.

Nate . . . Nate . . . Nate . . .

Somewhere deep inside he knew he had failed his son
over the years, being on the trail of outlaws more than
he'd been home. Serving process brought in most of their
money, and he had to ride all over the southern part of New
Mexico and down into Texas for that. He had been gone
and let Ruth raise their son.

But it had been too much for her, strong as she was, after
Patrick died. Or maybe it was the fault of neither of them.
A bad seed sometimes produced a warped, gnarled tree.

His son was the Sonora Kid. His son was a terrible,
cold-blooded killer. And his son hadn't even seen fit to

gun him down when he had the chance. It might have been payback for the moment in Mesilla when he had been unable to shoot Nate. That instant had come out of surprise. But even then, deep down, he had known the awful truth. He was clever enough to come up with a dozen different reasons why Nate wasn't the Sonora Kid, and he had run through all of them.

But Nate was. And he was still federal deputy marshal and empowered to arrest him and see that he was tried for his crimes.

Barker stared down into the canyon and the lengthening shadows that refused to betray any of the gang to him. He didn't have a rifle or six-shooter. Nate had kept them. If any of the gang chose to ride out, he could do little more than throw rocks at them. And if Nate returned, it would be to taunt him even more than he had. Nate had developed quite a cruel streak.

Barker wished the Sonora Kid had killed him, shot him in the back, clubbed him senseless, and left him to die. But Nate was far crueler than that now. Killing men had become easy and enjoyable for him, but not as easy or enjoyable as taunting his father and making him feel like a fool.

Twilight deepened into darkness. He strained to hear the gang at their campsite, joking, making crude comments, even shooting at anything moving through the night. There were only the sounds of night he had known all his life.

"You took my guns so I couldn't shoot myself," he said aloud. Tears streamed down his cheeks and left muddy trails. He wiped them on his sleeve, but more formed and flowed.

Had Nate been right that the disgrace of knowing his son was the most notorious outlaw in all of New Mexico would push him to suicide? He allowed as to how his son might know him better than he thought, but that would never happen. He loved Nate, in his own way, but he loved duty more. He had sworn an oath to uphold the law and would die before breaking it.

The sound of horses behind him caused Barker to clumsily stand and look northward. He saw nothing in the darkness until a glint of moonlight off brass caused him to catch his breath.

"Over here!" he shouted. "Just out of the canyon!"

The clank of gear and the sound of horses drew closer. Lots of horses. And then the thin sliver of moon showed an officer riding at the head of a long column of soldiers. Barker waved, took off his hat, waved that furiously, and finally drew the attention of a soldier riding to the side of the column. The soldier galloped toward him while the remainder of the troopers halted.

"Glory be," called Sergeant Sturgeon, "I didn't think we'd find you alive. Not after what your town's marshal had to say."

"I'm not giving up," Barker said, the words hollow in his ears. "I can't."

"I've seen men with a bug up their butt 'fore this, but from the sound of it the bugs oughta have eaten you all hollow by now. Marshal Dravecky made it out that you were mostly dead."

"The Sonora Kid and his gang are holed up a half mile into the canyon. Or they were last night. N-none of them's come out." Barker almost choked on that lie, but telling Sturgeon that he had spoken with the Sonora Kid required explanations he refused to deliver.

"You don't think you've got 'em all bottled up now, do you, Marshal?"

"They can go deeper into the mountains. They've had a day or so, but I think they're waiting."

"What for?"

"You. You and the colonel. The Sonora Kid wants to kill you all."

"That'll take some mighty fancy shootin'," said Sturgeon. Then the sergeant thought on this a moment and said, "They've got the cannon trained on the trail, don't they?"

"I'm surprised Dravecky didn't tell you. The howitzer wiped out most of our posse."

"All he said was that they shot you up good."

"Shrapnel. Was it the marshal who got you down here?"

"A boy a couple days back was shooed off by a guard. Another came, but the colonel wasn't takin' visitors." Sturgeon sounded bitter over this. "Then the marshal came, inquiring after a man named Cullen."

"He never reached Fort Selden," Barker said, knowing the outcome as surely as if he had watched with his own eyes. The way Dravecky had spoken before riding out had warned him that Cullen was unreliable. He hadn't known the surviving member of the posse at all but didn't see him as the kind to get involved more than he had been, trying to make an easy dollar a day. After seeing his partners blown up and shot down, he was likely a hundred miles away by now.

Barker considered him the lucky one.

"I'd better talk with the colonel 'fore he takes it into his head to charge on into the canyon," Sturgeon said. "You sure they have the howitzer?"

"Trained on the trail," Barker assured him. The sergeant nodded once, then galloped back to tell his commanding officer what he had found out. It took only a minute before Tomasson rode to talk personally with Barker.

"From what the town marshal said," Tomasson started without preamble, "you ran into a force you couldn't conquer."

"That's one way of putting it," Barker said. He still felt the outline of his son's boot in the middle of his back. If anyone had gotten walked over . . .

"What do you recommend? Should I send a couple scouts ahead to get the exact location of the howitzer?"

"Might not be a bad idea," Barker said. "All I knew was that it was firing from a ledge not too far above the canyon floor. And it was to the left."

"A quarter mile into the canyon?"

Barker nodded. He rested his hand on his empty holster. The habit of touching the six-gun's butt now drew attention to his condition.

"You require a sidearm, Marshal?"

"Reckon so. A rifle, too."

"I see your horse," Tomasson said. He started to ask another question, and Barker knew what it was. The colonel wanted to know how a deputy federal marshal could lose all his weapons but not his horse. That was the kind of story that would be good for a round or two of drinks if told with aplomb.

All Barker felt when he remembered he had lost his pistol and rifle was shame. His own son had taken them. If he neglected to tell the crowd at the Plugged Nickel it was his son and instead told them the Sonora Kid had taken the guns and let him live, he might get a third round out of them. Why would a *bandolero* like the Sonora Kid let a sworn enemy live once he had plucked his weapons from him and left him helpless?

The only answer Barker had for that was how Nate wanted to humiliate him further—and that meant something else awaited the unwary deeper in the canyon.

"Your scouts might try to sneak in on foot," Barker said to Tomasson. "Find out if the gang is even camped there anymore. They've had a full day to lose themselves in the canyons."

"Sergeant," barked Tomasson, "see to it. Three scouts, one down each wall and one down the center of the canyon, following the stream."

Sturgeon saluted and went to send the men into the shooting gallery. Barker almost volunteered to go but found movement a bit of a problem. He would only draw attention—and fire from the gang.

Would Nate congratulate any of his men who shot him? Or would Nate punish them for doing what he wanted to do for his own pleasure? Barker shivered.

"You needing a blanket, Marshal? It doesn't seem that cold to me yet," the colonel said.

"I'm just thinking on what it'll take to pry them loose. It won't be easy."

"Don't think it will. Here, take these." A private came up with a carbine and a pistol that barely fit into his empty holster. The pistol had been designed to ride butt forward in a cavalry trooper's holster. Barker almost asked if any spare holsters were to be had, then knew they weren't. The soldiers had come directly from the fort, so they hadn't been in combat and salvaging equipment off fallen comrades. He was lucky to get any firearms at all, since the soldiers traveled light and fast. Carrying extra rifles would take away from their ability to carry more ammunition.

"Thanks, Colonel." Barker hefted the carbine and then shifted the pistol around in his holster. It felt better in his hand than at his side.

"I don't want to pitch camp here," Tomasson said. "Pressing on in the dark is dangerous, though, without definite information about the gang. How many are there?"

Barker shook his head.

"Can't rightly say, but there are at least five. My guess, from the way they fired the howitzer and had two others on either side, is that there might be two or three more."

"Colonel! The scouts are back," came the call.

"So soon?" Tomasson frowned. "I need to find out if this is good or bad for our mission."

Three men drifted closer and then stood at what passed for attention among the scouts. Barker doubted they were soldiers, but rather they were recruited drifters who happened to know more about the territory than even the locals. One looked to be an Apache, but Barker couldn't tell.

"They cleared out, Colonel," the nearest man said. "From the destruction in there, they fired at least a half dozen artillery shells, then struck camp and hauled away the howitzer."

Another scout spoke up. "The outlaws have a full day's head start. But they're not going to be able to move real quick, not if they're draggin' the howitzer and its caisson down that rocky trail."

"Do you think they would abandon the weapon?" Tomasson said.

The scout took a few seconds to ponder on his answer, but Barker knew that the howitzer afforded added firepower and that meant increased destruction. All Nate wanted was to add to the blood he had already spilled into the arid New Mexico dust.

"They lugged it with 'em. Can't see any reason not to try to make it into Mexico with it."

"Mexico?" The question slipped from Barker's lips before he realized it.

"The Sonora Kid's from south of the border, so he wants a shiny toy to show off to his amigos there. Think how he could brag on stealin' one of our cannon," the scout said.

"That makes sense," Colonel Tomasson said.

Barker wasn't going to argue. They thought the Sonora Kid was a Mexican. Hope sprang up like a weed in a rocky crevice, but it soon died again. What good was it if the cavalry thought the Sonora Kid was anyone but his son? That changed nothing between him and Nate. Worse, it did nothing to wipe away the blood his son had spilled for the sheer thrill of it.

The vaquero might have called himself the Sonora Kid, but Nate had killed him and taken over leadership of the gang. Those were facts, and no mistaken identity would ever change them.

"You look peaked, Marshal. You want to stay behind? Go back to Mesilla?"

"I'm riding with you."

"I understand. You've tracked that bastard so long, you can't give up with victory so close at hand."

Barker touched the pistol crammed into his holster, then curled his finger around the trigger of the borrowed carbine.

"You have no idea how long I've tracked him, Colonel."

This got him another odd look, but Barker was past caring. He made his way downhill and stepped up into the saddle. He settled down with a soft moan. He hurt now. He would hurt a hell of a lot worse at the end of the trail, and not just from Nate crushing his laudanum beneath a cruel boot. Barker snapped the reins, and his dutiful mare once more entered the canyon where most of the posse had been killed. He tried not to look at the craters left by the artillery shells or the tatters of clothing and the bodies half picked clean by the animals.

The night hid most of the carnage, but the guilt—the shame—burned hot and bright in his breast.

"Up yonder, Marshal. That ledge. That where they fired on you from?"

The scout sounded a little apprehensive.

"It is. You picked the spot exactly." Barker had said the right words. In the dark, the scout hadn't been completely certain of the gun placement, but he relaxed when his guess was confirmed.

They slowly rode past the point of the ambush, finally on the trail after the fleeing outlaws. At the bottom of the steep-walled canyon only a faint band of stars directly overhead provided ghostly illumination. It had the feeling of an especially deep grave, and Barker looked up repeatedly, expecting to see giant shovels of dirt cascading down onto his head.

Eventually the moon rose high enough in the sky to add to the light, but the rocky trail still proved treacherous. When they came out into a broader valley, Tomasson called a halt.

"We camp for the night. Sergeant, set up guards. Double duty tonight. I don't want to get caught with my pants down."

"Right away, sir." Sturgeon looked over at Barker, then went to issue orders.

"We ought to keep going. They're slower, as long as they're dragging the cannon with them," Barker complained to the colonel.

"You're half-dead in the saddle. My men have ridden damned near fifty miles today to get here. We rest." Tomasson said in a softer tone, "We want to be ready for them. They're a treacherous lot. You know that. The more rested we are, the quicker the fight will be over."

"The quicker it'll be over," Barker said dully. He left the soldiers to pitching their camp and found a spot off to one side where he could be alone. Dismounting with his stiff back was a problem, but he finally kicked his feet free and simply fell down. The impact sent a harsh jolt up his back, but he gritted his teeth and endured it. He had to.

Tomorrow he would arrest his own son for crimes so terrible he could barely understand them.

23

BARKER SLEPT POORLY, YET THE SOUND OF THE SOL-
diers breaking camp woke him with a start. He sat up,
clutching the pistol and looking around wildly.

"Whoa, settle down," came Sergeant Sturgeon's soft
drawl. "I been watchin' over you all night. Their deaths are
weighin' down real heavy on you."

"Deaths?" Visions of the men his son had killed pa-
raded through his mind. Those on the stagecoach, Hugh
Dooley, Lieutenant Greenberg and the other soldiers, and
earlier. How many of the deaths he had attributed to the
entire gang were perpetrated by his son's own hand?

"The posse. It wasn't your fault."

"I led them into a trap. I felt in my gut that it was a trap,
and I bulled my way in and—"

"And the Sonora Kid could have been all the way into
Mexico by then. You were just overanxious, Marshal.

Nothin' more'n that. Now, get your gear ready. We're on the trail in ten minutes."

Barker saw that most of the soldiers were ready, though a few polished off cups of coffee and used the dregs to douse the flames of the campfires. He made his way to the stream and washed his face. Where tears had flowed before burned as the cold water touched his cheeks. He had no explanation for that. As he bent forward to drink, he saw a reflection in the water. He reached for his pistol, then stopped.

"Morning, Colonel," he said.

"Sergeant Sturgeon told me you'd come down here. Can I ask you a question, Marshal?"

"Ask away." Barker finished rubbing the cold, clear water on his face, then drank what he could. It settled to his belly in a hard, cold lump.

"How'd you get the boot print in the middle of your back?"

"You don't miss much, do you, Tomasson?"

"As commander I find myself ignoring much of what goes on, either because I have to or want to because it's not good for discipline to take every detail into account. Some of it I don't understand. That's a strange thing to admit, but it's true. These soldiers aren't like the people I grew up with back in Wisconsin. Their concerns are best dealt with by the noncoms."

"Sergeant Sturgeon is a good man."

"The best soldier in the field I've ever commanded. But while I ignore details, it's not necessarily true that I don't notice them."

Barker felt the weight of secrecy on his shoulders, crushing the very life from him. He wanted to blurt out that his own flesh and blood was an inhuman murderer, but that wouldn't ease the pain. It would only add to it.

"Your troopers are waiting for you to lead them, Colonel."

"The scout returned just after sunrise. We have a problem, Marshal."

"What?" His heart almost stopped beating.

"This valley leads away in three different directions. The scout knows the gang split up and went down at least two of them. He didn't have time to see if they might have gone down the third as well."

"You have plenty of men."

"I do, Marshal, I have plenty even if I divide my force into thirds, but my problem is somewhat different. Do I insist that you ride with me or with Sergeant Sturgeon? And if it's necessary for yet another contingent to break off, could I trust you with Sergeant Jefferson? He's new to the company, transferred in from Fort Davis only a week before . . . before Lieutenant Greenberg was killed."

"Depends on how much you trust me," Barker said, cutting to the heart of the matter. Tomasson might order him back to Mesilla, but they both knew that was not going to happen. Ignoring such an order would be easy for a civilian federal deputy, and Tomasson didn't want to spare a man to escort him back to town.

"That is a matter of some concern to me, Marshal. You are carrying a burden of knowledge I would share."

"If that's what it takes for you to trust me, you'll have to make your choice without knowing."

Tomasson looked hard at him, then did a sharp about-face and marched back to his command. Barker followed more slowly, wondering what the colonel would decide, but when he mounted and the officer gave the order to move out, he didn't even glance in Barker's direction.

Less than an hour later they reached the far end of the valley and the three paths breaking away. Barker knew that the scout hadn't made any mistake about the two trails, and he rode to the third. He crisscrossed the trail, hunting for any sign the outlaws had ridden this way.

"Well?" Sergeant Sturgeon trotted over and waited a few yards away.

"One rider. He tried to cover his tracks but there was . . . one rider." Barker looked into the distance and saw only the curve in the narrow canyon. The walls told him nothing. To find out more, he would have to pursue.

"There's no question that they split and went down both of the other trails. The deep ruts in the soft dirt near the stream show where the howitzer was pulled."

"That's the trail I'm following." Barker cast a glance over his shoulder, wondering if Nate had sent the rest of his gang down the other paths so he could escape this way. Nate had no loyalty to his men. He had shown that repeatedly, but something more told Barker he had made the right decision.

He had to follow the cannon, since that weapon afforded his son the best chance of killing huge numbers of men.

They rode back to where Tomasson spoke animatedly with his scouts. The scouts waved their arms about and looked madder than wet hens.

"What's the argument?" Barker asked.

"There's no doubt the cannon was drawn down the left-hand canyon, but I can't get a clear idea how many men went with it and how many took the central canyon trail."

"Most of 'em went down the middle, Colonel. We followed ten men. Six went down the middle."

"And four down the left?" Barker asked. "Or only three?"

"However many's left after the six went that way."

Barker considered mentioning the solitary rider he was certain had escaped, but finally he said nothing. He had made his decision. He followed the cannon.

"Sergeant," the colonel finally said, waving the scouts to silence. "You will take your squad and recover the howitzer. I will pursue down the middle since it is my opinion that is where the Sonora Kid thought to escape."

Barker frowned, not sure how the officer had come to that conclusion. Tomasson felt the man's eyes on him and responded.

"A coward and a killer like the Kid will want the most men around him possible, both for protection and to command. I don't know why the forces were split, since they are stronger if they remain in a single unit, but he is, after all, an outlaw and not a soldier."

Colonel Tomasson formed his company and rode away, leaving Sturgeon with Barker and a squad of men.

"They're the best there is at Fort Selden," Sturgeon assured him. "They're mine."

Barker stared at the ruts in the earth made by the mountain howitzer and knew his son was riding along this road. Colonel Tomasson had judged wrong what the Sonora Kid would do.

"It'll be hard if you lose any of them," he finally said.

"We're soldiers," Sturgeon assured him, then set his men on the road after the Sonora Kid.

"HOW CAN THEY MAKE SUCH SPEED PULLING THE cannon?" Barker asked, frustrated. It was nearing sundown, and they had yet to catch sight of their quarry.

"They don't worry much about takin' care of the horses

hitched to the carriage," Sturgeon said. "My guess is that horse—or horses—is 'bout dead by now."

"Their saddle horses should be tuckered out, too," Barker said. "That'll make it easier for us. They won't be able to run."

"Might make it harder. You corner an animal and it fights ten times as hard. Column, halt!" Sturgeon held up his gloved hand when he spotted movement ahead at the point where the narrow canyon widened into another valley.

Barker blinked and saw furtive motion. He slid the pistol from his holster since whoever'd come up was close. Real close.

"Don't go gettin' all antsy on me," complained the scout. He appeared out of the darkness. "I got some good news and some bad news."

"What's the good news?" Sturgeon asked.

"We finally run 'em to ground. The gang's camped not a half mile ahead."

"What's the bad news?" Barker had to ask.

"They're camped not a half mile ahead and they ain't makin' no effort to hide."

"It's another ambush," Barker said in a husky voice. Visions of artillery shells exploding all around and the sound of men and horses being blown apart returned to haunt him.

"That's the way I see it, too," the scout said, "but I don't know how it's intended. There's four men around the fire. If I'd wanted, I coulda snuck up and cut a throat or two."

"Did you see him? The Sonora Kid?" Barker's mouth turned as dry as the desert. He wasn't sure what answer he wanted to hear.

"If he wears one of them fancy sombreros with the big

brims, yup, I seen him. He was talkin' real loud and boastin' on all the men he'd killed."

Barker sagged a little. Then he sat upright and said, "We should hit them now, before they know we're here."

Sergeant Sturgeon stroked his stubbled chin and nodded.

"You got the right of it, Marshal. We're all tired from ridin' and trackin', but surprise can make up for that. If there's four of them, we outnumber them three to one."

The darkness would work against them but possibly it would be worse for the outlaws. The soldiers were trained, and Barker had to believe Sturgeon when he said these were the best troopers at Fort Selden.

"We need to take them fast. They might set up the howitzer."

"Might already have," said Sturgeon. "I would swing it around to cover my back trail as soon as I made camp."

Barker knew his son. Nate would not consider the safety of his men—or himself—until he had a drink or two or otherwise blew off steam.

"They're not soldiers," he said. "They're not you. Let's attack."

Sturgeon nodded, then motioned for his corporal to ride closer. The two spoke rapidly for more than a minute, then the corporal went to pass the orders along. Barker felt increasingly nervous about the skirmish. If they went in fast, there might not be much killing.

Even as that thought crossed his mind, he knew how wrong it was because of Nate. He would go down fighting, no matter the odds. Taking him alive would be impossible unless someone got close enough to capture him without filling him full of lead. Barker hoped he could do that, but he had to face the possibility that the first man he would ever kill would be his own son.

"Advance!"

The voice was low but somehow carried in the night. Barker jumped as if it had been a gunshot, then spurred his horse toward the outlaws, staying shoulder to shoulder with Sturgeon and another soldier.

"There's the camp," Sturgeon said. In a stentorian voice, he cried, "Charge!"

The soldiers galloped down on the camp. One man at the fire looked up, startled. He shoved back his serape and pulled up a sawed-off shotgun carried around his shoulder on a leather strap. Both barrels exploded, sending buckshot into the soldier at the far end of the skirmish line. Then the bandito died as half a dozen soldiers opened fire with their carbines. The attack carried through the camp. Hooves kicked up dust and coals, obscuring everything.

"Where're the others?" Barker shouted over the tumult of the attack.

The words were hardly out of his mouth when the howitzer fired. The shell crashed through the left flank and killed one soldier. The shrapnel took down another's horse and forced Barker to fight to keep his mare from rearing. The horse spun about, hooves fighting the air. When Barker regained control, he saw that Sturgeon had mustered his troops and continued the attack.

Barker looked around and saw only the dead soldier and another one wounded. The rest had surged past. He waited for a second, expecting a new blast from the cannon, but it never came.

The roar had died down, so he could plainly hear sporadic rifle fire. Mingled with it were the duller reports of pistols. Barker yanked out his pistol and made his way toward the fight by tracking the foot-long tongues of flame from rapidly firing rifles.

"Got one. The rest are running!"

Barker didn't know who had spoken, and it didn't matter. It was one of Sturgeon's men. The dust began to settle, and through the gloom he saw two of the buffalo soldiers swinging the howitzer about, aiming it down the trail at the fleeing banditos. Barker started to cry out to stop them, then any warning was swallowed by the throaty roar of the small cannon's discharge.

"Got 'em. Got 'em both!"

Barker stared in horror at the weeds burning alongside the trail where the artillery shell had struck. These might have been horse soldiers, but they also were good enough artillerists to have dropped the shell in exactly the right spot for maximum damage.

"They were lucky," Sturgeon said. "Sometimes, that's better'n being good." The sergeant slapped Barker on the shoulder, laughed, and rode off to assemble his men. They had to make a sweep of the area to be sure they had killed all the outlaws.

"Nate," he said in a voice so low it threatened to choke him.

The two soldiers who had fired the cannon were actively working to swing it back around and examine it. One looked up and smiled.

"They didn't harm it none, suh."

"I can see that they didn't," Barker said, his returning smile weak.

"Marshal, Marshal! We got all of 'em if you want to see."

Barker dismounted and walked slowly to the spot where Sergeant Sturgeon's men had laid the four dead outlaws. The one from the camp looked as if he were sleeping. The one killed at the cannon was cut up from a half dozen carbine rounds that had stopped his career as a gun crewman. The other two were in pieces. Only the serapes they had worn showed any connection between them.

"You recognize any of them?" Sturgeon asked.

Barker forced himself to look from their wounds to the slack faces. He sucked in his breath after examining the fourth outlaw.

"I don't know any of them." And he didn't. Nate wasn't one of the dead. He blurted out the question before he could stop himself. "Was there a fifth road agent?"

"Didn't see him during the fight, if there was any other," said Sturgeon. "Why are you thinkin' there was another?"

Barker wrestled with the answer. If Nate had escaped, he might reach Mexico and live out his life in peace, the law not chasing him down. But he had killed so many. The ache in the middle of Barker's back returned as a counterpoint to any hint of leniency. His son had done terrible things and deserved to be sent to prison for them. And he was a lawman entrusted by the United States of America to enforce the law. Nothing in his oath said "except your son."

"Have a scout make a circuit of the camp to see."

Sturgeon sent the scout out and then tended to hitching the howitzer carriage to the team of horses and being certain the caisson was properly attached for easy hauling.

"Getting back the cannon will make Colonel Tomasson real happy. I suspect by now he has run down the Sonora Kid and captured the rest of the gang. This is a really fine day, yes, sir."

Barker watched as the soldiers slung the bodies over the caisson to return them to Fort Selden for burial. The soldier who had died was not placed with the outlaws. Instead, his body was draped over one of the outlaws' horses and then lashed into place. Burial here made more sense, but

Barker knew the reason for returning both the outlaws and the soldier to the fort.

The cavalry did not leave behind their dead and wounded. And Tomasson wanted to gloat over the deaths of the banditos, possibly having pictures taken. Reporters would be notified and the telegraph would sizzle with the news until even General Sherman acknowledged the feat.

"Sarge," called the scout, riding up. "You ain't gonna believe this, but there was one of them killers that got away."

Barker stood a little straighter. Nate had escaped. Again.

24

"YOU SHOULDN'T GO OFF BY YOURSELF LIKE THIS,
Marshal," Sergeant Sturgeon said, frowning. "Let the bandito go. He's got a half day's start on you." The soldier
pointed to the sun just poking up over the distant high canyon wall.

"It's . . . the Sonora Kid."

"Colonel Tomasson said the Kid would ride with the big
part of his gang, down the other canyon. You ride with us
and you'll find that he's got the Sonora Kid in custody—or
maybe he killed him."

Barker shook his head. It wasn't that way. Nate would
have stayed with the howitzer because the most killing
could be done with that weapon. When the soldiers over-
ran the cannon so fast, he didn't have any choice but to run.
Once more, Nate had sacrificed his men for his own safety.

"I've got to get him. It's my job."

"It'll kill you, Marshal, it'll kill you dead."

"It already has," Barker said. He took what ammo and supplies that he could from the buffalo soldiers, then watched them rattle off with the howitzer and its caisson. In minutes he stood alone. The sun warmed the side of his face. He turned slowly so the sun applied some soothing heat to his back, then he bent, heaved his gear up, and saddled his horse. He patted the mare's neck. She had been a loyal, constant companion. More than his own family because he spent more time on the trail than at home.

That was his job.

Tracking down the Sonora Kid was a disagreeable part of that job, too.

He rode at a quick walk, making sure he didn't miss a single bit of spoor along the trail. Now and then he saw where Nate had passed by. A freshly broken twig, a hoofprint, piles of horse manure—he didn't miss a bit of it as he hurried along the trail that wandered through the canyon and finally opened out into a broad valley. The grass was sparse, and the stream he had followed down the canyon had run dry. The summer heat became even more oppressive, if that was possible, now that he was out of the canyon.

Barker slowly studied the terrain. Canyons from the north fed into this long, wide valley, but he doubted Nate had backtracked. Losing his entire gang would have spooked him. He'd hightail it for Mexico, where he could recruit more *bandoleros* and return to New Mexico Territory to prey on the stagecoaches and even the towns. Stealing the howitzer had shown Barker what his son sought most of all. Blood. More blood.

He might sate that bloodlust in Mexico, but Barker doubted it. The footprint in the middle of his back showed why Nate kept returning and why he escalated his butchery. He wanted to prove something to his pa. Barker held back tears as he wondered what he had done to make his son hate him with such venom.

Barker rode slowly to the middle of the sere valley and took his time to survey it. If he followed the lay of the land and continued south, that would eventually lead to Mexico. That was where Nate was going. He felt it. And less than an hour later, he saw evidence of a recent traveler. A fire had been built, then snuffed out. All around lay the scattered remnants of a hasty meal. Some flakes of oatmeal. Discolored ground hinting that coffee dregs had been tossed into the dry earth. The ground was cut up by a horse's hooves. With the wind that blew down this valley, evidenced by the way the trees all flagged northward, the man responsible had to be only hours ahead.

Barker ate in the saddle, drank what he dared of his precious water, and kept riding. He had a job to do.

By late afternoon he'd spotted a rider in the distance. The man wore a sombrero and rode hunched forward, as if he was injured. Barker's heart jumped when he considered that Nate might have been wounded in the fight, more than the leg wound he had sustained in Mesilla. For whatever reason, he hadn't thought of that before. Barker urged his horse to a quicker gait, seeing that Nate was heading directly for the border through San Luis Pass. He didn't have a good idea where that might lead, but it was close, very close to Mexico. Barker's badge wasn't any good in another country.

Whether Nate saw his pursuit or he just got lucky, he disappeared from sight. Barker whipped his horse and galloped for a spell, then slowed, walked the horse to rest it, and finally topped a rise. He spotted Nate immediately. Barker drew his rifle and sighted down the barrel, but his aim wavered. A thousand conflicting thoughts burned in his head. The range was too great. The barrel was short for such a long shot. He wasn't that much of a marksman.

He was pointing the rifle at Nate Barker.

He lowered the rifle and headed due south, toward the pass leading into Mexico.

Twice he had lost track of Nate and twice he had found the trail again. Barker's Spanish wasn't the best, but he got by, asking the farmers along the way if they had seen a man wearing a sombrero with a serape thrown over his shoulder. He thought this might be a foolish question, but each of the campesinos he asked had seen such a rider, and that kept him moving until he reached San Miguelito. The town looked to be the same size as Mesilla but without the large number of saloons. Only one cantina along the main road into town looked promising.

Riding behind the cantina, Barker found Nate's horse. He had spied the animal, though from the rear, for four days and knew it as well as he did any saddle horse. He checked the saddlebags, but they were mostly empty. Then he heard a ruckus inside the cantina.

It had to be Nate kicking up a fuss over some slight, real or imagined.

Barker dismounted, drew the cavalry pistol, and walked into the dimly lit cantina. It smelled of stale beer and pungent pulque. The air was cooler but heavy with smoke. Four caballeros smoked so hard, their heads disappeared in the clouds from their cigars. But Barker had eyes only for one man. At the bar, his back to the door, a man banged his fist on the bar. His sombrero was tossed back and hung in the middle of his back by a string. The serape over his right shoulder drew Barker's attention because he remembered the first outlaw in the camp and the shotgun he had carried slung around his shoulder. The serape might hide another scattergun.

Barker walked slowly. Something in his manner caused everyone in the cantina to fall silent—except Nate.

"Deaf? Tequila!"

Barker lifted the pistol, cocked it, and laid the muzzle against the man's head.

"I'll shoot if you move so much as a muscle, Nate."

"What is this?" The man threw up his hands, and Barker swung, catching him alongside the head with the barrel. Buffaloed, the man dropped to hands and knees. Barker reached under the serape and pulled out a six-shooter.

"You're under arrest."

"Why is this, gringo?" The man looking up at him wasn't Nate Barker.

Taken aback, he said nothing for a moment.

"You are the marshal from Nuevo Mexico."

"You're wearing the sombrero and serape," Barker said, fighting against his shock. "You're the Sonora Kid?"

"Ha! Do you hear this man? He thinks I am the Sonora Kid! Why not? I am Hector Rodriguez y Gomez, the greatest bandit in all Mexico! You take me back for a big reward?"

"You stole the howitzer?"

"*Es verdad*. I fired it twice! The posse died. Ah, you were with the posse? Why did you not die, too?"

Barker grabbed Rodriguez by the front of his shirt and pulled him to his feet, spun, and shoved hard to get him moving outside. The others in the cantina pushed away from their tables and reached for their six-shooters.

"Don't," Barker said, slowly moving the pistol in a

wide arc that took in all the men. When he saw he wasn't going to bluff them, he fired. The bottle of tequila in the barkeep's hand exploded, showering him with glass and booze. "That could be your head." He grabbed again to keep Rodriguez from running.

Outside in the hot sun, he shoved the Mexican around to the rear of the building, cocked his pistol, and stuck it into the man's face.

"Easy question. Are you the Sonora Kid?"

Rodriguez's eyes went wide with fear. Barker saw how he wanted to lie, to boast that he was, but there was the question of what would happen. He might die if he lied or if he told the truth. Face as white as a ghost, Rodriguez croaked out, "No. I am not the Sonora Kid. He is a madman, a killer, *todo loco*!"

Barker drew back a half pace, wondering what he ought to do. Rodriguez had been a member of the gang Nate rode with. There wasn't much question about that, and for his part in the killings he ought to stand trial. He had even confessed to firing the howitzer and killing several of the posse. That alone was reason for Barker to take him back to stand trial.

But it also meant that he had to stop lying to himself. Even with the evidence of Nate's boot in the middle of his back, he had held out a sliver of hope that the wild youth had lied about being the Sonora Kid. The evidence now was too great. Not only had Nate confessed, but everyone else in his gang who might have been the leader was dead or captured.

"Into the saddle. We're going back across the border."

"You are a lawman there, not here," Rodriguez said loudly. That tipped Barker off to what was happening. He spun, pressed hard into the adobe wall, and fired. A man who had been sneaking up from behind grabbed his arm, forcing him to drop a wicked knife. Barker didn't linger on the sight of the blood pumping from the man's arm. He turned back, six-gun cocked again, and aimed at Rodriguez.

"Mount up. We got a long ride ahead of us."

Rodriguez's horse died under him just as they crossed into the U.S. For one of them, it was an especially long walk to Fort Selden.

"SHOOT ME. I WILL NOT TAKE ANOTHER STEP," THE Mexican moaned.

"Tell me again," Barker demanded. "Tell me and we can rest. For a few minutes."

Rodriguez collapsed and glared up at the marshal. He would have spit, but his mouth was too dry. Barker took a swig of water, then handed the canteen to the outlaw. Rodriguez made a face but did not spit. The day was too hot.

"The vaquero, the one you call the vaquero," the outlaw said. "He was first the Sonora Kid. He and Nate were. . . . *simpatico.*"

"Two peas in a pod," Barker said, wondering if the story would be different this time. He had forced Rodriguez to tell him what he could since leaving Mexico. It always came out the same. The vaquero had recruited Nate—and it had not taken much effort. The lure of easy money had been too much. Worse, Nate's taste for blood had been whetted after the first stage robbery. He, not any of the others in the gang, had taken the watch.

"I don know this peas," Rodriguez said. He finished the water, then threw aside the canteen. Barker retrieved it. They were days from the fort now. The end of the road.

"Nate killed him and became the Sonora Kid. He took over his reputation."

"*Sí*," Rodriguez said in disgust. "But he soon built the reputation. He killed to become the Sonora Kid—and his every instant after the killing, he *was* the Sonora Kid. His Spanish was *muy malo*, even for a gringo. He killed men for telling him this."

Barker heaved a sigh and closed his eyes for a moment against the sun. He had forced Rodriguez to repeat the story many times, and each time the ending was the same. Nate had become the Sonora Kid. He hadn't even been content making his own reputation and had stolen one.

"So he went with the rest of the gang? Down the other canyon?"

"I fired the howitzer," Rodriguez said with some pride. "The Kid, he approved. He left me in charge of the big gun."

"While he escaped, knowing you couldn't drag the cannon fast enough to escape the soldiers," Barker said. Rodriguez shrugged. "He was likely killed. The colonel is a persistent man."

"The Kid, he escaped. He is like the air between your fingers." Rodriguez grabbed nothing in front of him and made a fist. "He will strike again!"

"If he wasn't killed—if you're right and he got away—I'll track him down and arrest him, just as I did you."

"You will not find him. He is too smart for you." The Mexican was smug, and Barker almost told him he would find his son and bring him to justice.

But he hadn't been able to say the words. He wasn't sure if he was ashamed or if he feared the outlaw would take pleasure in that knowledge. Maybe both. Probably both.

Barker got Rodriguez to his feet and back on the trail.

Getting through the mountains was easier than he'd expected. Following an unpolluted stream up one canyon gave them plenty of water and less rocky footing. When they emerged on the north side of the Peloncillas and found the road leading east toward Mesilla, luck was again with them. A rancher driving his buckboard into town sped them along the way, but once they were at the outskirts of Mesilla, Barker walked his prisoner to Fort Selden. It was petty, but he was not feeling inclined to make life easy for a man who had committed the crimes the bandito had.

"The fort's ahead. You'll have a nice cell in the stockade tonight. Food, a place to sleep."

"What is this celebration?" Rodriguez pointed. Red, white, and blue bunting had been draped from poles and across the low adobe walls circling the post. "They know I arrive and rejoice to see one such as I?"

"Shut up," Barker said. He tried to figure out what holiday it might be and couldn't. It had been almost two weeks since he had left Sergeant Sturgeon and struck out after the last of the Sonora Kid's gang.

The "last of the gang" echoed in Barker's head. His son must have died. The colonel had been right about Nate going with the larger part of the gang down the other canyon, but there was no way Nate would ever be taken alive.

That made punishment for Rodriguez all the more important. Somebody had to face justice, to have the crimes spoken of in public, in court, and judgment rendered.

He marched the Mexican into the fort amid boisterous celebration. No one paid him any heed; they were too busy dancing about and enjoying the festivities. A fiddler and a mouth harp player kept the music loud at the end of the parade grounds.

He looked away from the revelers and the musicians to

a gallows constructed nearby. A noose swung in the hot breeze—the noose he had made for the Sonora Kid.

The music stopped and a heavy drumroll quieted the crowd. They were celebrating because there was going to be a hanging.

Mason Barker went dead inside when he realized who was going to have his neck placed inside that noose.

25

"LOOKS LIKE A HANGING," RODRIGUEZ SAID, HIS voice small.

"Not your day," Barker said. He couldn't take his eyes off the dangling noose.

"Get over there." He started the outlaw toward the post stockade but was intercepted by two soldiers with rifles at port arms.

"Got another one of the gang for your commander," Barker said.

"You the marshal Sergeant Sturgeon's always goin' on 'bout?" asked one.

"I reckon so. Why don't you fetch him?"

It wasn't necessary. Sturgeon came marching over, stride long and smile bigger than looked humanly possible.

"You got him, Marshal? I have to admit to being surprised at that."

"It's not the Sonora Kid," Barker said.

Sturgeon motioned for the pair of guards to take Rodriguez away. The outlaw shouted and protested, but the soldiers brooked no argument from him. Barker was glad to be rid of him.

"The colonel had a good idea what went on in the son of a bitch's head," Sturgeon said. "He rode with his gang, thinkin' we'd go after the howitzer. That'd let him get away. Almost worked."

Barker had never been right about his son. He had never believed Nate would commit such vile murders, and he had tried to find ways to excuse him and alibi him as only one of the gang. Even the massacre on the hillside beyond the canyon—his back still ached from Nate's boot—had not been enough to sour him on finding ways to explain away the evidence. He couldn't lie to himself any longer.

"The colonel caught him?"

"You would have enjoyed it, Marshal. The Kid tried to use his men as a shield, then he tried to slip away and let them get killed. Some did, but the colonel was too smart. He had sent a detachment around 'fore he started the attack. Caught him good and proper tryin' to skulk off."

"Was he hurt?"

"How'd you know?" Sturgeon's bushy eyebrows arched and his mouth dropped open. "You just got in. Somebody in Mesilla tell you?"

"How bad?"

"Pretty bad, but he's up and walking. Almost had his leg shot off and some thought he'd lose it. No way will he ever walk right again and riding's gonna be a chore. Might have to ride in a buggy."

"Buggy?" Barker tried to sort it all out. Then he saw Colonel Tomasson being helped from his office by his striker. His leg dragged, and he leaned heavily on a cane.

Only then did he realize Sturgeon was speaking of his commanding officer and not Nate.

"It's likely he'll be mustered out. The colonel's fighting it, but word is that a new commander is on his way with orders tucked in his pocket. Might be Colonel Hatch himself what takes over command."

Barker had to ask the question that gnawed at his gut.

"What of the . . . the Sonora Kid?"

"Snared him as slick as can be. You need to get all caught up. Took you forever to catch that bandito and get on back here with 'im." Sturgeon looked around, lowered his voice, and asked, "You have to chase him into Mexico?"

"San Miguelito," Barker said. The Mexican town seemed a hundred years in the past, and he hardly remembered the long trip through the canyons of the Peloncillas.

"You'll catch hell for that, but not from the U.S. Army. If it's up to the colonel, he'll pin a medal on you for catchin' the last of the gang."

"The last of the gang," Barker repeated dully. He stared at the noose. A hot wind had picked up and set it swinging. He watched as it twisted and turned, its shadow slowly disappearing on the gallows platform as the sun neared the zenith. He jumped when the drumroll began again.

"Yes, sir, you made it to the post just in time," Sturgeon said with some glee. "You wouldn't want to miss this."

Barker caught his breath when four armed soldiers escorted Nate from the stockade. He took an involuntary step forward, then checked himself.

"What do you know of him?" he asked Sturgeon.

"'Nuff to give him a fair trial, even if he never gave us a name or where he was from. Truth is, he's a white man and the colonel has his doubts the owlhoot ever was in Mexico, much less hailin' from Sonora. His Spanish is mighty bad, too. Don't matter, though. He confessed to 'bout every crime 'long with bein' the Sonora Kid," Sturgeon said. "You've done good work, Marshal, trackin' down this one. He's a bad one, a real bad one."

The slow tattoo continued, the soldiers marching in a half-time cadence with it, Nate waving to the crowd as if he were some stage performer. When he reached the foot of the gallows, he paused. Barker saw the flash of fear on his son's face, then an arrogant sneer replaced it.

He might have been wrong about the fear. He couldn't tell. Nate took the thirteen steps up to the platform two at a time, then did a little dance at the top to mock them all.

The drumroll ceased and Colonel Tomasson stepped forward. All eyes shifted to him, all save Mason Barker's. He stared at his son, wondering what was running through his boy's mind. He was strangely unable to think of anything himself. Barker floated. He felt no emotion, no pain, no sorrow. Nothing.

"You have been tried and convicted by a military court," Tomasson boomed.

"Military court?" Barker turned to Sergeant Sturgeon. "He ought to have been tried in a civilian court."

"He killed the soldiers from Fort Union and bragged on how he personally shot Lieutenant Greenberg full of holes," Sturgeon whispered. "Crime against the military, a military court."

"But—" Barker cut off his protest. His mind sped away now, thinking of all the possible appeals. His son wasn't a soldier and couldn't be tried by a military tribunal. There had to be some way to . . .

He caught himself and forced back the tears. He was still making excuses for Nate and looking for ways to help a boy—a man—who no longer wanted his help.

Barker stared at Nate, who fought briefly as they tied his hands behind his back and pushed him into position on the trapdoor.

Barker heard Tomasson's condemnation and explanation of the charges but was again unable to understand the words. All he could do was stare at Nate.

". . . and may God have mercy on your miserable soul," the colonel finished. "Carry out the sentence!"

The executioner, a sergeant Barker had never seen before, draped the noose around Nate's neck. For a moment Barker closed his eyes. He had fashioned that noose . . . for the Sonora Kid. If he had only known!

"Do you have any last words?" the sergeant asked.

"I wish I'd killed more of you. You don't deserve my lead! You—"

Barker's intent stare somehow drew his son's attention. Nate broke off his tirade and again looked frightened and innocent.

Barker sucked in a deep breath as the trapdoor was sprung and his son dropped out of sight.

"That ends a whole bunch of killing," Sergeant Sturgeon said. "Come on over. I'm sure the colonel will want to speak to you."

Barker nodded numbly.

He couldn't be sure, but thought Nate had seen him and mouthed, "I'm sorry, Pa," just as the trapdoor opened. He wasn't sure, but he hoped it was so because he wanted it to be, like he had wanted so many other things for Nate.

26

IT WAS JUST PAST TWO IN THE AFTERNOON, DURING
the heat of the day, when Mason Barker rode into Mesilla.
His back hurt like fire and his legs had gone numb from
being in the saddle too long, but it was the cancer in his
soul that was the worst.

"There, there he is. Marshal!" called Gus Phillips from
the front steps of the Plugged Nickel. "Come on in. Drinks
are on me. For the rest of the week."

"For the rest of the whole danged year, you mean," corrected a customer who had followed Gus outside. "You're a
hero, Marshal. You're the best lawman in the whole danged
territory!"

The two men cheered, which drew more of the townspeople. When enough had gathered, a real cheer went up.

"What are you cheering about?" Barker asked. He wondered if he sounded as tired as he felt. Probably so.

"You caught the bastard. You saw the Sonora Kid hung by his scrawny neck."

"The soldiers at Fort Selden caught him and hanged him," Barker said.

"To hell with them takin' the credit. *You* were the one what run him to ground. *You* were the only lawman who knowed right off how dangerous the son of a bitch was right from the start."

"And you got the reward waitin' for you."

"Reward?"

"Halliday Stage Company posted a reward and so did the cavalry. Both of 'em is all yours. But you won't be able to spend a red cent of that reward, Marshal. Not in my drinkin' emporium. Come on in," invited Gus again.

Barker couldn't muster enough spark to tell them to all go to hell.

"Got business at the marshal's office," he said.

"Well, sir, you finish up with Dravecky and you get on back here."

"You got free drinks at the Lucky Lew," piped up someone Barker had never seen before. That drinking establishment might have changed hands while he was gone. It had been only weeks, but it stretched to a lifetime for him. A lifetime.

He snapped the reins and guided his horse through the adoring crowd until he reached the marshal's office that had been his headquarters before Dravecky was hired. The marshal came out and stood with hands on his hips, watching as he dismounted.

"You got quite a followin'," the marshal said, looking past Barker to the crowd in the street. They were dancing and joshing, waiting for him to return.

"Don't know why."

"You're the man of the hour. After all the killin', they needed to know it was over and done with. You stopped the Sonora Kid."

"Army did, not me," Barker said.

"That's not the way Colonel Tomasson reported it to Marshal Armijo. I don't know for certain, but the letter waitin' for you inside from Armijo might just be an offer to become his chief deputy."

"Do tell." Barker looped the reins around the cast-iron ring set in the corner of the building.

"You don't have to sound so excited. Come on in. I got a bottle of whiskey in my drawer, and it'd be an honor to share some of it with you."

Barker followed the marshal inside, then sank into the rickety chair across the desk from him. Dravecky shoved a stack of envelopes toward him and then fished around in the large lower drawer for the whiskey and two glasses.

Barker listlessly opened the letter from Marshal Armijo and scanned it quickly. As Colonel Tomasson had told him before he left Fort Selden after the hanging, he had recommended him to be Armijo's chief deputy marshal the day the Sonora Kid was tried and convicted. The letter was the offer. Barker read it again to be sure, then put it aside on the desk.

"Here. Drink up. To catchin' the bad guys." Dravecky hoisted his glass, waiting for Barker to acknowledge the toast. Slowly, Barker did so.

Their glasses clinked, and Barker knocked back the fiery liquor. It did nothing to ease his pain. Any of his pain.

"Good," he said, although he could not have identified what it was. Rye? Trade whiskey? Good Kentucky bourbon?

It hardly mattered as it settled in his belly and churned away there.

He opened the other envelopes. He might as well have had his entire life printed up in the newspaper. Each envelope contained a letter praising him and offering the reward money for capturing and bringing to ultimate justice one bandito, known only as the Sonora Kid.

"You take them letters over to the bank and they can give you cash money for 'em. They're what's known as letters of credit."

Barker tucked the letters into his coat pocket. His fingers touched the empty, cracked bottle there. It had been too long since he had eased his pain with laudanum, since Nate had mashed the bottle into the sand. But looking for more right now didn't seem right. He wanted to feel something, and if it was pain, so be it.

"I'm glad it worked out this way," Dravecky said.

"What? How what worked out?"

"You capturin' the Sonora Kid like you did and all. Your promotion to chief deputy means Mayor Pendleton ain't as likely to send me packin'. I've taken a likin' to Mesilla and want to keep on bein' town marshal." He smiled almost shyly. "Me and Griselda's hittin' it off real good, too."

"I'm not any competition," Barker said. "Never was, not now."

"It's neighborly of you to say that, but we know how the folks in town took to you and yours."

"Me and my family," Barker said. He looked sharply at Dravecky, wondering if the marshal was taunting him. The man's earnest expression told Barker that he didn't know the identity of the Sonora Kid. He was sincere in what he said.

If Barker never mentioned Nate around town, it was

likely nobody would inquire. He could always distract them with stories of how he caught the Sonora Kid. And they would never know.

"You have pen and ink?"

"Surely do. Too damned many reports to fill out. You won't believe this, but Pendleton wants me to keep track of what I spend on upkeep for the jailhouse. I had the Gunther boy sweep up, and Pendleton wanted that writ down so he could charge it off against some account or other. Said he was using double-entry books now, which sounds a powerful lot like a crime to me, but he said it wasn't."

As Dravecky rattled on, Barker carefully wrote his letter to Armijo on the back of the same letter offering him the job as chief deputy marshal. His hand shook something fierce, and he had to force himself to keep his normal hen scratching readable. He finally dropped the steel-nibbed pen, blew on the ink to dry it, then folded the letter carefully and tucked it back into the envelope.

"You wantin' that sealed? Here, got some sealin' wax."

Barker waited as Dravecky did the honors. He lit a match and dripped a couple specks of hot wax from a stick onto the back of the envelope so it was sealed.

"There," Dravecky said.

"One more thing." Barker scratched out his name on the front and wrote in Marshal Armijo's name. Then he handed it back to Dravecky. "Would you see that's sent when you can?"

"It'll be on its way to Santa Fe on the morning stage," Dravecky said, holding the envelope and beaming. "My pleasure to see to this, Chief Deputy Marshal Barker."

"That has quite a ring to it, doesn't it?" Barker stood. "Thanks for the drink. I'm heading home now for a spell."

"You certainly deserve a rest 'fore you get back on the

trail of the owlhoots. It's an honor knowin' you, Mase."
Dravecky stood and thrust out his hand. Barker shook,
then he left silently. Behind him, the marshal hummed to
himself and, from the sound of it, poured another drink.

Barker stepped into the saddle and turned his mare's
face toward the edge of town, where Ruth waited for him.
He hoped to hell he would know what to tell her before he
got home.

Don't miss the best Westerns from Berkley

....

LYLE BRANDT
PETER BRANDVOLD
JACK BALLAS
J. LEE BUTTS
JORY SHERMAN
DUSTY RICHARDS

....

penguin.com